THE
ANGEL
DECEPTION

David Leadbeater has published more than fifty novels and is a million-copy ebook bestseller. His books include the chart-topping Matt Drake series and the Relic Hunters series, which won the inaugural Amazon Kindle Storyteller award in 2017.

www.davidleadbeater.com

T0364467

Also by David Leadbeater:

To find out more visit **www.davidleadbeater.com**

THE
ANGEL
DECEPTION

DAVID LEADBEATER

avon.

Published by AVON
A division of HarperCollins*Publishers* Ltd
1 London Bridge Street,
London SE1 9GF

www.harpercollins.co.uk

HarperCollins*Publishers*
Macken House,
39/40 Mayor Street Upper,
Dublin 1
D01 C9W8

First published by HarperCollins*Publishers* 2025
1
Copyright © David Leadbeater 2025

David Leadbeater asserts the moral right to
be identified as the author of this work

A catalogue record for this book is available from the British Library

ISBN: 978-0-00-865991-2

Set in Sabon by HarperCollins*Publishers* India

Printed and bound in the UK using 100% Renewable
Electricity by CPI Group (UK) Ltd

MIX
Paper | Supporting
responsible forestry
FSC™ C007454

For my mum and dad. Thanks for always being there.

Chapter 1

Moloch fixed the horned mask firmly to his head and walked out onto the stage.

There was a collective, almost inaudible gasp. Before him stood a sea of guests, all wearing black robes, all with masks of varying shapes and colours fixed over their faces. Moloch saw white Venetian masks and African masks, many popular bird masks with the drooping snout, several ghost masks and even a rhinestone mask. He held up his hands for the utmost silence.

Before him stood an altar made of black stone. It was very old and adorned with twisted carvings. Moloch looked down at it. The face of the Devil looked back at him, twisted in hatred, eyes wide.

'Confess your sins,' Moloch said.

And one by one, the guests started to speak up. They spoke one at a time, but quickly, getting it out of the way. They confessed all the times they'd visited church, the Masses they'd heard, the moral and respectable deeds they'd done and the evil deeds they'd failed to do. They confessed to not striking a priest down when they had the chance, to cowardice in the face of good, and inaction towards their Lord.

'The long confession to our Lord has begun,' Moloch said.

It went on. The repentant spoke long and low and with regret in their voices, pouring their hearts out. From kissing babies to helping a friend out to failing to gamble, Moloch heard it all. He let the words wash over him in a wave of decadent affirmation, not letting any of it colour his actions.

A wooden Christian cross was brought out and laid on the floor in front of the altar. The guests proceeded to spit on it and then to trample it. They did this one at a time, lining up as Moloch watched. He committed the ultimate sin by lifting his cloak, unzipping his pants, and urinating on the symbol.

The sound of laughter and clapping filled the chamber.

They broke all the rules as Moloch started the Mass, reading his sermon. Black candles were laid out on the altar. The guests shed all their clothing and stood there naked, some on their knees, others on their tiptoes. Some slipped their cloaks back on but remained naked beneath. They all had knives, which they took out now to lightly cut themselves. Blood spilled on the floor. Instead of water, they drank whisky and doused the cross with it. A few of the guests ended up kissing and committed carnal acts. All this as Moloch ran through his short sermon.

At last, though, he was finished.

Next, Moloch held up something black and round, the size of a host. It was dried blood and on it was painted the image of the Devil.

'This is my body,' he said.

He handed it out, spread pieces among the small crowd. Each ate a small piece and then passed it around their brethren, sharing spit and flesh. Moloch waited until they had finished.

The atmosphere was heavy in the ritual chamber, and laced with tension. Moloch thought it was getting thicker and thicker, intensifying with every ritual that passed. Something had noticed them, he knew. Something was watching them, taking note. Was it pleased? Were they worthy? Was it satisfied with their supplications?

Moloch brought forward a black chalice. Inside was a vile-smelling liquid, something mixed with blood and urine. He gave the guests communion, one by one, and watched as they shook with pleasure. The atmosphere was crackling by now, the whole chamber on the edge of something.

In his way, this was what made Moloch decide to search for the Hellfire.

It was always like this. The Black Mass they performed was always the same, and it always ended the same. Years ago, it had been incredible. They couldn't wait for their regular meetings. But as the months had passed, as the rituals became constant, identical, one after another after another, Moloch had grown restless. He needed something more. Something that would take their cabal to the next level.

He let the delicious image of the Book of Baphomet eddy through his thoughts, savouring it. He had time. He didn't have a lot of time, but he *did* have time. The great book had always been important, always been at the forefront of everything he did, but recently he had decided to use it for even greater purposes. To plumb one of its greatest secrets.

It would have vast consequences for the cabal. Incredible consequences.

Moloch shivered with excitement, anxiety, and anticipation. He was a tall man, thin-faced and clean-shaven. He usually wore his hair short and was always dressed in expertly tailored suits. He was relatively wealthy, owning an extensive property on an estate in the countryside that had come in very handy for the cabal's monthly rituals. Moloch spoke well and came from a highly educated family, money having dripped down favourably from his ancestors. He enjoyed being the head of a secret cabal.

The cabal was powerful. It consisted of high-flying influential men and women from the upper echelons of life: bankers, solicitors, celebrities, doctors, lords and their ladies, and so very many more. When they met, they were a prevailing entity, a weighty and formidable unit that could achieve almost anything.

And that was why Moloch wanted to take it to the next level.

He wanted the Hellfire.

The time had come.

He turned now, beckoned to Smithson. The man disappeared, then returned carrying an inert figure. The figure was clearly a naked man. Smithson laid him out on the altar, spread-eagled, and then backed away.

Moloch stood over the body.

'*Ave Satanus*,' he said.

The chant was repeated back to him and then picked up again and again. It rose and swelled and rolled through the chamber and against the ceiling. It became a tidal wave filled with every sin imaginable, a gluttonous, carnal chant that filled every ear and mouth. The masks waved before Moloch as the terrible excitement rose and as he brandished the gleaming knife.

He held it high above his head, point down, held it above the chest of the motionless man. The blade flashed with reflected light.

Moloch looked out over the crowd. His face stretched in a rictus of pleasure, his eyes flashed with violence. This was the best part.

The drugs were wearing off. The man on the altar was stirring. His right hand flexed, his left arm shifted. He swallowed, still barely able to move.

Moloch wanted him to see. To really *see*.

The moment stretched. The knife wavered. He wanted to bring it plunging down, to feel the power. The man's eyes were flickering.

Almost . . . almost . . .

And then they opened.

Bright blue, they shot wide open and fixed firmly on the point of the blade. Moloch waited until recognition set in, until fear started to coil. Then, with all his strength, he brought the blade plunging down.

It struck flesh and slipped right through, passing straight into the man's heart. There was a gasp. The eyes flew wider still, now filled with terror, and then they went out. Moloch was staring right into them when they expired. He drank it in. This was his reward for being the leader. These moments of expiration were his and his alone.

There was a cheer, the sound of clapping and whooping. It was a blasphemous act, and they revelled in it. The moment of the man's passing was marked with happiness and laughter, with joy. After that, they started a prayer, *their* Lord's prayer.

It began:

'Lucifer, grant me the knowledge to understand your ways,
Power in your name to fight against the light,
Praise be to Lucifer.
Their God is but a trophy,
Not the rapture in the darkness that is you.'

And so it continued, verse after verse. The supine man was dead. Moloch left the blade sticking out of him, occasionally dabbing his fingers in the leaked blood. He revelled in the raised voices, in the chant and the prayer. It had been a good night.

The cabal was stronger than ever.

Now, with the onset of Hellfire, it would expand exponentially and take on the world.

Chapter 2

Sally Rusk sat in the back seat of the car, the blue tips of her hair hanging over her laptop as she bent over her work. She was finishing writing an invoice for the team's latest job and was just about to send it.

'That's done.' She pressed the button and then closed her laptop, satisfied.

'Easy enough,' Hassell said.

They had just transported an ancient relic from Edinburgh to London, deposited it with the Natural History Museum, and were now trying to negotiate Cromwell Road and the other tributaries of South Kensington. Quaid was driving, and he wasn't happy.

'But you're never happy,' Mason was telling him.

'You should be,' Sally told them. 'We just completed our first job for the Natural History Museum. That's a major client.'

'Maybe they'll give us free tickets to look round,' Roxy said, having eyed the majestic building as they passed.

'You'd just get lost in there,' Mason told her.

'Maybe that's the idea. It'd keep me away from you.'

Sally tuned the banter out. Since they'd started the new company, Quest Investigations, their client list had been steadily growing until they now boasted some major movers and shakers in their list.

Sally sat back, satisfied. She was happier now than at any time since her father died. When that happened, during her search for the Vatican secret, she'd met Mason and Roxy for the first time, got to know and trust them. She'd had to grieve her father's murder on the run, amid the action. When the dust had settled, she'd realised that she now had all his wealth to contend with, along with his old, rambling country house and everything inside it. Sally had fought her father for years, rebelling against privilege and golden handshakes, and now she had inherited it all.

But it was what she did with it that mattered.

Sally was twenty-eight, a brunette, with those characteristic blue tips that showed her rebellious nature. She'd softened them since her father died, but couldn't quite bring herself to lose them even now. She was a champion fell runner and was learning unarmed combat from Roxy and Mason to better help defend her team. She was getting good at it too; the lessons were paying off, though she hadn't had much real-world action yet. The last five or six months, working with Mason had helped her deal with a new life, a new situation. It had helped all of them.

They were all at least half broken, she reflected.

Roxy Banks was a hard-hitting, rum-soaked loose cannon, still trying to find the woman she might have been if a CIA-type organisation hadn't whisked her out of college and turned her into a kind of assassin. She'd quit that organisation when she realised what it was doing to her and had embarked on a quest to find the softness of youth. Only then would she be able to face her family again.

Then there was Mason himself, the de facto leader of their little group. Mason blamed himself for the deaths of two friends whilst on a mission in Mosul. Mason was ex-army and had fought long and hard for his country. After Mosul, though, nothing had been the same. Mason now just wanted to do good to atone for what he saw as his past mistakes. He was coming to terms with the losses, but there was still some way to go.

Sally patted Quaid on the arm. 'How's your left foot?'

'Eh? It's fine, why?'

'It wouldn't be in this stop-start traffic if this car wasn't automatic.'

'Ah, yes, bollocks to that. I'd be happy with the pain just to drive a proper car.'

Quaid was stuck in the past with his love of older things. The modern world and all its accoutrements were passing him swiftly by, and it didn't bother him one bit. If it could be done old-school, Quaid was your man.

Still, Sally knew that, deep down, he was trying.

The car inched its way out of South Kensington and then London and wended its way down some twisting, tree-lined country roads. For a few months now, the team had lived together at Sally's house simply because it was the easiest way to do things. They didn't seem to get on top of each other and were always on hand when a job came in. Sally knew it wouldn't stay like that for ever, but it was good whilst it lasted.

Soon, they were pulling into Sally's driveway and crunching along the gravel to park outside the front door. Her father's house was long and rambling, with rows of windows and a thatched roof. Inside, there were many rooms, several he'd never even used, and he had three studies. Sally had barely scratched the surface of his old belongings and wondered if she should even bother. She had her own life to live.

Her father had been a professor with great connections, most of them fostered by his wealth. He'd looked into the provenance of ancient relics and had left copious notes of his adventures through the years, some of which helped Sally and the team even now with their own tasks. She had copied all the notes onto a computer and carried them with her always. She called them the Rusk Notes.

Quaid turned the car off, the sudden silence loud after the long drive. Sally felt worn, as if the journey had leached all the energy out of her. She packed up her laptop, grabbed her rucksack from the boot and went to the house, unlocking the front door. The others followed in their own time. Soon, the lights were on, the heating on high, and a pleasant fire crackled in the living room. Quaid ordered takeaway, and they were soon sitting in the living room, pizza boxes balanced on their laps, drinks to hand. This was how they decompressed.

'Good job, well done,' Quaid said. 'Although I don't think that curator liked us.'

'I think he thought it was overkill,' Sally said with a shrug. 'All of us at once. Maybe it was.'

'We could take on more jobs if we split up,' Mason said around a mouthful of pizza, which he washed down with a swig of beer.

'That works when the jobs are . . . light,' Sally said. 'But what happens when they get hairy, like our most recent adventures in Japan and China, like when Marduk attacked the Vatican, like—'

Mason held up a slice of pizza. 'Okay, I get your point.'

'Stick together,' Roxy said. 'I like it better that way.'

Sally looked at the raven-haired, black-eyed American. 'You've changed,' she said.

Roxy sat back and nodded. 'I'm trying. You know I am. The more barriers I build between this life and the last, the better.'

'And what's up for us next?' Hassell asked.

Sally took a sip of her red wine before answering. 'A choice between a trip to the Museo Nacional de Ciencias

9

Naturales in Madrid or the Victoria and Albert Museum in London.'

'That's not a choice,' Roxy said. 'One's a holiday. The other's right next to where we've just been.'

'Big client, though,' Sally mused.

The evening stretched before them. The fire crackled in the hearth, the coals splitting and snapping. A warm glow infused the room, spreading among them as the conversation turned. Eight turned into nine and then half past. They talked about their last mission in Japan and China, the different cultures they'd come across and the characters they'd met. Quaid tried to steer the conversation away from Luciane and Anya, two female acquaintances who'd helped them, the latter of which kept popping up in Quaid's life and then leaving with nothing getting resolved. Sally thought the two loved each other, but only from afar. It was an odd relationship.

Around a quarter to ten, with the wind increasing in velocity outside and starting to snap about the eaves and batter the windows, with a rain shower spattering against the glass, and the flames in the hearth roaring, Sally heard a familiar noise.

Her phone was ringing.

She put her wineglass down on the table with a clink and fished the device out of her pocket.

'Hello? Who is this?'

The others looked over expectantly, hushing with respect, the fire reflected in their eyes.

'Sally Rusk?' a deep man's voice asked.

'Yes.'

'Oh, hello, it's Jonathan Jacobs here. I am . . . was . . . one of your father's friends. And, of course, yours.'

Sally frowned. She remembered Jonathan Jacobs. He was her godfather, and a good man. Most of her father's friends were brash and privileged people who thought they were aristocrats, but Jacobs had been one of the better, easier-going ones.

'Hello, Jonathan. What can I do for you at this time of night?'

'Please,' he said. 'You have to help me. If you don't . . . they'll kill me.'

Chapter 3

Sally gripped the phone tighter, then pressed the button for the speakerphone and placed the device on the table.

'Wh . . . what?'

'It's just . . . a mess. It's become the most terrible mess of my life. I don't know why I even started doing it. It was . . . a whim, a fancy. A way of whiling away the long, cold nights after Margo died. By the time I realised he was taking the whole thing too seriously I was already compromised. He films the whole thing, you see. And the years, they pass in the blink of an eye and, before you know it, you're in so deep you can't get out.'

Sally was having trouble following him. 'Slow down, Jonathan. What are you talking about?'

Jacobs took a deep breath and went silent for a while. 'Sorry,' he said finally.

'What's the problem?' Roxy asked him. 'Who's trying to kill you?'

'Well, no one yet, but they will. Just as soon as they find out that I've betrayed them.'

Sally spread her hands wide. None of this was making any sense, and she saw similar blank looks on the faces of her friends.

'Maybe start from the beginning,' she said.

'Yes, that sounds better. From the beginning then. You see, I have a friend called Moloch. Well, he calls himself that, but his real name is Nathaniel. This man, he's charismatic, fascinating. He draws you in. He drew me in. He had a vision, you see, a vision to form a cult. Or a *cabal,* as he calls it. At first, as I said, it was a way to while away the evenings. We talked behind closed doors, decide who we were going to invite into the fold. Only the most powerful, those who could keep our big secret. But there was nothing bad at first, nothing against the law. It was just a bunch of men and women wearing cloaks.'

Sally blinked. 'Cloaks?'

'This is where it gets delicate, where you must suspend your disbelief. Am I on speakerphone, by the way? Is anyone else listening?'

'Just my team.'

'I see. Do you trust them?'

'With my life.'

'Then I will have to do the same. Literally. So, years ago, Moloch and I kind of . . . became Satanists.'

Sally swallowed hard. Roxy looked exasperated. 'You *kind of* became Satanists? How the hell does that happen? It's not like I *kind of* bought a dodgy magazine, is it?'

'We actually just fell into it. We were reading one night, came across an article, and followed it up. We dabbled. We laughed at it, were appalled by it. And then everything changed.'

'Moloch?' Mason asked knowingly.

'Yes, Moloch. He actually *became* a Satanist. He started taking it seriously, researched it thoroughly, started acquiring all the right paraphernalia and conversing with other groups. Moloch used them to build up his own cabal, used me to help bring the right people in, promoted me through the ranks. Even then, at first, it was disgusting but largely innocent.'

'Disgusting?' Roxy said.

13

'There are certain rituals when it comes to devil-worshipping that you can't get away from. Things that include bloodletting and urine and hindquarters. I'll spare you the details.'

'So a throwaway hobby suddenly got very serious,' Mason said.

'Yes, exactly. And I was neck-deep in it, unable to get out. But it got worse. I won't go into the awful scenarios. The problem is, Moloch really believes it now. He truly believes, in his madness, that he can summon the Devil.'

'You say you got into this when your wife, Margo, died?' Sally asked.

'Yes. As I said, at first, it was a way to while away the time. But then, I couldn't get out. Now, well . . . I'm terminal . . . I'm dying. I've found out I haven't long to live.' He paused for a while, collecting himself. 'And I just can't live with the shame. I have nothing to lose anymore, and can't bear to stay silent anymore. Especially in light of the Hellfire.'

'Hellfire?' Sally repeated.

'Moloch knows the Hellfire is out there. It contains something he needs, something vital. When he gets it he will use it to perform a terrible, deadly mass ritual. Multiple victims. We can't let him get that Hellfire.'

'Why not go to the police?' Quaid asked.

'They are compromised too. I know some of Moloch's guests belong in the high echelons of Scotland Yard.'

'But why come to me?' Sally asked, shaking her head. 'This isn't what we do.'

'Because of your father,' Jacobs said, and his words electrified her.

Sally sat straight up. 'My father? What of him?'

'Your father was helping me get out by putting all of his considerable knowledge towards investigating the cabal. It is low-key at the moment, but still powerful. It consists of commissioners, politicians, solicitors, newspaper owners, money men, influential people from all walks of life, who help cover it up and keep it safe.'

'Wait. My *father* was helping you?'

'Yes, I brought the problem to him some time ago. He was helping me wend a path through the immense danger. Basically, he was investigating the cabal and its members and trying to link them to their crimes.'

'Is devil-worshipping a crime?' Hassell asked.

'A good question. One of the oldest notions of connections to crime is demonology. Satanism is a complex belief system, as complex as any spiritual belief. I mean, the occult is the influence of supernatural powers. A ritual is a series of acts. It is not exactly a crime in itself. But when it comes with a belief in Satanism law enforcement is forced to look at it. If individual crimes have been committed. That's where the objective lies and where any investigation should focus.'

'They worship an occult figure they call Satan,' Roxy said evenly. 'How can that be a crime?'

'It isn't,' Jacobs said. 'But it's the things they get up to in said rituals that might constitute a crime.'

'Like what?' Sally asked.

'I'll get back to that. First, your father was helping me. He made an extensive study and copious notes. We pored over them, trying to find a way to take the cabal down. But they are so well protected, they exist under a shield of authority and law and influence that you wouldn't believe.'

'I haven't found any of these notes,' Sally said quickly, then thought that she hadn't been looking all that hard. And it had been a busy six months.

'He made them. I can tell you where they are. I'm still stuck here, you see, and things have gone from bad to far, far worse.'

'In what way?' Quaid asked.

'With Moloch,' Jacobs said. 'He has a new undertaking, the Hellfire and this artefact it contains, and it's something that could affect the world.'

15

'A new undertaking?' Roxy asked.

'Moloch has the original Book of Baphomet in his possession. He acquired it from a languishing group of Satanists at some cost. There are two more copies, by the way, one of which your father has.'

Sally shook her head, finding it hard to come to terms with this new view of her father. The only way she could process it was that he was trying to help a friend. And at least, this time, it was a good friend, someone worthy of his efforts.

Jacobs continued, 'Moloch has decided that all the wealth, power and influence that surround him aren't enough. He wants more. In his own words, he wants to take the cabal into the stratosphere. Expand exponentially.'

'How is that even possible?' Mason asked.

'He's found a way to do it,' Jacobs said. 'And it's straight out of the Book of Baphomet. Some say is the Satanist's manual. It's not a grimoire or a dictionary of demons or a reference book, it's more like a *guidebook*. Something put together by Satanists down the years, something to hold their knowledge.'

'Who is Baphomet?' Mason asked.

'Baphomet is a deity associated with the Knights Templar,' Jacobs said. 'They worshipped it and, later, it became incorporated into various occult traditions. Baphomet is associated with the sabbatic goat and has been called both a deity and a demon. The image of Baphomet is the classic image of the horned devil with the goat's face and black angel wings.'

'Nice,' Roxy said tightly.

'But we digress,' Jacobs said. 'Within its many pages, the Book of Baphomet contains a reference to this thing called Hellfire. This Hellfire will give Moloch the means to influence governments.'

'He's already doing that, isn't he?' Sally said.

'Not to this extent. We're talking policy-making, behind the scenes, all-powerful influence the like of which nobody should have full control of, never mind an avaricious Satanist.'

'So what is this Hellfire?' Mason asked.

'Hellfire is a collection of gold and precious metals and gemstones and rare earth elements the like of which has never been known,' Jacobs said. 'A raw, vast treasure that has been accumulated over centuries by various Satanic groups and then hidden away. The Book of Baphomet holds clues on how to find it.'

'So Moloch wants more wealth?' Quaid asked.

'In a nutshell,' Jacobs said. 'And he's determined to get it.'

'What's this artefact he needs to commit the terrible atrocity?' Mason asked.

'That I don't know.'

'My father has a copy of the Book of Baphomet?' Sally asked.

'Yes, one of the only three known copies.'

'You still haven't told us why your life is in danger,' Mason pointed out.

'It's simple. I want out. I've wanted out for years. I can't go on being witness to all the sacrifices. And if I try to leave openly, Moloch will have me killed.'

'So my father was looking for leverage?' Sally said. 'And you've turned to us to carry on the cause?'

'I have nowhere else left to turn. Your father made good progress. Yes, I'm hoping you will carry on where he left off but, with Moloch's new obsession with Hellfire, it's now much more urgent. We can't allow him to obtain it and turn a modest cabal into a leading power. They are ruthless, they are killers, they are immoral.'

'And you can't go to the cops because some of them are cops,' Roxy said.

'I thought I'd already covered that, but yes. They hold many aces.'

'Has Moloch started searching for this Hellfire?' Mason asked.

'He's actively recruiting a team now, as we speak.'

'What kind of team?' Hassell asked, no doubt remembering the team he'd been a part of that had robbed the Vatican. Hassell had been unknowingly working for the man who ordered the murder of his girlfriend. Since then, Hassell had resolved that issue by killing the man, but his demons were anything but exorcised.

'Capable, fit, intelligent. Probably ex-military. He wants someone who can follow clues and jump straight onto the next ones. He wants someone like you, I guess.'

'I'll check our emails,' Roxy said drily.

'This is no joke.' Jacobs misunderstood her sarcasm. 'If Moloch gets that Hellfire, there'll be no stopping him and no way out for me short of death.'

Sally was already raking the ceiling with her eyes, as if trying to peer through the plaster to where the Book of Baphomet might be hidden.

'We're on it,' she said tightly, thinking of her father's hidden quest, Jacobs' situation, Moloch's hunt for power. Jacobs was right, it couldn't be allowed to happen. And if her father had cared enough about Jacobs to put himself in danger, then she had to see this through. She wouldn't let the man be murdered.

Jacobs was sighing with relief. Sally ended the call and then rose to her feet.

'Looks like the day isn't over after all,' she said. 'In fact, it looks like it's just beginning.'

Chapter 4

Moloch sat in the restaurant of a hotel near London, alone. He owned the hotel and had closed the restaurant doors and sent the staff home at ten so that he could have it to himself. Moloch had perched himself on a bar stool and was currently eyeing up the pale and amber liquids that stood on the other side of the bar, wondering which one to try next. He was on spiced rum, but there were so many good ones to choose from.

He let his foot kick back and forth, at peace. The seven men and women he'd chosen to search for the Hellfire would be here soon, and he would have to explain exactly what they needed to know. No more. No less. And he would have to be very careful about what he said.

The restaurant clock struck 22.15. He knew his new recruits wouldn't be late. And sure enough, there soon came a knock at the closed restaurant door. He saw shadows standing outside. He slipped off the bar stool, walked over to the door, and unlocked it.

'Come inside,' he said.

He turned away so that they could follow him to a large table. He took a seat, offered them a drink, and fixed one for everyone. Then he went and sat at the head of the table, studying the faces before him.

'You are here because you have already been well paid,' he said. 'Now, I will give you a reason to stay and work for me. Of course, you're all bloody mercenaries.' He laughed. 'And that reason is more money. I'm offering a quarter of a million each for what should be no more than two weeks' work.'

He had them. He saw their eyes shining.

'Let me continue,' he said. 'I'm looking for something. That something holds great value to me and my . . . friends. I can't go get it myself, so I need to employ a team to do it for me. That's where you come in. There's a book . . . but wait. I believe you are in charge?'

A well-built man with short-cropped dark hair, striking blue eyes, a hook nose and an easy, confident manner held up a hand. 'I am, Boss,' he said. Interestingly, Moloch noticed, the man wore a golden crucifix around his neck. It unsettled him and made him not want to look the man in the eyes, but he couldn't let his personal convictions impede something as incredible as the quest he was about to offer.

'And you are?'

'Ed Bullion, Boss.'

'Right, Mr Bullion, I will address all questions to you and maybe you could pass any team issues to me personally.'

'Just call me Ed, Boss.'

'I prefer to keep this on a formal level, at least from my side. Now, let me tell you a story. There is a book called the Book of Baphomet. Inside are many interesting ideals and values that, to you, are not important. What is important is the treasure called Hellfire, and a man named the Duke of Adlington.'

Bullion nodded for his team. 'Go on, Boss.'

The 'Boss' thing was going to get on Moloch's nerves after a time, but he let it go for now. Moloch was desperate

20

that nothing go wrong with this mission and therefore had decided it couldn't hurt to give them the full background. 'The Duke of Adlington was a very wealthy landowner back in medieval times. He owned a vast estate and guarded his riches jealously. He was a hard man, hard on the servants, his vassals, his own men, even his family. It was said the Duke lived his life in winter, never once setting foot in the spring. He was a fighter, a warrior, a man who took everything he wanted. The king at the time, seeing a powerful ally, always came down on his side, feathering his own nest at the same time. Adlington was a man first into battle, last to leave the field, and he wielded his sword with gusto. He was a blood-spiller, and a hoarder of treasure. Everything from jewels and gemstones to gold and more. They said his castle was filled with it, and that only made him long for more. The man's eyes were ablaze either with anger or with bright reflections of his vast treasure.'

'Sounds like my kind of man,' Bullion said, grinning.

Moloch took a moment to look over the assembled team. There were two women and five men, and to him, they all looked pretty much alike. Short hair, hard faces, hard eyes, musclebound. They lounged with ease and looked like they had plenty of energy and could handle themselves.

He went on, 'But age comes to us all and it came to the Duke of Adlington with a vengeance. At age fifty, he started feeling the consequences of all those battles, all those old wounds and broken bones. At sixty, he almost drank himself to death. He lost interest in everything except his treasure, and those around him started drifting away to find better lodgings. It was at the age of sixty-five that he lost it all.'

'How?' Bullion asked.

'That would be where a band of ancient Satanists come in. Hunted by the church, persecuted, they were on the run most of their adult lives, living rough, living hard.'

'Satanists?' Bullion fingered the golden crucifix at his throat.

Moloch glared at him. 'Are you a religious man?'

'Not especially, Boss.'

'Then why do you wear that . . . thing?'

'This?' Bullion held out the crucifix towards Moloch, much to his distaste. 'It's . . . a present from my girlfriend.'

Moloch didn't believe him. The way his fingers had gone straight to the crucifix when he heard the word 'Satanist'. It had undone him. But Bullion didn't need to know he was working for a Satanist, did he? At least, not yet.

'The group of Satanists came across Adlington's castle. They were a large bunch, and savage by now. Attacking the castle, they murdered the guards, found Adlington, and strung him up in his own tower. They tortured him for days, made him a part of their bloody rituals. It is said they conjured the Satanic master on the fifth day.'

Bullion now stared at him. 'The Satanic master?'

Moloch realised he'd gone a little too far. 'Whatever you want to call him,' he blustered. 'The Devil. Satan. Lucifer.' The one Moloch firmly believed he was in touch with and would grace him with his infernal presence soon.

'Crackpots,' Bullion said.

'Indeed,' Moloch drew the word out, reining in emotions of anger. 'Anyway, these people took over the castle, murdered whoever was left inside, and called it home. They would have been as shocked as anyone to find all that treasure.'

'Christmas come early,' one of the so far voiceless women put in.

'The Satanists hoarded it too, now rich beyond their wildest dreams. They bought an army big enough to protect the castle and were never bothered by anyone. Obviously, they didn't let it be known they were the very Satanists once pursued across the country.'

'But it doesn't end there,' one man said.

'You are right, of course. The Satanists crawled through their treasure room, draping themselves in gold and precious gemstones. They revelled in it. They'd never seen so much wealth in one place. They believed their master — the one they worshipped — bestowed it upon them for a lifetime of reverence and adoration. The Satanists came to believe that they'd earned it. From him.'

'Mad bastards,' a man said.

Moloch wanted to stab him through the hand, or, better still, the heart. The words went against everything he believed. Instead, he went on, 'All good things end and nothing lives in permanence. It was decades later when the Satanists themselves found their fortune moving into shadow. Their leader could see their downfall approaching. Townsmen were becoming suspicious. Others had moved close and now a town had sprung up close by, a religious town as many were back then. The Satanists knew their days were numbered.'

'So what did they do?' Bullion asked.

'After their religion, the next important thing to them was their gold. And other Satanists, of course. They contrived a way to hide the gold, find the Book of Baphomet and make two copies, and then enter the clues into the book. It was the best way to safeguard their treasure and leave it available for future generations.'

'You're saying a bunch of Satanists hid their gold and then wrote down a series of clues so those who came after could find it?' Bullion said.

'They hid it well somewhere in England,' Moloch said. 'That's the belief.' Feeling dry of mouth, he walked over to the bar and poured himself two more fingers of spiced rum. He didn't offer the mercenaries another drink. His mind was awash with thoughts of the Hellfire, and the secret it contained that he so desperately needed, and the last time he had conversed with his master, which had been so utterly satisfying.

'And now you want us to find it?' one woman said.

'How did you come by this Book of Baphomet?' Bullion asked suddenly.

Moloch stiffened. He had his back to the men and women, which was just as well, because they couldn't see the sudden expression of indecision that crossed his face.

'Inheritance,' he lied. 'On my mother's side. That's where all the stories come from, too.' He didn't need to tell them he'd gleaned all the information from the book itself. That might further reveal his secret.

'And how do you know it's all true?' Bullion asked. 'For all we know, it's a crock of shit.'

Moloch turned around. 'Follow the clues,' he said. 'That's all I'm asking. If it turns out you get to the last clue and there's no treasure, you will get paid anyway. I can't be fairer than that.'

'You keep mentioning the word "clues",' Bullion said. 'Can I ask more about that? Are we talking written instructions, riddles, that kind of thing?'

'You've been reading too many books,' Moloch said. 'The clues are in the form of the written word like a scroll and a map, and they're hidden in Satanic relics. We're talking the Crown of Beelzebub, the one true inverted cross, the altar of the Day Star, and many more.'

The mercenaries looked pleased. They all nodded. Bullion rose to his feet and held out his hand. 'How about that first clue?' he said.

Chapter 5

First, Sally ran straight up to her father's main study, the conversation with Jonathan Jacobs buzzing through her mind. It seemed impossible in this day and age to hear of an active cabal of dangerous Satanists, but she knew they existed. They were powerful, and, like many religious sects, they thought they had a right to rule the world.

She burst into her father's study, took a long look around the room. It was messy; the walls lined with overfull bookcases, the sturdy wooden desk awash with paper. She had already been sorting through it and knew there was nothing relating to Jacobs or a cabal – on the surface, at least.

Now she had to dig deeper.

She sifted through the papers, trying to find a neat sheaf or a folder, anything that might point towards the cabal. Behind her, Mason and Roxy walked into the room. Quaid and Hassell hovered at the door.

'Can we help?' Mason asked.

Sally looked from the solid dark oak bookcases to the long, low table in the room's far corner to the leather-topped desk.

'Have at it,' she said. 'You heard what Jacobs said. My father has been investigating a Satanic cult that apparently murders people. That wants to take its influence to the next level. That might even murder its own members if they decide to leave. This is one evil cult, and we don't know who we can trust.'

The team split up, searching the room. It went quicker with five of them, and Sally was soon sighing and biting her bottom lip.

'Nothing,' she said.

'He wouldn't leave something like that on full display,' Quaid said.

Sally looked at him. 'Of course. The safe.'

Mason shook his head. 'The safe?'

'My father has another study upstairs. It contains a safe.'

Hassell smiled. 'I'll go get my tools.' He paused. 'Unless you know the code?'

'Go get your tools.'

It wasn't a fancy safe, just a steel box painted white with a key lock. Sally did not know where her father had secreted the key, so Hassell got to work. Whilst working for the criminal called Gido, he had become an infiltration expert and knew how to accomplish anything, from picking locks to entering buildings.

Mason handed Sally a mug of hot coffee, something to keep her going. She took it, sipped it, still reeling over the revelation that her father had been investigating a deadly cabal for a friend. Yes, that friend was in danger, but still . . . her *father*? Of course, she knew from long association that it was the investigative side of things that he loved. Maybe that explained it a little.

Cracking the safe didn't take Hassell long. Soon he sat back on his haunches and opened the door. Then he looked up at Sally.

'All yours.'

Sally crouched down and looked inside, angling her phone torch to see better. The safe was half-full of papers and she could see the bound edge of a large book in there, too.

Reaching in, she pulled the whole pile out.

A squall of rain spattered the windows of the study like a salvo of bullets, making them jump. It was late now. A fervent wind gusted outside, howling around the brick walls and blasting through the eaves.

Mason made a fire in the room, and soon the hearth was crackling, flames leaping. Quaid made space on the table and Sally dumped the whole pile of paper onto it. Next, she turned her attention to the book.

It was bound in black leather, dusty and untitled. A gold band ran down the centre. Everyone pulled up chairs and sat around the table.

'You think that's the Book of Baphomet?' Roxy asked.

'One way to find out,' Sally breathed, and opened it.

The first page struck her in the face. It was off-colour, more cream than white, and bore the very title she had expected.

The Book of Baphomet.

2/3

So this was the second copy, she thought. The medieval Satanists had made three copies in total. It wasn't a thick tome, but it was larger than a regular hardback and felt heavy when she hefted it. It occurred to her that the heaviness could be because of the deep and terrible matter that it contained, but she decided that thought was a little too deep and cast it away.

Another squall of rain struck the windows, startling her. She looked up. 'We don't have time to read this thing properly,' she said. 'Or, to be honest, the inclination. But we do need to know about the Hellfire.'

Mason was skimming through a pile of papers and notebooks. 'There's a lot of research here,' he said. 'On various people. Most with question marks after their name. We'll google them later, but my guess is most of these will be prominent people, or people with means.'

'Your father was just scratching the surface,' Quaid said, also searching.

'He hadn't been at it long,' Sally said in unconscious defence of her father.

She turned the pages of the book. 'It's written in Middle and eighteenth-century English,' she said. 'I've come across it before. First there's a recipe for turning a normal drink into one that one would consume at a Black Mass. It starts, *"Take the rootes of fennel, a reasonable quantitie, steep them in white wine. Let them lay a night and distil them into water and add your blood . . . "* It just gets worse from there.' She turned another page. 'More recipes. Some of mixing blood, some on making the host out of . . . well, we'll skip that. It appears to be a hash of instructions.' She flicked through the pages, searching for Hellfire.

The book flicked off plumes of dust as she worked. The others all perused the various papers and notebooks.

'Did Jacobs say the leader of this cabal is called Moloch?' Mason said suddenly. 'Your father has a lot of information on the man. Owns an estate outside London. Family money. Keeps himself to himself. Doesn't appear to run any businesses. Has the means to do everything that Jacobs is suggesting.'

Sally turned page after page, her eyes scanning the text as quickly as she could. When she came across drawings, she couldn't help but take them in, shuddering inside. Invariably, they depicted Satan ministering over his minions, committing heinous acts and being royally worshipped. There was lots of blood and entrails and other grinning demons around, and Satanic artefacts such as thrones and inverted crosses and swords. She tried to ignore the drawings, but knew at least some of them would stay with her for the rest of her life.

'Any luck?' Mason asked after a while.

She shook her head. 'Going as fast as I can. This stuff is hideous.'

The night spun by, punctuated by the rain and the furious wind. The fires in the hearth blew this way and that, and the coals popped like firecrackers. They all drank tea or coffee and shared a plate of sandwiches. There would be no sleep tonight.

Hellfire.

The word popped out of the page at Sally. It sat in the middle of several long paragraphs and was repeated several times. Quickly, she scanned the text.

'I have it,' she said. '"*We hid the Hellfire beyond all sighte of human man. Only ye daemons know its resting place and they will say nawiht.*" Wait, let me go through this first so that I can recite more clearly.'

She flicked through the old text, nodding, taking it all in before looking up again. 'Basically,' she said, 'it describes the vast treasure, explains the state of mind of the Satanists at the time – that they were fearful of losing it and the castle. Those were their reasons for hiding it. It explains that a series of ancient Satanic relics holds various clues to the whereabouts of the treasure. It is a hunt, a quest. A strange one at best. Each relic has a piece of a map that, when fixed together, points to the resting place of the treasure. It also has a scroll, a set of instructions, that leads to the next clue.'

'And if Moloch gets it, we're doomed,' Quaid said.

'The world will be a poorer place,' Sally corrected him. 'And many more people will die. We can't let that happen.'

'And we can't go to the authorities,' Mason said. 'Because we don't know who we can trust.'

29

'Perhaps some of my own contacts could help,' Quaid mused. The ex-British army officer had amassed a wealth of contacts during both his army days and later, when he'd helped distribute much-needed goods to the poorer parts of the world, which was how the team had found him in Bethlehem.

'Maybe later, if we're forced to. For now, can you be sure one of them isn't involved?' Mason asked. 'Absolutely sure?'

Quaid pursed his lips, thought about it and then said, 'Of course not.'

'Then it's up to us to help Jacobs and find the Hellfire before Moloch does,' Mason said and sat back in his chair, looking around. 'Agreed?'

At the table, everyone nodded.

Chapter 6

Inside, Sally felt as if she was being tugged from pillar to post. It wasn't all that long ago that she had rebelled and left her father behind, moved on to other things that involved helping those who lived on the street. She had felt fulfilled during those days, not happy but content. As the years passed, though, she started to feel a yearning for the old family values. She hated the wealth, the ostentatiousness, the hangers-on who greased around you because they thought they might get a piece of it. She hated that most people thought she'd been born with a silver spoon in her mouth. That wasn't Sally. It wasn't what she wanted.

Sally had reconciled with her father, and agreed to work with him again because she enjoyed the job. She worked for a renowned professor, above all else, and that was all that mattered. She didn't need to think about the other side – the wealth. Sally could lose herself in her job. And that was what she did.

Until they visited the Vatican in Rome.

After that, it all came crashing down for a while. Her father was murdered in front of her eyes and she had met Joe and Roxy and . . . well, that adventure was history. Sally had always despised most of her father's friends. They were shallow and showy and snobbish. But here she was, agreeing to help one of them and potentially risking her own life and her friends'.

Was it what she wanted?

It was damn complicated, she thought. That's what it was.

She continued flicking through the book, hiding her feelings from the rest of the team. They all seemed ready to head out at a moment's notice, ready to hit the road in search of the Hellfire. Not her. Not yet.

She had to talk to Jacobs again.

Sally checked the time: past two a.m. If he was asleep, she would wake him and hope that he slept alone.

She jabbed in the number and waited. After four rings, a hoarse voice came over the line.

'Yes?'

'Jonathan, it's Sally.'

'You shouldn't be ringing me. It's too dangerous for me. Wait for me to call you.'

'In the future, I will. Do you have any more information?'

There was the sound of rustling and a deep sigh as Jacobs sat up in bed. He took a drink of something and then said, 'You know it's almost three?'

'We've been working on this thing all night. Trying to decide what to do. Now, do you have anything else for me regarding this artefact Moloch needs?'

'I'm sorry, I don't. I do know that it's an imperative part of the puzzle. I also know Moloch went out last night because I heard him go and waited until he got back so that he'd talk to me about it. I didn't mention it earlier, because he only explained when he got back. The man has recruited himself a team.'

'Already?'

'You remember I told you he was actively trying to recruit a team to search for the Hellfire? Well, he's got it.'

'That was quick.' Sally had thought they'd have more time.

'Seven of them. Five men, two women. All ex-military. Mercenaries, I guess. They've been tasked with finding the Hellfire.'

'Any idea who we're up against?' Quaid said, no doubt thinking he could use his army contacts to read up on them.

'No names. Moloch's too guarded for that, too clever.'

'But he doesn't know you're working against him,' Mason pointed out.

'I'm still alive, aren't I? Look, these guys are planning to hunt down the relics, get the maps and piece them together. Are you?'

Sally nodded to herself. 'We are,' she said, finally deciding. Despite her misgivings, it was the best and only course of action. The right thing to do.

'Do not ring me anymore. Let me call you.'

'Well, it's not like I imagined you'd be sleeping alongside Moloch,' she said with a touch of exasperation.

'Nevertheless. Sometimes his rituals go on long into the night. In any case, it's not worth the risk. You know he's talking about holding a very special Black Mass when he acquires the Hellfire. A terrible ritual.'

Sally nodded. 'In what way is it special?'

'Bigger. Deadlier. More terrible than anything he's ever done. Everyone involved. Something that will include new incantations and harsher justice. That's his word, not mine. When he murders a person, he sees it as justice.'

'Why?'

'Because he's a mad fucker,' Roxy said.

'The Satanist in him sees everyone who doesn't worship the devil as an agnostic. And an agnostic, I'm afraid, is an enemy. Someone to be reviled, to be . . . killed, if possible. By their disbelief, they are refuting the devil and all his trappings. Moloch and many others around the world see their deaths as glorious.'

'Like I said,' Roxy murmured. 'A mad fucker.'

Sally agreed, but she still had another question for Jacobs. 'And what camp do you fall in?' she asked.

'Me? Oh, Sally, I've never been a staunch believer. I fell into it, as I explained. And once you're in, you can't get out, as I've also mentioned. He has as much video evidence on me as anyone. I think those who worship the devil are the true manifestations of evil in our world.'

Sally was glad to hear it. She ended the call and looked around the table. She tapped on the page of the book.

'I've got something very interesting to show you,' she said.

Chapter 7

Joe Mason sipped hot coffee and waited. It had been a long day, and it was far from over yet. Never could he have imagined on waking the previous morning that he'd be discussing Satanists after midnight into the next day. The team had finished one job only to fall straight into another.

Mason listened as Sally continued.

'The Book of Baphomet not only gives a background for the medieval Satanists, the story of the Duke of Adlington, and other material – it also gives us the first clue. That's where we get started.'

'Do you think we could get some sleep first?' Roxy yawned.

Mason tended to agree. They'd be no good running on empty. 'Maybe we could reconvene in the morning,' he said. 'Find out where we need to go and then get at it.'

The team agreed to a break and drifted off to their rooms, leaving Sally alone in the study, the area illuminated by a single Tiffany lamp. Mason took a last look at her before leaving the room.

'Get some sleep,' he said. 'There's too much information to take in here and now.'

'This is my father's work,' she breathed. 'He got a lot done in a short period. I have to continue it now. For him.'

'You think he'd have wanted that? Considering the danger? Might this mission put you in too much danger?'

'As Jacobs' goddaughter? I don't think so. . . Yes, it's dangerous, but that wouldn't have bothered my father personally. He was helping a friend out.'

Mason nodded and left her to it. What she did with the rest of her night was up to her. He wandered downstairs, fixed himself a vodka and topped it up with cola. He took the drink to his room and climbed into bed. He couldn't stop thinking.

All this talk made him focus on the change in his life since they started chasing the Vatican Book of Secrets. Before that, he had been working for a private security firm, taking on jobs that he wasn't happy with, but working for a woman who knew of his harsh past and respected that he brought with him a plethora of demons. He'd been trying to overcome that past, moving on, moving forward. But it was only when Mason had met Roxy, and then the others, and they had embarked on their own missions, that he had started exorcising those demons. He still wasn't there, not by a long shot, but he could feel the healing inside, feel it starting to take hold.

He sipped the drink, felt a familiar numbness that he used to look forward to. Not anymore, though. He didn't need it anymore. Tonight's drink was purely recreational.

He lay down, closed his eyes. Months before . . . this would have been the time he dreaded, the time when the old memories of what had happened in Mosul caught him in their unbreakable claws. They would churn and they would twist in his gut and cause his mind to reel.

Mason fell asleep in just a few minutes.

* * *

36

He woke early, showered, and went down to breakfast. The team appeared, one by one, all looking bleary-eyed and tired. Most were in their dressing gowns. Sally, when she entered the kitchen, wore the same clothes as the night before.

'Get any sleep?' Mason asked.

'I got some shut-eye at the desk,' she said.

Mason saw the tiredness in her eyes and handed her coffee. Soon, the entire team was seated at the table and eating breakfast.

'Right,' Sally said. 'We're all here. We're all rested—'

'Speak for yourself,' Roxy muttered.

'Shall we continue?' Sally went on. 'We have a big day ahead of us.'

Mason waved his spoon at her. 'What do you have in mind?'

'The Book of Baphomet holds the first clue, as I said. Do you want to hear it?'

Everyone leaned forward expectantly.

Sally spoke clearly. *Part of the old display at Holyrood, the item that doesn't quite fit in the throne room.*

Mason frowned. 'It's vague. How would we know if an item doesn't fit?'

'I thought the same,' Sally said. 'But then I thought we should look at this from the point of view of the people who wrote it.'

'Satanists,' Quaid said.

'Exactly. Clearly they've tampered with something at Holyrood. And though the current displays in the throne room date back to the twentieth century, they repurposed their exhibitions time and time again. Whatever is in there would have been used previously.'

'What is Holyrood?' Roxy asked.

'Well, it's called Holyrood House, or Palace, occasionally Castle. It was originally a monastery in 1128, so it has an excellent history. It's closely tied with Scotland and was the home of Mary, Queen of Scots.'

'Bloody hell,' Quaid said. 'We've just come back from Scotland.'

Sally shrugged. 'These days, Holyrood serves as a royal palace but is still open to the public. It has a royal collection and regular exhibitions, which is why all its vast array of treasure is constantly repurposed. There is a description of the throne room and its exhibitions in the Book of Baphomet that will enable us to compare notes when we arrive.'

'You're taking that damn book with you?' Roxy shuddered. 'I hate it. It looks and feels all wrong.'

'It does feel a little . . . menacing,' Mason said.

'Oh, I agree. The book is a mini-demon. But we have no option. The Book of Baphomet stays with us.'

'Where exactly in Scotland are we going?' Hassell asked.

'It's just outside Edinburgh,' Sally said. 'I think we should get another train. It has to be the fastest way.'

Their last mission to Edinburgh had involved arriving on a train at Waverley station and had turned out rather well.

'A train it is.' Hassell took out his phone and booked the tickets.

The team finished breakfast and then started to get ready. Sally drifted off upstairs and came down a quick twenty minutes later, showered and dressed. They packed rucksacks with essential gear and then stared at each other, all of them thinking through a thorny problem.

'Do we take our weapons?' Quaid voiced it.

'It's not an official job,' Sally said. 'We don't have a client as such.'

'She's right. If we end up having to use them, we've no comeback. No one to officially back us up,' Mason said.

'And yet there's a seven-person mercenary team out there searching for the same thing,' Roxy protested. 'It makes sense to take the guns.'

'We have permits.' Sally was clearly on the fence with this one.

'It's loose,' Mason said. 'The fact is, we're not on an official job.'

'We take them,' Roxy said. 'Better to have them than not. I'm not going up against a bunch of enemies unarmed.'

The consensus was that the weapons should go with them. Mason was dubious, but gave in to the others. Sometimes you go with the flow, and this was a team, not a dictatorship. They took a few minutes to unpack their Glocks and store extra magazines, checking and cleaning the weapons before putting them away. He looked around the kitchen and realised that the team was ready to go.

'Last question,' he said, addressing Sally. 'Since you stayed up all night researching, do you have any idea how we're gonna find this map and clues? I mean, a physical location for them.'

Sally smiled. 'None at all. My guess is there's a secret compartment somewhere. But we'll have to see.'

Mason followed Quaid out the door. The team piled into their car and got settled for their long journey north, which would start at the railway station. The prospect of going up against Satanists wasn't a pleasant one, but this Moloch clearly had to be stopped before he killed anyone else or extended the reach of his cabal exponentially, and they had to save Jacobs' life. They had taken the man at face value, but none of them believed someone Sally knew so well and who clearly had feelings for his goddaughter, and who Sally's father had been helping, would be untruthful with them.

They drove away in the early morning light, rushing from a haven of safety towards a world of potential violence and angst and fear. It was what they did. Through the hell of the last half year, they had become a tight-knit team that took on any problem, put their lives on the line for the greater good.

Mason thought this as they drove into a spectacular sunrise, the darkness at their backs.

Chapter 8

Sally explained a little to them as they approached Scotland by train. 'Holyrood Palace was built in the twelfth century. It's now a modern house with central heating, electric lighting and renovated kitchens. King Charles III spends one week there each summer, known as the Royal Week. It stages investitures, banquets, dinner and garden parties and is open to the public. It's a three-storey-plus attic classical-style quadrangle layout, with towers to north-and south-west, turrets, and Doric columns, and bears the carved Royal Arms of Scotland.'

They arrived at Holyrood at around 3.30 p.m., having coasted into Waverley on the hour. They approached the grand house amid bright sunlight and drizzle, bending their heads into the rain. They found out there were seventeen rooms open to the public, but, of course, they were only interested in one. So, ignoring the state apartments with their Baroque ceilings and Italian paintings, and the Great Gallery, the largest room in the palace, they made their way directly to the throne room. They were in a hurry, didn't have time to waste. All they had were the packs on their backs, the guns at their waistbands.

The palace was busy. Droves of tourists filled all the open spaces, flitting this way and that. Conversation drifted from wall to wall, most of it respectfully low. There were couples and families with small children, men and women, young and old, a vast cross-section of people. The team tried to thread their way through the throng.

'Gonna be hard to spot an enemy in here,' Roxy said under her breath, looking from face to face. 'But if that new team's involved now, they could be anywhere.'

Mason just managed to catch her words above the hubbub. 'Keep your eyes peeled. It's likely they're here.'

'Or they've already been and gone.' Quaid shrugged. 'Who knows?'

Mason said nothing as they walked along a wide gallery with black carpeting toward the throne room. There were numerous paintings on the walls, statues to the left and to the right, and though there were many people standing around them, he saw nothing untoward, and carried on walking with a single-minded intention. The others spread out and followed, watching their backs.

Mason kept a careful eye out for guards and staff, seeing only a few, which was good. There were guides showing groups around, but palace employees were scarce. It didn't surprise him. Budgets were always being tightened.

'Throne room dead ahead,' said Quaid, pointing to a sign.

Mason walked as fast as he dared, not wanting to draw attention to himself. He reached the throne room and stopped before it, letting the others gather around, pretending to study an old Italian master that hung on the wall just outside.

'We ready?' he asked.

Sally nodded most eagerly.

They entered the throne room one by one, stepping carefully. There was a bright red carpet, a carved white ceiling, a chandelier, padded seats, and paintings on the panelled walls. The throne room was used for receptions and state occasions. The chief feature of the room, standing at the far end, was a pair of thrones commissioned by King George V in 1911.

Sally didn't need to consult the book. She already knew by heart what it said about Holyrood. 'The thrones and the paintings,' she said. 'They've been in situ for decades. That's what we need to concentrate on.'

The team split up. They moved about the room, scanning the walls and heading towards the two thrones. They squeezed around people, moved past them, and tried to get closer. Mason stared at the nearest painting without knowing what he was looking for.

Part of the old display at Holyrood, the item that doesn't quite fit in the throne room.

He leaned in, studying the picture of a man in a kilt. At first, he concentrated on the painting's golden frame, wondering if it might contain a special carving, but the antique-style frame was uniform all the way around. Next, he focused on the man and then the background. Was there a bloody Satanic church standing there, he wondered, an inverted cross almost impossible to see? Anything that didn't fit in?

Mason saw nothing. He moved on, now staring at a painting of a lone man that hung above a golden antique clock. He took a moment to scan the room. Nothing stood out . . . not even the tourists. They wandered back and forth, a constant stream entering and exiting the room. Could their enemies be close? Maybe.

Where next?

He studied the painting. The background was pretty simple, a Doric column and a wall, a patch of sky. He concentrated on the man's clothes, wondered if something might have been added to the sleeves or the trousers.

Nothing stood out. Was Mason even doing this right?

He wondered about the two thrones. Perhaps there was a carving . . . maybe even on the backside. That would make it incredibly hard to locate in a room full of people. But they'd deal with that problem if it jumped out at them.

He went back to the painting, guessed there was nothing to find, and moved on. The others were doing the same, covering the room between them.

Sally, in her usual manner, was rechecking everything the others had already checked. Nobody minded. It was what she did, and how she worked, and Sally was very good at her job.

Another few minutes passed, and he stopped in front of one of the red velvet-topped seats. He bent down, examined it carefully. Nobody stared at him, taking him for just another interested tourist. The legs were ornate and curved and smooth gold. There were no carvings, no marks, nothing. Mason straightened up again.

As he did so, Roxy passed close by. 'I'm not feeling this,' she said.

'If only we knew what we were looking for,' Mason said.

'The Book of Baphomet seemed pretty sure about it,' Roxy said.

Mason nodded. 'There will be something,' he said.

'How do we know someone hasn't removed it?'

'Because Sally knows what's been moved and what hasn't,' he said. 'She already told us what to look for. Keep looking.'

They went back to it. Minutes passed, long minutes when they all examined the paintings and edged closer to the thrones. Mason now studied a painting of a woman with long, curling black hair, wearing a white frock, standing in front of a wide vista. She might have been on a rolling hill or a grassy bank. He couldn't tell because the painting cut her off at the waist. It was a dark, blustery day, it seemed. There

44

were flowing dark clouds above her head and darkness among the trees at her back. She was holding onto a white hat that had slipped slightly from her head. There was a bright smile on her face.

Mason peered closer. Was he seeing things?

Something seemed off with the painting, but at first he couldn't quite pin it down. It was nothing more than a feeling. He squinted, wishing the painting wasn't in a darker corner of the room.

He looked up at it, staring hard, wondering if he'd found something.

Minutes later, Roxy joined him. She, too, glared at the painting.

'You thinking what I'm thinking?' he asked.

'I hope not. I was thinking how cute that guy with the tight pants looks over there.'

Mason rolled his eyes at her. 'Focus,' he said. 'Something here feels off.'

Roxy focused her full attention on the picture. She shook her head. 'It's a little dark,' she said. 'Apart from that . . . '

Mason stepped away, looked at the entrance and exit doors for a while just to grab a different perspective. Then he turned back to the painting.

He saw it almost immediately.

'There,' he said. 'Look.'

Roxy stared at him, then at the painting. To Mason, it was now clear. The darkness in the sky, the blackness between the trees. It wasn't random, but formed a very subtle pattern – a shape behind the woman. Two long curved horns. It only became apparent when you squinted at the painting or studied it as long and hard as Mason had. But the shape was unmistakable.

'Crap,' he said.

He traced the pattern in the air so that Roxy could see. Right then, Sally came up to them.

'How are you doing?'

'This could be it,' Mason said. 'Do you see what I see?'

He didn't want to point it out to her. He wanted her to spot the anomaly for herself. The more he looked at it, the more obvious it was. And now, as he stared at it, he couldn't believe nobody else saw it.

Sally peered hard, leaning forward, the blue tips of her hair hanging low. She had her hands clasped behind her back. All three of them were so close Mason could smell a mix of perfume and body spray, of recently washed hair. He waited patiently, hoping that she would see what he did.

And finally, she leaned back.

'Horns,' she said.

Chapter 9

'I see it now,' Roxy said. 'Damn, that's spooky as hell.'

Mason took it all in from further back now, letting tourists walk between him and the painting. It was so clear when you knew what to look for. The horns rested in the air above the head of the smiling woman, misty and black and dangerous-looking. It totally transformed the painting, adding a heavy air of menace and jeopardy. It almost felt as if the woman was being watched over by the Devil himself.

One by one, they got the others over, asked them to look, and one by one, they all agreed. This was the anomaly, the one thing that didn't quite fit. In a way, it could be viewed as a Satanic relic too, a brilliant one because it had existed here for years and had remained in place, unmolested, even unnoticed. He wondered how many Satanists had visited over the years, to gloat.

'What do we do now?' Quaid asked.

'We do what we've done many times before,' Sally told him. 'We create a shield and search the object.'

Mason viewed the room. It was still busy, which was both a blessing and a curse. The busyness would help shield their actions, but it also added many more eyes to the mix. Still, there was no way around it.

'No guards, no staff,' he whispered. 'And no mercenaries so far. We're golden to go now.'

The team stood in front of the painting, and Sally, as she stepped forward. Mason had spied only one CCTV camera, and that was out in the hallway, above the door, so they should be fine in that respect.

Sally got started as Mason watched. She started by testing the frame, her fingers brushing and curling around it. She was careful not to move the frame for fear of setting off any alarms. She ran her fingers up and down, searching for anything that might feel out of place. She worked from left to right, moving from the top of the frame to the bottom.

And then she stood back.

'Take a break,' she said.

They didn't want to stand in front of the painting for too long, figuring that might attract attention. They moved back, let other people take a gander at it. So far, their search had gone unnoticed. Mason was highly conscious that there might be another team close by, his heart beating rapidly.

'I saw someone suspect a few minutes ago,' Roxy whispered to Mason. 'I don't like the feel of this.'

'Stay on it,' Mason told her. 'Keep it quiet for now.'

They moved back in, creating another shield around Sally. This time, she went further, brushing her fingers across the glass that protected it, peering around the back. She still didn't move it for fear of setting off an alarm, but she did everything but.

'How we doing?' Quaid asked anxiously.

'I've found nothing.'

'It has to be in the frame,' Hassell said, who knew something about hiding things because of his old profession. 'Can you find a place where it's—'

'Chunkier,' Sally said suddenly. 'Yes, I can.'

She stepped back, then leaned in again. Mason counted the seconds that they held the protective shield. Again, they couldn't hold it for too long. Roxy was watching the exit and entrance doors, looking out for staff and guards and mercenaries, but, so far, she'd seen nothing problematic.

'Hurry,' he said.

Sally reached out, curled her fingers around the right-hand side of the frame near the bottom and placed them in the depressions of the moulded frame. She pressed and stroked and flicked her fingers around.

'Move,' Roxy suddenly said.

They parted. Sally stepped away quickly from the painting. Mason turned to see a guard enter the room and start sauntering past. He didn't look at them, didn't suspect them of anything, but his eyes searched the walls and faces as he went by.

'It's nothing,' Mason said. 'Just a random patrol.'

The guard lingered near the exit door for a while, just watching and getting a feel for the room. Then, he turned around and was gone. Just as Sally was preparing to turn her attention back to the painting, a staff member entered the throne room and started answering visitors' questions. Minutes passed. The team abandoned the painting for a while and turned to other items in the exhibition, sauntering around the room. They split up, left by the exit door, and then returned.

Finally, the staff member drifted out of the room and entered the next.

Now they came together again and took up their original positions. Roxy watched the doors. Sally went straight for the frame of the painting.

Again, she curled her fingers around it, searching. Mason, listening hard, heard nothing above the general chatter, but he saw her face change.

And he saw a wedge of frame slide out, a piece that measured about eight inches by three.

Sally stared at it, shocked. 'Oh, my,' she said. 'It's real,' as if she couldn't quite believe her eyes.

'Take it,' Mason said.

But Sally had other ideas. She quickly felt inside the chunk, found that it was hollow, and pulled out two pieces of paper. One was a yellowed scroll, the other a ripped sheet. She felt around a little more, found nothing, and pushed the wedge of frame back where it belonged.

She stepped away from the painting. The thing presided over them in all its dark glory, a threatening vision of darkness and evil, but only if you looked at it the right way. Mason couldn't look at it any other way now. It was like one of those optical illusion pictures showing a face within a face, a wicked trickery.

They withdrew from the corner and left the room, walking over to a row of windows where there was more natural light. Sally had the scroll and the piece of torn paper in her hand. She unhooked her backpack, put them in a small leather box to keep safe, and then put the pack back over her shoulders.

'Ready,' she said.

'We're not gonna look at it?' Quaid asked.

'I think we should leave this place as quickly as possible,' Sally said.

Mason guessed she was probably right. There was no telling if a member of the public had spotted and reported them. No telling if security was already on its way. And no knowing where Moloch's mercenaries were.

They fell in and started walking away from the throne room. Mason was quite pleased with the way things had gone. They'd found what they'd come to find and had encountered no resistance along the way. A successful mission. He wondered what was in the scroll, what the torn scrap of paper meant.

They walked along a hallway, a row of windows to their left against which a shower of rain pattered. Long rivulets ran down the glass, obscuring the view of the gardens outside. They moved with a purpose now, eager to get to a place where they could inspect their prize. It was as they walked along this passage that Mason saw the three men following them.

He turned to Roxy. 'Six o'clock,' he said. 'You see them?'

She turned casually around, looked back at him. 'They were in the throne room with a few others. I saw them watching us, but then they turned away. I didn't think—'

Or had she been thinking about something else, Mason wondered. He knew that Roxy sometimes got so involved in her own self-analysis that she could miss something. It had happened once before and it was why she'd initially been presented to him by his boss as a loose cannon.

'You didn't think?' he asked. 'What exactly were you thinking?'

Roxy's eyes were wide. 'A lot of introspection,' she said. 'I've done it again, haven't I?'

'Maybe,' Mason knew he couldn't blame her. Roxy was as fallible as anyone else, just as he was. They all fought their own demons, wrestled with them every minute of the day. A mistake was a normal thing to make.

Instead, he concentrated on the three men following them.

'You say there were more initially?'

'Yeah, I saw a group of seven come in, saw them look over at us and then disperse. If they're the mercenaries, then they're good. They must have left the rest of their crew back searching the painting and sent these guys to keep us in sight.'

'Also, they must have known what to look for,' Mason said. 'If they are working for Moloch, then he must have vast resources.'

'Well, he is a Satanist,' Roxy said. 'He must have a tonne of books, charts, scrolls, papers. You name it. And if these old Satanists wrote the Book of Baphomet, you can be damn sure they wrote something else.'

Mason kept a guarded eye on the men following them. They were tall and broad and walked with a purposeful gait. Their faces were severe, and they didn't look at any of the items on the walls, the statues, the display cases to the right. Mason didn't catch their eyes, didn't want them to know they'd been seen, but moved forward briskly so that he was among his team.

'We have company,' he said. 'The mercs. And I think they know that we've got the . . . prize.'

Sally turned, and Mason impeded her gaze. 'Don't look,' he said.

'What the hell do we do now?' she said.

'Whatever we have to do to get out of this alive,' Mason said.

Chapter 10

Mason stayed at the heart of his team, guiding them towards the exit of Holyrood House. Using mirrors and display cabinets, he monitored their followers. The three men stayed at the same distance, not watching them outright but flicking their eyes towards them time and time again. For now, they didn't try to close the gap.

As he watched, Mason saw one man put a finger to his ear, saw his lips move. Clearly, they were using some kind of comms system and were staying in touch with those in the throne room. A door was coming up. Mason and his team pushed through it, closely followed by the three mercs.

They would be at the exit very soon. The merc with the finger to his ear was still talking. Mason saw his reflection in various glass cabinets. Roxy had drifted to the left, Quaid to the right, and Sally was leading the way. Hassell remained a step ahead of Mason, ready for anything.

There was a commotion from way back down the other passage. Mason saw it through the doors they'd just pushed through as other people opened them. He turned, staring just like everyone else. It appeared that the other four mercs were rushing to join their colleagues.

Not good.

'I think we've definitely been rumbled,' he said. 'They know we have the items.'

'There's nothing they can do here,' Sally said.

Mason wasn't too sure about that. These were mercenaries they were dealing with, men and women who didn't play by the rules.

'They'll try anything,' Roxy said. 'Watch your six.'

They walked on, increasing their pace. The entrance hall was ahead, awash with tourists. Sally left the plush carpeting and walked onto a polished floor and started making her way through the throng, moving as efficiently as she could. The mercs, all seven of them now, followed at a distance of maybe twelve feet, one of them talking into a mobile phone.

Mason readied himself. There was no way they were going to get out of this without a fight. He positioned his right hand near his gun, not really expecting to use it in this crowded place, but highly unsure of what was about to happen.

Sally whipped out her phone and called for an Uber to meet them outside. Arrival time, eight minutes.

Tension thickened the surrounding air. Mason's expression was grim. He waited for something to happen. They headed for the front doors. It was edgy, taut and nerve-wracking as they crossed the lobby and pushed outside into the drizzle-laden day.

A bracing wind struck them, making them shiver. The parking area was just ahead, where they could wait for their taxi. Were they going to get out of this without an encounter? Mason doubted it, but they were getting closer and closer to a getaway.

Moments, stretched thin and taut, passed as if they were stepping through molasses. Outside, with the drizzle, there were very few people milling around. Mason got a clearer picture of what the mercs were up to.

They didn't want to cause a scene. As he'd expected, they were concerned about not drawing attention to themselves.

They approached the parking area where the Uber would collect them. Here, there were even fewer people, just a few parties hunched over, pulling their jackets over their heads or raising umbrellas for the short walk to the building.

Mason slowed.

'Stop,' came the voice he had been expecting.

He turned. They were standing along a wide row of cars, with vehicles on either side. There was no sign of their car yet, but then only a few minutes had passed since they'd booked it. The man facing him had short-cropped hair and striking blue eyes. He was well-built and stood with a calm manner, confident. Curiously, around his neck glinted a gold crucifix, a sight that made Mason's brow furrow, considering who this man worked for.

Quickly, he assessed the situation. Two women and five men faced them, every one looking capable.

'Can I help you?' Sally asked.

Roxy and Hassell were standing to Mason's left, ready to act. Quaid stood to his right. Sally was a step behind, looking over his shoulder.

'Bullion. Ed Bullion,' the man said with a forced smile. 'Just hand over whatever you took from the house and you can go.'

'What are you? Security?' Quaid asked.

'Something like that.'

'We'll take our chances,' Mason said.

'This doesn't have to turn nasty,' Bullion said, then frowned. 'Who the hell are you guys, anyway? What do you know?'

'We're the A-team,' Roxy said.

Mason spread his arms. 'We're nobody important. You guys need to walk away.'

Bullion's mouth stretched into an easy smile. 'We do? I've asked you very nicely for the piece you stole. I'd advise you to hand it over.'

'Our ride will be here soon,' Sally said. 'You should stand aside.'

There was a moment of stretched silence and tension, a loaded few seconds where nobody moved. Mason could feel his heart beating double time. It was Quaid who broke the moment by inching aside his jacket so that Bullion could see the butt of his gun.

'Walk away,' he said.

Bullion didn't react. If anything, the eyes went cooler; the face hardened ever so slightly. 'A deterrent only,' he said. 'No way you're gonna use that here against unarmed men and women. They'd throw away the key.'

'I'm authorised to use it—' Quaid began, but then everything went crazy. Bullion had clearly had enough. He struck out like a snake, surprising Mason with his speed. The blow landed on Mason's left temple, knocking him to the side. He staggered, put a hand on the car beside him for balance. Bullion stepped towards him.

'Last chance,' he said.

But they didn't even have that. Bullion's team, taking the blow as a sign, were attacking now. They swept by Bullion, down the lane between parked cars, and leapt at the team. Roxy was first in their way and started lashing out, catching a man in the stomach and a woman across the forehead.

Mason struck out at Bullion. The other man covered up, moving backwards. Mason redoubled his attack, using Bullion as a punchbag, coming in from left and right with hard punches. Bullion backed up for a few feet and then stood his ground, taking the punches, warding them off, and then coming back at Mason. He stepped in, grabbed Mason by the arms, tried to hurl him off his feet.

Along the aisle, Hassell and Quaid fought hand to hand with more mercs. They spun and staggered and thrust them away. Hard punches were thrown. The air was full of grunting and tension and painful gasps. It was all close-quarter work. Time and time again they came up against the hard metal of the cars, bouncing off.

Roxy grabbed her opponent by the jacket, swung and hurled him against the nearest car. There was a loud thud as he struck and then bounced off. Roxy still had hold of him. She spun again, effecting the same manoeuvre. This time the guy's spine struck the car, making him cry out sharply. He slithered to the ground. Roxy turned to see a merc striking at Sally, bringing her to her knees. Roxy leapt at the man, hooking an arm around his throat.

Mason had two hands on Bullion's jacket, as did Bullion on his. They were locked together, shoving, pushing, trying to hurl each other off their feet. Mason fell back against a car, turned swiftly and threw Bullion against it. The window shattered, loud in the sweaty, drizzly day, but there was no one around to hear. Right then though, the strident alarm went off, turning some heads. Bullion's fingers slipped away from Mason's jacket and he fell to his knees, clawing at the car.

Mason took advantage. He stepped away and kicked Bullion in the ribs. He came in to knee him in the side of the head, but Bullion dodged at the last second. Mason's knee hit the car, sending a jolt of pain through him. Glass from the broken window trickled down over Bullion's head.

Hassell and Quaid were holding their own with the mercs, but barely. They were standing back to back, the cars on either side, trying to make headway against their opponents but failing. Neither Hassell nor Quaid was a true fighter, and the mercs were well trained. They didn't rush in, didn't try to finish it quickly, but were waiting for that opening they knew would come against less experienced opponents.

Roxy choked the man who had been beating on Sally. He collapsed to the ground. She turned to see the other man she'd decked, saw him clambering to his knees, and gave him a kick to the head. He went down too. She turned to Sally.

'You okay?'

'Yeah. Let's get these bastards.'

Roxy grinned. That was her kind of talk. She ran at the men and women who were accosting Hassell and Quaid, going through them like a bowling ball, scattering them. On the way through, she landed several hard blows.

Mason took hold of Bullion, hefted him, and threw him across the front of the car. The man rolled and came down hard on the tarmac on the other side. Mason quickly followed. How far did they take this? He glanced around quickly, took in the full scene. It almost looked like a stalemate, but the mercs were better trained, he knew. At the moment, Roxy was making the difference.

Bullion struggled to his feet just as Mason reached him.

'Call your people off,' he tried. 'Let us go.'

'Give me the items you stole,' Bullion grunted.

Mason smacked him on the chin, saw him go down.

'No chance,' he said.

Bullion kicked out at his legs. Mason wasn't quite fast enough to get out of the way. The blow took his legs away, and he landed in a heap beside Bullion. An elbow struck his face, sending his head back against a car's tyre, the rubber hard against his skull. Mason saw stars.

'Give me the items,' Bullion growled.

Mason struggled upright. A fight could turn that quickly. He'd miscalculated, given his opponent a chance, and now they were at the same level. He berated himself, tried to regain the advantage. He launched himself at Bullion, leading with an elbow that rattled the man's skull and made him slump.

'Not today,' he muttered.

Standing up, he raced towards the fight.

Chapter 11

Roxy and Mason ploughed through their opponents. The mercs backed away or collapsed to their knees in the melee. Hassell and Quaid punched out too, striking skulls and chests and thighs. It was a mess, a chaos of grunting, moaning, heaving, bloodied bodies. They rebounded off cars and slithered down their bonnets, smashed windows, left dents in the wings. Sally got involved too, calling on her newly learned fighting skills, but looking way out of her depth. She got hit twice in succession and then crawled away, coughing.

Mason knocked one man down and then threw a woman on top of him. Tangled, they lay in a twisting heap. Roxy felled her opponent at that moment too, and both Hassell and Quaid stepped away from their own.

There was finally a small amount of space between them all.

At that moment, Mason spied a large black SUV pulling into the car park outside Holyrood House. That would be their Uber, he knew, an outsize vehicle to take them all. He assessed the situation. If they ran for it . . .

There were only two mercs currently standing. He leapt at one, Roxy at the other, beating them to the ground.

With a grunt, he kicked them to make sure they stayed there, at least temporarily. He received a punch to the thigh and the knee in return, and staggered slightly. He looked at Roxy.

'Go.'

Everyone heard him; they all saw the black Uber outside the building. As one, they turned to run.

Someone grabbed Mason's heel. He tripped and went sprawling, scrabbled along the tarmac and forced himself back to his feet. His hands were scraped bloody, but he kept running. Behind him, he heard men and women clambering to their feet.

'*Run!*' he cried.

As one, they raced toward the black Uber. To Mason, it felt bizarre. Running for a taxi to make a quick getaway. But they were new to this. Maybe next time they'd make sure to rent a car.

They flew through the aisles of the car park, closing the gap to the Uber. Mason could see the driver staring at them strangely, as if wondering what all the rush was about. This probably wasn't something he saw every day. As Mason ran up to the car, the driver got out.

'You guys seem awful keen,' he said in a Scottish accent.

Mason looked back. The mercs weren't chasing them. Instead, they were climbing into a silver seven-seat car, a Kia if he wasn't mistaken. Mason pursed his lips. That wasn't good.

'You're gonna have to stay here,' he told the driver. 'I can't risk your life.'

The man's mouth fell open.

'Sorry.' Mason pushed past him. Quaid ran around the other side, sliding in behind the wheel. The others yanked open doors and climbed in. The driver just stared and only when Quaid started the engine did he act.

'Hey, hey, you can't—'

'It's for your own good,' Mason said, closing his door. He couldn't risk the driver's life and didn't have time to explain that the mercs were intent on giving chase.

The driver banged on the window, shouting now.

Quaid turned the car around and started heading along the driveway that led away from the impressive house. The silver Kia was already on their tail. Quaid accelerated up the driveway, passing a car on the way in, heading for the gates. He flicked the wipers on, getting rid of the drizzle that coated the windscreen.

'Put your damn foot down,' Roxy said.

Quaid threaded the car between the gates. The Kia was right behind them. Mason turned. He could see Bullion in the passenger seat and the face of the female driver and the shapes of the others.

Quaid hit the main road and floored the accelerator. The car leaped forward, engine roaring. Mason fell back into his seat and then leaned forward again. He swivelled to look through the rear window. The Kia fell back immediately and then put on a surge, but wasn't gaining on them.

The road rolled and swooped before them, a narrow country road lined by hedges and the occasional tree. They held on as Quaid pushed it. He used both lanes, able to see that there was no traffic coming towards them, clipping the apexes and pushing the vehicle as hard as he dared. The roads were slick, and once the back wheels started slipping, making the car drift. Quaid controlled the skid and slowed down.

Still, they had put a sizeable gap between them and the Kia.

Mason cursed as they came up behind a slower-moving car. Quaid, checking ahead, was forced to slow as a vehicle came towards them. The Kia crept closer. Now, it was right on their tail. Quaid overtook the car and pulled back in, trying to create another gap between them and the Kia, but it passed with a similar manoeuvre.

'We can't do this all the way into Edinburgh,' Hassell said.

Mason agreed. Ahead, the roads were already looking more built up. The Kia was right behind them, giving no quarter. It seemed prepared to stay glued to them all the way through Edinburgh.

The road was becoming busier.

Mason knew they had to end this. He turned and said as much to Quaid. The other man shrugged in frustration. What could he do?

'If I slam on the brakes, we could all plough into the nearest wall,' he said.

Mason cursed. They *had* to get the silver Kia off their scent. He couldn't see a way to do it. Then his worried eyes met Roxy's.

'There's always a way,' she said.

She scooted over to the nearest window, climbing over Sally's lap to do so. She hit the power button for the window, letting it slide down. Then she unholstered her gun.

'Roxy,' Mason warned.

'Trust me.'

He did. She was as good as it got. Now she turned in the seat and thrust her head out of the window. A snapping gust of wind filled the car. Quaid was swivelling his head to see what was going on.

'Watch the road,' Mason said. 'The last thing we need right now is an accident.'

Roxy now leaned her top half out of the window. She brought the gun up. Instantly, the Kia dropped back, but not fast enough. Roxy showed them no mercy. She fired two shots, one at the passenger-side tyre and one at the windscreen. Both shots struck true. The Kia immediately swerved and bucked in the road, its back end coming around. It stopped suddenly, temporarily standing on two tyres, and then settled back, rocking.

The doors flew open. An angry Bullion could be seen shouting after them. Other mercs stepped out of the car. Mason couldn't see anything inside through the shattered windscreen.

Quaid slowed.

'Keep going,' Mason said. 'Don't slow yet.'

'Don't wanna get stopped by the cops,' Quaid said.

Mason nodded in agreement as Quaid slowed to the speed limit. The Kia fell back and was soon lost to sight.

'We have to ditch this thing as soon as possible,' Hassell said. 'The cops will be aware it's been stolen by now.'

Mason pointed at a street up ahead. 'Just pull over to the kerb. We're clear now. There's no need to risk anything.'

They stopped the car and climbed out. Sally found out where they were on the map in relation to Waverley and pointed them in the right direction. They hefted their backpacks and started walking. Sally soon ordered them another taxi from a different app.

Mason felt irritation that they'd had to fight their way out of Holyrood. They had got unlucky coming across the mercs right at the end there, but he'd never known an op yet to run smoothly. There was always a hiccup. He turned to Sally.

'Are the clues safe?'

She patted her backpack. 'Safe and sound.'

'We really should look at them before we leave the area,' Quaid said. 'For all we know, we could be heading right back here.'

Mason smiled at that. It was typical, practical Quaid. But they couldn't start checking out the clue sitting in the back of a taxi. They would have to wait until they reached Waverley station.

'That was . . . surreal,' Sally said.

Mason knew exactly what she meant. At first, when they entered Holyrood, he hadn't even been sure they would find anything. In the end, they'd had to fight their way out of there. And now at least they knew what they were up against, and that they could best them.

'Waverley station,' the taxi driver said, pulling up at the kerb.

Mason opened the door and climbed out, always moving forward.

Chapter 12

They found a busy restaurant in Waverley and settled down at a large round table in the corner. Mason sat with his back to the windows that looked out onto Princes Street, currently crammed with tourists and locals and workers, strolling along and minding their own business. Inside, there was a low hubbub of chatter and laughter, the clinking of pots and pans from the kitchen, the clear voices of the serving staff, the shout of one of the chefs as something went wrong, the calm movement of managers watching over everything. Mason ordered beers all around, and then they opened the menus. They were all starving.

'Feel like I haven't eaten in days,' Quaid said.

The others nodded. The drinks arrived, and they ordered their meals. Then Mason sat back and eyed Sally.

'You ready for the reveal?' she asked, with a twinkle in her eye.

Mason was happy that she, and the others, had recovered from the fight so easily. They'd taken a few good hits, Sally as much as anyone, but it didn't seem to have fazed her. He smiled now as she reached down to undo her backpack.

Mason took a long swallow of beer. The liquid felt good going down and helped soothe a few of the aches he'd earned from the fight. His head was banging. He made a point of swallowing a few painkillers and offering the packet around. Everyone took one. They were all smarting.

Sally laid the leather box on the table. All eyes turned towards it.

First, she opened the box and then took out the yellowed scroll, which was wrapped with a red ribbon. Next, she took out the thickish sheet of torn paper. Sally laid both items on the table and sat back, staring down at them.

She reached out for the scroll first.

Around them, the excited chatter of the restaurant continued unabated. People came and went, some carrying armfuls of shopping bags, others just a rucksack or nothing at all. Servers flitted from table to table. Mason thought they were anonymous enough to be safe here and knew there was no way the mercs could track them.

Sally untied the red ribbon and unfurled the scroll. It was covered with black spidery writing, some of it quite faint. Sally reached into her rucksack and came out with a magnifying glass.

Roxy stared at her. 'Really?'

'It's part of a researcher's arsenal. I wouldn't go anywhere without one.'

Sally bent over the scroll, reading to herself for a while. Eventually, she sat back, frowning. 'Well, that's concise,' she said.

'Is it the clue to the next Satanic relic?' Quaid asked.

'Yes. Basically, it's a sheet of directions. I mean, normally, we're used to a few words, maybe a line, but this . . . well. It's actually too much.'

'Why too much?' Hassell asked.

'Too much information, I mean. You can't take it all in. Like I said, it's a set of directions. It begins *White Scar Cliff, Whitby. There is a doorway half up the cliff. Enter at your peril and tread carefully. At the first junction, turn left, walk*

66

for . . . ' She paused and let out a long breath. 'And so on, and so on. It's very comprehensive.'

'Does it say what the next Satanic relic is?' Mason asked.

'Yes, it does. We're looking for the Day Star Altar.'

'That doesn't sound very Satanic.'

Sally shrugged. 'I'll have to do a little research. The fact of the matter is that we're headed to Whitby next, which is on the north Yorkshire coast of England. I think we're going to have to get a train somewhere and then hire a car.'

Hassell immediately fished his phone out and started working that out. Sally took a few photos of the scroll, then rolled it up and placed it back in the leather box. Next, she reached out for the torn piece of paper.

Mason could see already what it was.

'I guess this is the map, or part of it,' Sally said. 'It's quite detailed. See? Hills, maybe mountains. Rivers. A road or two. It could be anywhere, I guess.'

'But when pieced together, it should give us a proper location for the Hellfire,' Mason said.

'You guys,' Roxy said. 'Have you considered that if we found this clue it means Moloch hasn't? He's a clue down already. Maybe he'll give up.'

'I doubt that,' Sally said. 'It's not that difficult to piece together and follow a map with just one part missing, and there are apps available now that can scan geographical points and *tell* you exactly where a place is.'

'There are?' Quaid asked wonderingly and then shook his head. 'Kind of takes all the fun out of it.'

'But it also helps to make the whole thing easier,' Sally said.

'Can we try it with that piece?' Mason asked.

'We could, but I think we need more detail. The more detail, the better. Right now, it could throw out hundreds of results.'

Their meals arrived, hot and sizzling. Sally put the map away and stuffed the leather box back in her bag. The team tucked into their dinners, finished their beers and then looked to Hassell.

'Where are we going, bud?' Roxy asked.

'The best route I've found is from Edinburgh straight down to York. No stops. The city of York is forty-six miles from Whitby. If we hire a car in York, we can drive to Whitby in just over an hour.'

'Then we should get a move on,' Sally said.

By the time they arrived in York, it was late and they were forced to find a room for the night. They rented a car and a few rooms in a hotel on the outskirts of York, and bedded down for the night. Early the next morning they breakfasted and then resumed their journey, following the sat nav directions to Whitby.

In the front seat, Mason yawned and then turned to Sally. 'You mentioned something about this next Satanic relic. The Day Star Altar?'

Sally clutched a takeaway cup of coffee and took a sip before answering. 'It's from Isaiah 14:12. *"How you are fallen from heaven, O Day Star, son of Dawn. How you are cut down to the ground, you who have laid the nations low."* It's Satan being portrayed as the day star because he was once an angel, bold and bright and beautiful. The day star is a lesser light or, perhaps, a lesser being. Satan presents himself as a source of light, but it is all false. He is a light, yes, but he is not the greatest light, nor even close.'

'So it's an altar upon which they worshipped Satan,' Mason said dryly. 'That'll do.'

'It is far more than that. It is an abomination to God,' Sally said. 'Satan has set himself up as a bright, heavenly being, but he is nothing compared to God or Jesus.'

The car cut through the early morning, wending its way along the A64 through small villages Mason had never heard of. Halfway there, they got a call from Jonathan Jacobs.

'I have a few minutes,' he said breathlessly. 'How's it going?'

Sally launched into a description of their trip to Scotland and ended up explaining the next clue. She told him they were on their way to Whitby right now.

'That's perfect,' he said. 'Are the clues . . . umm, concise?'

'They're pretty damn good so far,' Sally told him. 'We have the first piece of the map, too.'

'Then it just might be possible to find the Hellfire,' Jacobs said.

'You sound as if you doubted us,' Mason said.

'It's not that. It's incredulity from my end. When you hear of something legendary, something mythical, and then find out it's real . . . well, it's hard to quantify. I'm trying to come to terms with the fact that the Hellfire even exists. I—' Jacobs went quiet suddenly, as if listening.

'Are you okay?' Sally asked.

Silence for a minute. Then Jacobs came back on the line. 'Paranoia,' he said. 'I thought I heard something from this end.'

'You should take care,' Quaid said. 'Your position there is . . . dangerous.'

'Oh, I know, I know. But you are making progress. That is good. Good to know. I will call you when I can.'

Jacobs ended the call. Mason saw a sign flash by, a sign that told him Whitby was twenty-one miles away. He turned once more to Sally.

'I'm guessing you know where White Scar Cliff is?'

She nodded. 'It's an obscure cliff on the seaward side of the town below the church of St Mary. It's unreachable, save for a treacherous path that runs down from the top of the cliff. We have to go up to go down.'

'But it's definitely there?' Mason, though he believed in the validity of their quest, still wasn't sure the medieval Satanists were wholly on the level. Everything about the Hellfire was based on Moloch's utter belief in them. 'At this point, I'm not entirely sure we should be taking on this mission. It's for free. The risk level is high.'

'How can we not?' Sally said. 'My father took it on. My godfather needs our help, or he might be murdered. And these Satanists . . . if they get what they desire their reach will be incalculable. And all that doesn't even take into account how bad a bastard this Moloch is.'

Mason inclined his head. Sally made a good argument and raised a point he couldn't refute. 'Do we believe everything he says?' he asked.

'What reason would he have to lie? And he convinced my father . . . ' Sally let that hang as if daring Mason to dispute it.

In the end, he just nodded. Sally's logic was clear. 'And you're sure this White Scar exists?' he repeated.

'It exists,' Sally nodded. 'But it's not gonna be an easy trek.'

At that, Roxy snorted. 'That's just another Thursday,' she said, and grinned.

Chapter 13

Moloch reeled in shock.

He stared at the phone in his hand, not quite believing what he was hearing. 'There was someone *else?*' he breathed.

Ed Bullion, the leader of his mercenary team, answered immediately. 'Another team,' he said. 'Damn good one too.'

Moloch found he couldn't speak. Ice had spread through his body and was now turning his legs to jelly. He sat down in his chair with a thud.

Another team?

'Tell me about them,' Moloch said.

Bullion did, and Moloch listened intently.

How could it be? He'd babied this project from the start, told only his most trusted colleagues, kept it close to his chest. It was his pet project, the one that would leapfrog the cabal into the upper echelons of society, into the stratosphere, as he was fond of thinking. The Hellfire quest was everything to him.

And now someone else was muscling in on it.

'Boss?' Bullion was saying.

Moloch had forgotten he was still on the phone. He closed his eyes now, still in shock. The words just wouldn't come. He sat there for a few moments longer.

'Boss?'

Now, finally, Moloch managed to push the numbness aside enough to speak. 'Did they . . . best you?'

'Of course not, Boss. But they're slippery. They got the clue. Got clean away with it.'

Moloch closed his eyes, heart hammering. This was about as bad as it got. He couldn't see straight. He took a deep breath and tried to focus on the moment.

'Do you have any idea as to the clue? Did you even see it?'

'No. We got nothing. They must have hidden it in one of their backpacks.'

Moloch could rant, he could rage, but it would get him nowhere. He had to face facts; the first clue was gone, and he did not know what it said. They had failed at the first hurdle. There was no going forward from this.

'Stay in play,' he said. 'I will contact you soon.'

It was clear Bullion and his team could be of no further help for now. They had failed. But then, they hadn't known about the other team either, had they?

Where had it come from?

Moloch tried to calm himself down, but it was no good. The flames were inside his brain, rising, eating away all conscious thought. The dream of Hellfire was teetering, but he knew, just *knew*, that the Devil was close to being summoned. It was all a matter of that final ritual. And not just that. The ritual had to be completed on a certain day on a certain night, and that night wasn't far away. Moloch was on the ropes here. He needed the Hellfire, needed the artefact, and he needed to summon Satan.

He screamed. He walked over to the window of his office and screamed again. He looked out over the estate grounds without really seeing anything. What next?

Moloch knew exactly what to do next.

He left the office, slammed the door behind him and made his way down to the bowels of the house. Through basement after basement he walked, and came eventually to a locked wooden door. He produced a key, unlocked and opened the door, and went through into an arched, brick-walled space and then a fantastical doorway. On a hook beside the door was a set of black robes, which he donned. He flicked up the hood.

Moloch walked to the centre of the room. Positioned here was a black stone altar, its hard surface awash with terrible carvings. A hierarchy of demons, their snarling faces taking up one entire leg of the altar. The face of the Devil himself, carved into the surface, horns and all. Witches and unnameable beasts and serpents with knives for tails. Moloch knew the altar intimately. It was his own personal platform.

He took his time, tried to slip into the ritual. Behind him, on the floor, was a pentagram, also crammed with hellish designs. His mind was already quieter, calmer. He let the ceremony take over. From a cage in the corner, he took a dead animal, a cat, and laid it out on the altar top. He placed a hand over it, said a few words.

'*Ave Satanus.*'

Moloch moved to the left side of the room and opened a drawer. Inside lay a knife with a red jewel-encrusted hilt and a razor-sharp blade. He removed it, held it up to the light, watched it gleam with promise. He walked back to the altar and held the knife poised above the dead animal.

Moloch brought the knife down sharply. As he did so, he recited a prayer to Satan.

'*Hail Satan, punish those who cross my path, lead me to treasures, feed my desire, indulgence and spite. I've sacrificed everything for a glimpse of your might.*'

Moloch breathed deeply, smelling the odour of the dead cat, the aroma that permeated the room, the true stench of success. His mind was unfettered, free. It was clear, and all he could see was a bright future. The Lord Satan was showing him the way forward.

Moloch brought the knife slashing down again and again. The more he disfigured his prey, made it different from what it was, the more the Lord would welcome him. For long minutes there was nothing but Moloch and the knife, and the bright way forward.

Eventually, he stopped. He was out of breath, breathing raggedly. The misshapen lump before him lay as it should do, in sacrifice. Someone, later, would clear it up. Moloch backed away from the altar, arms raised.

'*As we wait for Heaven to collapse,*' he chanted, '*we kneel in prayer. As we wait for your light to shine, we drink of your wine.*'

And he uncorked a cup of fresh blood and washed it down with wine. He took a long swallow. The heady mixture soothed him. For the first time since he'd received the phone call from Bullion, he felt clearheaded.

The ritual had cleansed the confusion from his body. Moloch stood for a long while, lost in silent prayer. Eventually, he sighed, knowing he had to return to the real world. He removed the robe, washed his hands, left the room, and started making his way back to the upper floors. It was as he made the journey back to his office that the answer hit him.

Praise be to Satan.

CCTV.

It was everywhere throughout the house, apart from at basement level, and its presence was unknown to all but a couple of trusted operators. Those operators could hardly be the mole he now believed was hiding in his own cabal. There could be no other answer. There was a traitor in their midst. Someone was feeding Moloch's own information to another team. *That* was how the team had beaten his own to Holyrood.

But . . . Moloch paused in his deliberations. *That would mean the presence of a second book of Baphomet.*

There were two copies and the original. All three were stored in the house's library. He hadn't checked on them in many months, perhaps more than a year. Moloch saw a way of confirming the mole in the house. Immediately, he altered course, heading for the operations room. He followed a winding route through the house, nodding to the few staff and guards he met along the way. He barely saw any of them, tunnel vision having taken over.

Moloch came to the operations room. They kept the door deliberately locked but he had a key. He entered and started quizzing the men about the library.

'How often do people go in there?'

'Rarely, sir. The cleaners mostly. A couple of guests.'

'Show me the logs.'

The men pressed a few buttons on their keyboards, brought up a new set of screens. Moloch leaned against a metal filing cabinet as they worked, looking over their shoulders. It was a small room, stuffy, packed with gear. There was barely enough room to swing a dead cat, he thought with a private grin.

One technician pointed at his screen. 'You see these timelines here,' he said. 'All about the same time, twice a week. That's the cleaners.'

'You can ignore those for now. I want something that doesn't fit.'

'Motion sensors are pretty sensitive in there,' the other man said. 'Let's have a check.'

Moloch waited as the men brought up twenty-seven events. Of course, some of them would be him, but he couldn't recall exactly which ones they'd be. Moloch asked for all of them to be viewed.

It took a while, and Moloch saw himself at least ten times coming in and out of the library, perusing the shelves at his leisure. Others included guests who just took a wander through and a guard who used it as a shortcut. Moloch stored that bit of information for later. He knew exactly where the three books of Baphomet were stored and he kept an eye on that area.

As it turned out, only one man reached up to remove one of the books. And that was many months ago.

Jonathan Jacobs.

Moloch felt his fists turn into hammers. His lips tightened into thin lines. For a while, he couldn't speak.

'Rewind that,' he said finally.

It was unbelievable, but it was true. One of his most trusted allies, one of the long-time members of the cabal, was working against him. He had stolen one of the books. Did he want to summon the Devil first? Was he looking for the Hellfire too? But the timeline was off. Jacobs had stolen the book months ago. How did that correspond to what was happening now?

For now, it didn't matter. Jacobs was the rat. Jacobs was the reason some rival team had got the second clue to the Hellfire. The reason Moloch was in deep shit.

'That's enough,' he said, and walked out of the room.

Moloch returned to his office study. He believed that the ritual had brought him closer to Satan, believed that the great dark deity had handed Jonathan Jacobs to him on a plate. The question now was what to do with Jacobs.

There was only one answer.

With a single phone call, he summoned Jacobs to the house. At first, he was reluctant, but Moloch spun him some story about trying to fit in an extra Black Mass that month. Jacobs really had no choice. He said he'd see Moloch that very afternoon.

Moloch passed the time in deep thought. He knew what he wanted to do to Jacobs, knew he couldn't do it. He tried to remember facts about Jacobs, about his late wife, and thought about how he was going to handle the meeting.

Late morning came and went, and then Jacobs was pulling up the long gravel driveway. He parked his black Bentley outside the door, got out, rang the bell. He was greeted by a man wearing a tux who showed him up to Moloch's study.

'Welcome, welcome,' Moloch greeted him grandly, and then pointed to a comfortable leather wing chair. 'Won't you take a seat?'

Jacobs muttered something about being short of time, about being ill, about the state of the traffic and the time it took him to reach Moloch's home. Moloch smiled tightly through all of it, noting the look on Jacobs' face.

The man looked scared.

And so he should be, Moloch thought. The bastard had betrayed him. He should die for that. No, not just die. The man should be sacrificed to his master in a most elaborate ceremony.

Moloch would save that for later.

For now, he leaned back and rested the palms of his hands on the table. Might as well get straight to the point.

'How long have you been working for the enemy?' he said.

Jacobs went white. 'I . . . I'm not sure I follow.'

'I know what you're doing. You stole one of the books of Baphomet. You are searching for the Hellfire. You sent a team to retrieve the first clue.'

Jacobs goggled at him.

'Why, Jonathan? Why would you do such a thing to me, to the great Lord? Why did you become the traitor that you are?'

Still, Jacobs stared at him, eyes full of horror. The man's mouth opened, but nothing came out. His eyes darted from left to right, as if expecting an attack from any angle.

Moloch smiled grimly. 'You're either working for someone else, or you are the instigator of a plot against me. But I found you out. You're mine now.'

'Please . . . ' Jacobs finally said. 'I don't mean any harm. I just want out.'

'Out? There is no out. You're well aware of that. And, Jonathan, you have done me a great harm. You're trying to steal the Hellfire from me.'

'You don't need it.'

'Don't *need* it? Perhaps not. But I *will have* it. Do you plan to keep it for yourself?'

'Nothing like that.' Jacobs stared hard at the floor.

'Then why, for Lucifer's sake? Why?'

Jacobs spread his arms. 'It's simple. I believe the Hellfire will give you too much power and influence. It is not right. And that final ritual . . . it's brutal. I can't let a man like you have it.'

'A man like me?' Moloch was trying to quell seething emotions.

'A man who worships Satan as seriously as you do. I mean, Christ, don't you remember how all this began? We were a small cult, just three of us at first, and we went down to your basement to do a little chanting. We found a few robes, put them on, ordered a few fake artefacts off the internet. Played at it. There was debauchery when the women joined and that was fun, but now . . . now . . . I believe you've gone quite mad.'

It was a frank speech, and hard for Moloch to take. It was true they'd started out low-key, barely believing in what they were doing. Everything was a game at first, just a way to pass the time for wealthy layabouts. Moloch had laughed along with the others even as they chanted, as the shadows moved.

Or at least they told themselves the shadows were moving.

It was only when Moloch started getting the dark dreams that he changed his mind. The dreams brought Satan to him, night after night. It was a time of promise, of dark seduction. Moloch then looked more deeply, concealed his burgeoning belief from his friends, and started expanding the cabal.

He found others like him, others who *believed*.

He showed them a new truth, gave them bloody ritual and a dark anchor to cling to. He showed them that worshipping the deity in the darkness was right.

'You betrayed the cabal,' he said. 'You will answer for that.'

'There are others who want out,' Jacobs blurted.

Moloch glared. 'Names.'

'I won't tell you. I don't even know if it's true.' Jacobs tried to cover for his brief outburst.

Moloch let it go. He had Jacobs just where he wanted him: terrified, almost out of his mind with worry, destabilised.

'You're working for me now,' he said.

Jacobs swallowed hard. 'I don't understand.'

'You've never heard of a double agent? Well, that's what you are now. You're working for this other team, but you're also working for me. If they get to the clues first, you will find out a way to reveal them to me. That should be easy for a turncoat like you.'

'You want me to betray my team?'

'I'm telling you that's exactly what you will do. No questions. If I think you're lying to me, you will be the immediate sacrifice in a very intricate Black Mass. The central character, if you know what I mean. Not only that, but I will include Sally too, your goddaughter. Wherever she is, I will find her, and I will feed her to Satan.'

Jacob's eyes instantly went wet and huge. They gazed at Moloch with something like terror and hatred. 'Please . . . ' he said.

'There is nothing else to say. You will feed me everything that they tell you, everything they're doing, and you will fish for more. Yes, it is the clues that I will need most, but, as I said, you are mine now.'

Moloch smiled grimly into the horror-struck eyes in front of him. He drank it in. It was one of the most incredible sights he'd ever seen. It filled him with glory, with arousal, with love for the master who had led him to this point in his life.

Hail, Satan, he thought.

Chapter 14

Mason stood in the graveyard that surrounded Whitby Abbey, his face scoured by the high winds. With many other tourists, they had climbed the 199 steps to reach the heights of the abbey. The way up had been lined with people coming down, with people sat on benches taking a breather, with snap-happy tourists standing on the steps and clicking photos of Whitby itself lying sprawled out below.

Mason stood amid the gravestones, studying the lighthouse and the harbour. The abbey sat at his back, a ruin that presided over the nearby lands where once Captain Cook had learned seamanship and, supposedly, Dracula had come ashore.

Sally was close by, referencing the map on her phone to other screenshots she'd taken that showed the way down White Scar Cliff. She spent quite a bit of time getting it right and then led them towards the retaining wall that encircled the graveyard.

Once there, they hopped over it and approached the cliff edge.

'Yeah, I'm about twenty feet off,' Sally said with a shrug. 'You can see the trail over there.'

Mason turned. The cliff edge just seemed to vanish, to break away. He moved as close to the edge as he dared, looked down. It fell away at a sharp incline, broken rocks and shrubs and jutting boulders all the way to the frothing seas below. Mason stepped back and shook the sense of vertigo out of his head.

They all followed Sally to the spot she'd pointed out. Here, a step led down the cliff and, when they jumped down on to it, they found a series of steps that wound around the outside of the cliff. The steps were ragged and cratered, uneven, and there was no handrail of any sort.

Mason took a deep breath and led the way. They moved down step after step, feeling exposed. The wind battered at them as if trying to pluck them off the cliff, howling around their bodies, playing with them. Up here, they could smell the sea salt too, but could feel no spray. It was too high. Mason kept his eyes on the steps, not on the deadly drop.

Still, he struggled with their quest. Sally's reasoning was sound, but Mason couldn't get used to the fact that they were chasing a bunch of Satanists, men and women who were killers. Should they risk the police? It was only on Jacobs' say-so that they hadn't. But then again, Jacobs was at the heart of all this, in the very same room as the Satanists.

They descended slowly, one at a time. They spread out all along the winding steps. Mason leaned into the cliff, away from the drop. A powerful gust of wind made him grab hold of a tuft of brush and hang on.

'Shit,' he said.

From behind came Roxy's voice. 'Are you fucking kidding me? Keep going. I almost crashed into you.'

'I almost fell off the bloody cliff.'

'Oh, stop moaning and move.'

Mason let go of the brush, fixed his eyes firmly on the next step. Adding to the problem was the fact that the steps weren't regular. Some were close together, others required a long stride to reach. He took his time. When he came to a larger step, he glanced back along the line, saw everyone descending steadily, carried on.

'Stopping for a moment,' he shouted out.

He looked up, and then down, figuring they were approaching the halfway mark of White Scar. Here, he could hear the roar of the waves, the crashing of water against rock. It rolled up the cliff face in a tumultuous upsurge. Strong winds buffeted him.

He went on and finally saw a break in the rock ahead. It wasn't exactly a door; it was more like a cave entrance. But it was wide enough to accept a person.

Was it all worth the risk? This was a wild quest, following old clues to track down ancient Satanic relics. But, as he often reminded himself, they were a team, and the team were all on board with this.

Before climbing up to the abbey, they had found a shop and purchased several items they thought might come in useful. Those items were stowed in their backpacks. Mason now took a heavy-duty flashlight out of his pack, stuck his head inside the entrance, and looked around.

The flashlight illuminated black, slick rock walls that formed a cave entrance. Inside, the ceiling was only a touch taller than Mason, giving a claustrophobic feeling. He walked in and looked around. At the far end, he spied a tunnel leading away into darkness.

'Why here?' he said suddenly as the others crowded around. 'The altar, I mean. Why this place?'

Sally was looking at the photo she'd taken of the scroll on her phone, reading the directions. 'It's a Satanic cult,' she said abruptly. 'To exist, they need to perform their rites in out-of-the-way places. Somewhere like this is perfect for them. I can imagine them clad in their robes, maybe carrying flaming torches down that cliff side, ducking into here and then making their way to the altar, fires burning. They would gather around it and do whatever they do before making their way back out. The altar, I imagine, will be too big to move.'

'Let's hope we don't bump into any of them,' Roxy said. 'As you know, creeping around old ruins like this isn't exactly my favourite sport.'

'But you do it so well.' Mason smiled at her. 'And with such grace.'

Roxy gave him the finger. Mason got a good look around the cave as his colleagues shone their torches all around. There wasn't much to see; it was a simple cave entrance. He gestured towards the tunnel.

'I'm guessing we go that way.'

Sally nodded. 'Straight on until we reach the first junction. But be careful. It mentions the word "pitfalls".'

'That's just great,' Mason said. He led the way, ducking into the tunnel, which was a narrow rock-lined passage about the width and height of a doorway. Jagged rock closed in on him from all sides as he pointed the torch at the floor, which, so far at least, was an unending stretch of rock.

They walked steadily, in silence, sweating in the close confines. Mason could hear nothing but the sound of their own feet, their breathing, the rustling of clothes. When he stopped occasionally, listening, silence reigned. He realised he was going to have to get behind Sally and the team, be just as invested as they were. Yet again, he tested Sally's reasoning and could find no issue with it.

They moved on, finally coming to a junction. Here, three tunnels branched off, two to the left and one to the right. Sally consulted the scroll.

'It just says go to the left. But there are two tunnels to the left.' She bit her lip.

Roxy peered forwards. 'Choose the biggest. That's my motto.'

Mason tried to ignore her, but her saucy grin, amid all this misery, was uplifting. Still, he managed not to smile.

'Furthest left, I guess,' he said. 'That makes sense.'

'Shall we start leaving the markers behind?' Quaid asked.

They had purchased dozens of small glowsticks that they could lay on the ground to easily indicate the way back. Mason took out a bag now, cracked one, and laid it in the passage that they had just traversed. He then led the way to the furthest left-hand tunnel.

It was even narrower than the last, the rock far more jagged. Mason got a couple of scrapes through his clothing and narrowly missed banging his head on a low-hanging lump. The going became harder. His backpack felt bulky and weighed him down, but it was essential. He shone the torchlight ahead, barely making progress.

Behind him, the others complained. His flashlight picked out the rough rock, the narrow way ahead. Finally, it picked out a solid wall.

The tunnel was blocked.

'Crap, we chose the wrong one,' he said.

Sally peered around him, again consulted her scroll. 'The directions aren't exactly Google Maps,' she said. 'Let's just turn around and go back.'

'Wait,' Mason said. 'Let's not be too hasty.' He surveyed the wall, making sure there wasn't a small way through. All he found was solid rock. Eventually, he brushed himself off and turned.

They made their way back to the junction and chose the other left-hand passage. This one was slightly wider than the last, a fact which Roxy pointed out immediately. They left glowsticks behind as they followed the tunnel's winding course. Mason led the way at a steady pace, conserving energy. After about ten minutes, he stopped and took a water break. The others did the same.

He peered ahead. 'What's next on the list of directions?' he asked.

'Next junction, take the middle tunnel.' Sally shrugged.

Which is what they did, still leaving their glowsticks to point the way back. As he walked, Mason noticed some deep depressions on the floor that looked like they had been made with a pickaxe, or something similar.

'Here's your first pitfall,' he said. 'A maze of ankle-breaking holes. Watch your step.'

Mason picked his way through. The Satanists, of course, would know the way by heart, but he had to tread carefully. A broken ankle down here would prove very difficult to deal with. Not only was there the way back through the tunnels to consider, there was the long climb up the cliff face.

Mason negotiated the deterrent. He stepped between the holes, taking his time. The team spread out, concentrating hard. After a few minutes, Mason came to the end of the maze of ankle breakers and exited through an archway.

Ahead were three passages.

He chose the middle one.

Chapter 15

Mason wondered just how deep they had to go into the cliff. They'd already been walking for almost a half hour, slowly, carefully. He was sweating and his shoulders hurt. His eyes ached because he was straining them in the torchlight. And he was constantly alert to any pitfalls. This wasn't all plain sailing. This was a hard slog.

The next obstruction came just after they entered the middle passage. This tunnel was wider and more airy, but as monochrome as the rest. It ran straight for almost a hundred yards before Mason came across the pitfall.

'Whoa,' he said, seeing it. 'That's nasty. Be careful here, folks.'

Ahead, taking up half the path, was a hole in the ground. Mason walked gingerly to the edge, looked down, saw nothing but endless blackness. He picked up a rock from the floor and threw it in, but never heard it land.

'A bottomless pit,' Roxy groaned. 'That's all we need.'

Mason looked to the left. Half the path led around the hole, but it was a tight fit. He moved as close to the wall as he could and started putting one foot in front of the other. His right boot came down on the edge of the hole, making him swallow. Slowly, he walked forward, dreadfully aware of the open drop to his right. The one advantage was that the ground was firm and level.

From the depths of the pit came a keening wind, something that sounded like a voice rising from the throat of a demon from Hell. It curdled the air to his right, set the hairs on the back of his neck on end.

It took him eight steps to circumvent the pit, but, finally, he was past. The mournful sound drifting from its depths stayed with him, though, making him shiver.

He turned to the others. 'Be careful,' he said.

It was a deadly passage. Mason's heart was in his throat as first Roxy and then Sally made the journey past the pit. When they arrived at his side, he patted their shoulders. He couldn't help himself. There was a certain terrifying helplessness in watching your friends skirt a deadly, bottomless hole in the ground.

Next came Hassell and then Quaid. There was no sound other than the doleful, keening resonance drifting up from the pit. Both men made the journey safe and sound and were then standing at Mason's side.

'And the problem now is, we do that all over again,' Hassell said with a shiver.

Mason had already thought of that. He placed a glowstick close to it to better mark it and then turned to carry on along the tunnel.

'Onwards,' he said. It was now, as he left the latest challenge behind, that he realised they were on to something big here, something vast and deadly. It wouldn't be so well guarded and hidden unless it was vital. This Hellfire, this artefact, it was everything, Mason realised, as he followed his team deeper into the caverns.

The passage started widening, opening out above and to the sides. Mason followed a proper path now, lined with boulders. He shone his flashlight up and to the side and determined that the passage was now at least twenty feet wide and high, and growing larger. They ploughed on, following everything the scroll told them to do, taking every junction, every turn, leaving glowsticks in their wake. Soon, Mason found they were beginning to ascend.

Their path became a trail that clung to the side of the cliff. To their right, the ground fell away, and they were walking with utter emptiness on one side and the jagged cliff on the other, along a path perhaps three feet wide. They struggled up and up as the path grew steeper.

Minutes passed. Mason could no longer see the ceiling. There was a sense of vast emptiness to the right, a void into which, if you fell, you would never return. The floor was as jagged as the walls, with enough hazards to make his heart-rate double.

Up they went, the path winding around a curving wall. Mason's right boot slipped off a rocky protrusion, skidded towards the drop. He sank low, balanced, caught himself and called back a warning. It was like walking on uneven spikes. He kicked debris towards the drop as he went, saw it go over in a stream. And even as they walked, more debris collapsed off the rock walls, trickling down the cliff ahead to rest in heaps on the path.

Mason carried on, checking with Sally to see just how far they had to go. Her reply was encouraging: only a couple more twists and turns ahead. A worry was that they would have to do this all again on the way back.

And suddenly, a cry rang out. Mason whirled. He saw Sally slip sideways and roll towards the steep drop. Her hands flung out, her face struck the ground, and she tumbled. Hassell, right behind her, reached out but failed to grab her.

Sally fell towards the drop.

Mason launched himself through the air, bypassing Roxy behind him. He hit the ground hard and reached out, desperate to cling to any part of the falling woman. His hands brushed her fingers, slipped away.

Sally reached for him. Their hands touched briefly. Then Sally went over the cliff edge.

'No!' Roxy shouted, on her knees.

Hassell and Quaid were scrabbling towards the edge. They couldn't see Sally anymore. Mason was right there, on his knees.

Looking straight down.

And staring Sally in the face.

She was clinging onto the ledge, fingers splayed across the rock. There was a shelf below her she'd gained purchase on. Her eyes were wide, her nostrils flaring. Mason reached down with both hands.

'Grab my legs,' he yelled.

First Roxy and then Hassell threw themselves across his legs, grabbing hold. Mason clutched Sally's wrists and looked her in the eyes.

'Trust me,' he said. 'I won't let you go.'

He started hauling her up, saw her boots leave the shelf. Now she was dangling in the air. He pulled on her wrists, dragging her back over the edge of the drop. Sally came up an inch at a time, first her forehead and then her face. Mason pulled and pulled, wriggling back as he did so, grateful there were two of his friends holding his legs.

Sally slid up and over the ledge. Her face was pale. She was shaking. Mason stayed on his stomach and held her close, his heart thudding. There had been a moment there when he'd thought he'd lost her, a terrible, ice-cold moment. He looked her in the eyes.

'Don't ever do that again,' he said.

Sally gave him a weak half-smile and lay there for a while, collecting herself. Mason sat up, breathing deeply. The others crowded around. It was a sombre few minutes filled with relief, but also with the cold knowledge that the job they did was extremely dangerous. They were always in peril.

They waited for Sally to rise and say she was okay to continue. Then Mason led the way again, clearing the rubble as best he could, kicking it over the edge to his right. Their progress was punctuated by the constant waterfall sound of plunging debris. They were all doing it to prepare for the way back.

After some time, they reached the top of their ascent. Mason looked back. It was a long way back down the path they'd traversed, never mind the drop. Mason ignored it and looked ahead, wondering where they were supposed to go next.

There was no tunnel. Just a craggy rock face.

Sally consulted her phone. 'At the top of the long ascent, skirt the rock and do not drop. The great altar will be dead ahead.'

Mason didn't like the sound of that. He skirted the rock, came around a bend, and then saw the way ahead plunged into darkness. He focused his flashlight on the rock wall and made a face.

'Damn,' he said.

A narrow ledge clung to the side of the rock, leading off into darkness. They would have to walk along the ledge to gain the far end. The ledge was so narrow they could only step onto it sideways, with their backs to the wall.

He didn't need to tell everyone to be careful, but he wanted to. He felt responsible for them these days. Not that long ago, Mason had vowed never to lead a team again. Now, he'd found an impressive set of people and actually enjoyed it. But that didn't stop him from worrying about what would happen if one of them . . .

He didn't complete the thought. Instead, he stepped out onto the ledge, pressed his back to the rock, and started sidestepping around it. In front was nothing but a vast space, the long drop just beyond his toes.

He shuffled around the ledge. The others joined him, a long line making the crossing together. Everyone held their breath, moving slowly and with care. Sometimes the tips of their toes were over the drop and the rock face behind them offered no real purchase. Again, a mournful keening sound came up from the depths, enveloping them as if trying to draw them down. It wrapped Mason's consciousness in desolation.

He kept going, coming at last to the end of the ledge and seeing a path ahead. He stepped on to it, breathed a deep sigh of relief, and then moved forward to make room for the others. When they were all across, they paused for a while, catching their breath and letting their heart-rate decrease. Mason's mouth was dry, and he broke the water out again, taking a long swallow. They paused to eat energy bars and other provisions, sitting with their backs to a wall and their feet pointed firmly towards the wide path that would lead them to the Day Star Altar.

It was Mason who rose first. Sally read from the scroll again, indicating that the altar should be dead ahead. Mason, conscious of the trials they'd already been through, hoped at least finding and then accessing the altar would be easy.

But when he started forward, and they shone their flashlights ahead, they saw that that was very much not the case.

'Bollocks,' Quaid said.

Chapter 16

Mason found his eyes travelling up and up.

The Day Star Altar was oblong, obsidian-black, and perched on a ledge. It was obvious now why it had never been moved, and any Satanists would have to come to it. The altar stood halfway up a steep wall. There were hand- and foot-holds leading up to it, but the wall was steep and precarious. And it was about twenty feet up. The ledge it perched on looked like it could hold only two or three people at a time.

Mason looked at his team. 'Who's gonna make the climb?' he asked.

Hassell stepped forward immediately and then Sally. Maybe her background as a fell runner would help her. Maybe not. But at least she looked confident again after her earlier near-miss.

Mason volunteered to be the third to go up. He took off his pack and laid it on the ground, resting his flashlight on top. They would depend on those who were staying behind to light up the wall for them from below. The flashlight beams were strong and wide enough to do the job.

Hassell approached the wall first. He found a hand-hold and hauled himself up, then found purchase for his feet.

Sally came next, following the same route. From Mason's vantage point, the way to the altar didn't look too difficult. But, he imagined, once you were on the wall, it would feel scary as hell.

He followed Sally, put his fingers into a niche and took hold, pulled himself up and found a small protrusion where his boots could balance. Gradually, he started climbing the wall.

Hassell moved from small ledge to small ledge, shifting left and right. He ascended with confidence, seeing the next outcrop or hollow and utilising it. He tried to do it slowly enough that Sally, following, could use the same route.

Down below, Roxy and Quaid lit up the wall as best they could, playing their flashlight beams steadily across its surface. The bulky black altar loomed above them all, presiding over the drop. Roxy kept half an ear to their rear, remembering that they weren't the only ones on the trail of the Hellfire. The mercenaries might have missed out on the first clue, but she didn't trust them not to pick up the trail. There were ways and means. For now, though, she heard nothing but the sound of her friends climbing the wall.

Mason reached up for another hand-hold, hauled himself up another few inches. His fingers ached from gripping, his face throbbed from where he'd scraped the wall. It was a short climb, yes, but it was an arduous one. A look up, and he saw Hassell approaching the ledge where the altar sat. Hassell had to reach out to grip the edge and then drag himself up and over the lip. Below him, Sally rested for a minute.

Mason was inches from her boots. He paused, breathing through his mouth and trying to relax.

Sally reached out, gripped the lip of the ledge. Hassell bent down and helped to haul her up. Two minutes later, Mason was with them. They paused for a moment, catching their breath, on their knees.

Mason congratulated them. He saw a look of excitement enter Sally's eyes, and then she rose to her feet.

'The Day Star Altar,' she said. 'We need it.'

They slowly stood and confronted the altar. It stood about four feet high, long and oblong and as black as Lucifer's heart. The body was carven with evil sprites and fanciful demons; the surface bore Satan's face and shoulders. The legs were intricately designed, twisted and intertwined like the tangled roots of a tree. They rested on four clawed feet with red rubies for toes, the feet matching the Devil's hooves. Carvings covered every square inch, but Mason didn't like to look too closely.

'Now what?' Hassell asked.

Sally nodded, as if she knew exactly what he meant. 'We search the whole thing,' she said.

Mason went to the edge of the wide ledge and called down to Roxy and Quaid that they were safe and about to carry out their search. He pulled a torch from his pocket and started using that. Though the two flashlights helped light up the whole place, they weren't as bright as direct torchlight.

He examined the surface first. There were old stains here, dark and swirling. He tried not to think about what they might be. Being in the altar's vicinity, in the presence of a Satanic relic, was making his stomach churn. It gave off a strange resonance, as if imbued with horrors of the past and demanding more. It was an evil thing, something best left forgotten, as it no doubt had been. Being this close didn't feel right. Mason's nerves, already on edge, thrummed with distaste.

'It feels . . . alive,' Sally whispered. 'As if it's aware of our presence.'

Mason wanted to tell her to stop, but he felt the same. Of course, what she said couldn't be true, but its very proximity, the purpose it was used for, the hell they'd had to endure just to get here – it all contributed to unnerving and disturbing him. He tried to tune the emotions out.

Hassell took the left side, Sally the right. Together, they passed their hands across every inch of the Day Star Altar, searching for a nook, a depression, anything that might come loose. Hassell started at the clawed feet, ran his hands over the rubies, and then worked his way up. Sally began at the top and worked her way down. Mason touched the top, cringing, feeling odd depressions and raised surfaces and just knowing that he was touching old, dried blood.

They worked as a team. Soon, they had all finished and stood there looking at each other.

'Nothing,' Mason said.

'We go again,' Sally said. 'Take your time. There *has* to be something here.'

Time passed slowly as they changed positions and restarted. It was a thankless task, and a tough one. They'd come all this way to gain this prize. They couldn't go back empty-handed now.

Mason took the left side this time, ran his fingers over the intertwined surfaces, delved into the spaces in between. He felt under the claws, in the recesses around the rubies, and right at the top, where the legs were attached. Sally examined the surface and Hassell took the right side.

As he worked, Mason heard a click. He looked up in surprise. Sally's face was just as shocked as he was.

'You found something?'

'I think so.'

It was on the top of the altar. Mason rose to take a closer look. Sally had been rubbing her hand around the carving of Satan, and had reached his eye. When she pressed the centre, something had clicked.

There was now a small depression in the pupil.

Sally stretched out her fingers, gripped the edges of the eye with her nails, and lifted. She brought up a long cylindrical tube carved from the same black stone as the altar. She held it up before them.

'It's open along one side,' Hassell said.

Sally reached in, grabbed hold of something, and brought it into the light. Mason caught his breath. It was a long yellowing scroll, like the one they already possessed, and another sheet of thick, torn paper. Sally grinned at both Mason and Hassell.

'We have it,' she said.

In preparation, Sally had made the climb with an almost empty backpack. Now, she took her leather box out of the backpack, put the two items inside, closed it and replaced it in the backpack.

'Let's go,' she said.

'You're not gonna read it?' Hassell asked.

'I always find that's best done in comfort and without the threat of someone else turning up.'

Mason nodded, glanced towards the rim of the ledge, and started walking. A sudden itch began in his spine and travelled the full length. He'd turned his back on the altar, on the exquisite darkness it represented. There was a whisper in the air, a sound of almost stifled shushing. It drifted over him now, playing around his ears, and made him go cold. Mason turned to the others.

'You hear that?'

'What?' Hassell asked.

It was all in his imagination; he knew. It was the unease, the old bloodstains, the presence of a terrible artefact. He steeled himself, then lowered his body off the ledge and concentrated on getting back down to the ground in one piece.

Behind him, Sally and Hassell made the same descent. Together, they climbed down and met their colleagues. They spoke in whispers, and it wasn't because they were trying to be quiet; it was the close presence of the dreadful relic.

Mason thought about the long journey back.

'Take a moment,' he said, privately wanting to get away from the place as soon as he could. 'Because the return journey isn't gonna be easy.'

And finally, with the whispering presence of something unknown invading the air all around them, they hurried towards the ledge around the rock and the way out.

Chapter 17

It was mid-afternoon by the time they were back outside the cave and ascending the cliff to the abbey. Mason was bruised and weary, concentrating on putting one foot in front of the other. He had exited the cave first and started climbing the steps, at first keeping a wary eye out for their enemies.

'It looks like we've thrown them off.' Roxy, behind him, was clearly on the same wavelength.

Mason shielded his eyes against the glare of the sun. 'Don't jinx it,' he said.

They trudged up and up, plucked at by the wind. The drop to the North Sea below beckoned alarmingly. Mason took his time. For hours, they had lived with the sensation of constant peril. All he wanted now was to reach safety.

At last, they reached the top of the steps and stood on wide, solid ground. The abbey lay ahead, surrounded by the graveyard and a lot of tourists. Mason found a spot in the grass to sit for a while, and the others joined him.

'That was intense,' Roxy breathed.

Sally stayed on her feet, looking around. 'We should keep moving,' she said. 'I know Moloch's men can't possibly have this clue, but I still don't enjoy lingering here.'

Mason nodded and pulled himself to his feet. 'Let's go find the car.'

They strode past the abbey, descended the 199 steps and made their way through the streets of Whitby, back to the car. Once safely inside, they all uttered a sigh of relief.

'No mercs,' Quaid said. 'Just the way I like it.'

Mason started the car and drove off. The roads were narrow and packed with traffic. They passed hotels and fish and chip shops and dozens of places that sold souvenirs, especially those made of jet, which is mined in Whitby. Soon, though, before the five o'clock rush hit, they were on their way back along the A64 towards York.

Mason felt himself shudder, still perturbed by the intense sensations exuded by the Day Star Altar. 'Remind me why we're doing this,' he said half seriously and with a shiver.

Sally turned to him, a hard expression on her face. 'For my godfather. To help and save him. And for Moloch's future victims. Not only the ones he'll kill at the big ritual when he finds Hellfire, but those at all the other rituals to come. Not to mention to stop these devil worshippers from becoming more powerful.'

Mason nodded, signalling that he'd not been entirely serious, and perhaps Sally had overreacted.

In the back seat, there was an atmosphere of tense excitement.

'Show us the prize,' Quaid said.

Sally had her backpack between her legs, in the footwell. She reached down now, grabbed it, opened it, and pulled out the leather box. She rested the box on her lap and lifted the lid.

Inside sat the scroll and the piece of torn paper. Sally took a cursory look at the map, knowing it couldn't really help them at this point, and then turned her attention to the scroll. It was wrapped in a tiny red ribbon, just like the last.

Sally plucked at the ribbon, untying it. Then she unfurled the scroll and smoothed it out over her lap. Just like the last, there was a lot of black, spidery writing upon it. She took out her magnifying glass and tried to make sense of it.

Just then, her phone started ringing.

Mason kept driving, glancing at her in the rear-view mirror. Sally shook her head at the bad timing and looked at her screen.

'Jacobs,' she said.

She answered the phone. 'I'm not sure if you can call that good or bad timing,' she said breezily.

'I have some time,' Jacobs said. 'I'm alone and in no danger at the moment. Tell me what you have.'

'Moloch suspects nothing?' Sally pressed him.

There was a momentary silence before Jacobs said, 'He . . . trusts me,' he stammered. 'We've been together for a long time now.' His voice sounded dry and scared.

'Still . . . you have to be careful, Jonathan. You said so yourself, Moloch is a violent man.'

'And also incredibly baffling,' Roxy said.

Jacobs spoke up. 'I am being careful. More than you know. Moloch has learned that there's another team on the trail of the Hellfire and he's not a happy man. He said – well, I believe – he's exploring other avenues to find the Hellfire.'

'Other avenues?'

'Don't ask. They're hopeless.'

'He doesn't suspect you?' Sally pressed again.

Another long silence. 'I'm . . . safe.'

Mason joined the conversation at that point. 'My worry is that he'll find out who the other team is,' he said. 'Maybe track us that way if he has the resources. Is there any sign of that happening?'

'Nothing like that. Moloch may have the resources to track you, maybe to even use facial recognition software to pinpoint you, but if he does, he hasn't mentioned anything.'

'Does he usually play his cards close to his chest?' Hassell asked.

Jacobs conceded that one. 'I guess he does.'

'Just something to bear in mind and keep an ear out for,' Mason said.

'I'll do that.'

By now, Mason was approaching the outskirts of York, wide fields spreading out to both sides. The road had turned into a dual carriageway where he made good time, but now turned back into single-lane, causing a traffic snarl-up. The car crept along for a while before approaching a large roundabout. Mason turned right to head around the ring road.

Sally was still staring at the scroll, the phone in her left hand. 'We've successfully found the second clue inside the Day Star Altar in the White Scar cave. It wasn't easy, I have to say.' She let out a long, tense breath.

'You mean you had trouble finding it?'

Sally recounted the rougher parts of their journey. Jacobs held his breath as he listened, perhaps living vicariously through them.

'Sounds intense,' he said. 'But you have the scroll?'

'Yes, and the map.'

'What does the scroll say? That would be useful to know. For me . . . I mean.'

Sally hesitated. 'I haven't got that far yet.'

'Is it with you now?'

'I was actually just about to decipher the writing when you rang.'

'Oh, that's good. We can do it together.'

Sally turned a wry look at the rest of the occupants of the car. 'Well, yeah, I suppose we can do that.'

She turned her attention back to the scroll as Mason drove the car around the ring road, found the correct roundabout and started heading towards the centre of York to their car hire centre. Thank God for sat nav, he thought. The traffic grew thicker the further they got into York and he settled back for a long, creeping drive punctuated by red lights and pedestrian crossings and four-way junctions. He listened as Sally discussed the contents of the scroll on the go, speaking louder so that Jacobs could hear her clearly. So far, it had been an interesting mission. They had been successful, but not without a few hiccups along the way. The only shadow was a big one – the spectre of Moloch and his Satanists hanging over it all. The last thing Mason wanted to do was to confront a bunch of would-be devil worshippers, and maybe he could avoid that. He *hoped* he could avoid that. If they could keep the mercs at bay and continue finding the clues, then they could locate the Hellfire, and everything Moloch was doing would be ineffective.

Then, they could find a way of stopping him.

Stuck in traffic, Mason listened as Sally spoke to Jacobs.

Chapter 18

Ed Bullion thought this a thankless task.

The six other mercenaries he commanded were of the same opinion, but they voiced it only once. What he said went, and what Moloch told him to do, he would do. The money was too good to disobey an order and get fired. And if Moloch wanted to waste an expensive resource this way, then let him do that.

They were inside the Whitby cave. Even though they were certain the other team would already have been here, Moloch had insisted they find the Day Star Altar, *just in case*.

Just in case of what? Bullion had wondered. The other team got lost, couldn't find their way out, were lying at the bottom of a deep hole? It was unlikely, but he guessed it was almost possible.

Their problem was that Jacobs didn't know the full clue. It was too long. All he knew was that the Day Star Altar was inside the cave in Whitby.

Still, Bullion's team had been sent to do their best and, on arrival, had found something rather useful. Bullion had seen them first – glowsticks lying on the ground. Glowsticks to light the way forward, and back.

Bullion had grinned, his face lit like a spectral ghost in the half-dark. 'We caught a break,' he told the team. 'We can follow these.'

The team murmured an agreement. *The team,* Bullion thought. What had they landed him with? Well, there were two men, Carrier and Jefferson, who were the spitting image of each other, both ex-military, buzz cuts, broad shoulders and tight T-shirts, who walked like they had medicine balls between their legs. There were two more men who were the exact opposite of each other. Carlisle was tall and skinny with no sign of obvious muscle and a high degree of intelligence. Basher was short and squat and muscly, slightly overweight, carrying it well, and possessor of the dumbest brain Bullion had ever encountered. You had to tell the man everything twice and even then the glimmer of understanding was like a fading light bulb. Then there were the two women. Slater was easygoing, capable, and listened to orders. She could take a punch and come back slugging, as had recently been proved in Scotland. Tomkinson was as hard as they came, surly and quiet. She did the job, but she didn't like it and wasn't afraid to show her feelings. Bullion wondered if, in a previous existence, she'd been passed over for promotion more than once. Her respect for authority was practically non-existent.

Bullion led them now into the dark depths of the cave, using the glowsticks. They took their time following the twists and turns, not expecting any encounters, but ready for them just the same. They carried illegal Heckler & Koch dream machines, as Bullion thought of them, and Glock handguns. Moloch certainly had powerful resources. They also carried military knives at their waistbands. Down here, in the caves, they weren't burdened as they had been inside the Scottish house. Down here, they could use their weapons to their heart's content. Well, maybe not quite, he thought. There was always the chance of ricochets. But he trusted his team to bring a high skillset to proceedings.

Which was how Bullion liked it. The loss they'd experienced in Scotland still smarted. Bullion was a proud man, proud of everything he'd achieved in the military and how he'd acquitted himself afterwards. He'd started off as a team member in a mercenary crew, but his exploits in the field, in Syria and Iran and Afghanistan, had turned him into a leader, a commander of his squad. Bullion had always been a go-getter. In school, he'd been captain of the football team. Once, during a skirmish with the enemy in the mountains of Afghanistan, he'd successfully led a four-man team through the hostile elements and back to base, earning the praise of everyone involved. His leadership had been flawless. Eventually, though, Bullion found he wanted more.

Money, that was.

He had needs, expensive needs. Bullion loved to gamble, but he wasn't stupid enough to get himself deep into debt. He preferred using hard cash and, once it was gone, as it always inevitably was, he would be done for the evening.

The answer came to him one dark night as he lay in mountain grit, his face an inch from the rock. He decided to get out of the army as soon as he could, get into the mercenary game, and use his downtime to hit the tables. It was the perfect solution, for him at least.

His mind flicked through these memories as he trudged at the head of his crew through the cave. He negotiated a few dangers, kept it together and then came at length to the Day Star Altar. There was no sign that any other team had already been here, save for the glowsticks. Staring up at the altar, he wondered if it was even worth taking a look.

But he knew what Moloch would say, and Moloch was paying him the big bucks to get this whole thing done quickly.

They spent some time climbing up to the altar and then even more searching it. Moloch stayed grounded, letting his team get on with it. In the end, they found the secret compartment, found it empty, and had to assume that the scroll and the map had already been removed, as they had known it would be.

And then they started on the long journey back. Bullion found, to his consternation, that the glowsticks were dying, becoming a faint flicker. It was an anxious time as they quickened their pace, still trying to avoid any pitfalls. But they made their way out into the dark night.

After they'd climbed the steps, Bullion led the way into the ruins of the abbey. The moon was bright, casting the buildings in a spectral glow and shining through the gaps in the walls. Bullion, bathed in the stark light, leaned against an empty window and made the call to Moloch.

'Boss,' he began. 'We're out.'

Moloch actually sounded peaceful when he answered, an emotion Bullion had never seen in the man. 'Tell me all about it.'

Bullion gave him a potted version of the journey, wondering what the hell was going on. This was a little unnerving, and the spooky, ethereal moon didn't help. Bullion knew who he was working for, knew what they did, and his right hand slipped unconsciously to the crucifix he wore around his neck, touching it gently.

Why do you wear a crucifix? people often asked him. It was unusual in his line of work. He never told them anything.

'Tell me about the Day Star. Did you get pictures?'

Bullion answered in the affirmative. The team had been tasked with taking pictures of the altar from every angle imaginable. Purely for Moloch's own pleasure, of course.

'Can it be removed?' he asked.

'Impossible,' Bullion said. 'It's too heavy, too bulky, and the distance is too far. Not to mention the hazards along the way.'

'Still, there are people who would take the risk,' Moloch mused.

Bullion wondered if Moloch considered *him* one of those people. Probably. Look at the wild-goose chase he'd just been sent on.

'I don't recommend it,' he said.

'Where are you now?'

Bullion told him.

'The abbey?' Moloch said with emotion in his voice. 'That would be a perfect place for our needs. I would love to conduct a Black Mass there.'

'It's been done at some point,' Bullion said, referring to the altar and whoever had used it in the past. 'Maybe it could be done again.'

'Perhaps. That's something to think about. But there is no rest for the wicked. I need you to get on the road right away. Time is of the essence.'

'You never mentioned a time constraint.'

'Well, there is, believe me. A big one. You need to get moving.'

'You have new intelligence?' Bullion felt his heart leap.

'My new rat has proven himself useful already.'

Bullion liked the sound of that. He had been worried that this, the big payday, might be cut short and there'd be less gambling for him to enjoy. Now, he really had something to look forward to again.

'In what way?'

'Get on the road. I'll call you back with the information later.'

Bullion pocketed the phone, feeling lighter now than he had before he made the call. This had all turned out better than expected, and it might even give them another crack at the other team. Bullion wanted that almost as much as he wanted the payday.

The team were standing around, waiting for their orders, some more alert than others. Bullion gathered them with a few short words.

'Looks like we're back in the game,' he said. 'The boss has a new lead. And he seems in a hell of a hurry.'

'A new lead?' one of them asked.

'That's all you need to know. We'll get further instructions soon. We might even get another opportunity to take that other team down. Don't fuck it up next time.'

He turned and started walking away from the ruins, heading for their vehicle. The team packed away their guns, hiding the H&Ks under long jackets and putting their Glocks in their backpacks. Bullion wondered briefly if he was stepping in the footprints of the other team. Had they come this way earlier today?

It didn't matter.

Bullion was ready for their next meeting.

Chapter 19

Jonathan Jacobs wondered how the hell he was now going to turn the tables on Moloch.

Was there such a thing as a triple agent?

Jacobs was in his late fifties, old enough to know how the first ravages of age affect your body, but not old enough that those ravages were too debilitating. He was most energetic in the morning; by mid-afternoon, he was wilting. And these days, half-nine was an agreeable bedtime. There was a time, not too long ago, when it had been midnight.

But Jacobs was currently sloughing off the tiredness. It was night, and he'd been ordered to stay over at Moloch's for a few nights so the man could keep track of him. He'd lost track of the time, and he was standing in a blind spot between cameras trying to listen in on Moloch's latest phone call. The evil man was talking to his mercenary leader, Ed Bullion, and was imparting information that Jacobs had learned earlier.

Jacobs' heart twisted when he thought of it. His soul grew blacker than it already was. He had enlisted Sally Rusk's help. He had turned to her in desperation, as a last resort, just a few months after her father had died. The death of Pierce Rusk had shocked him. At first, he'd thought

Moloch might even be involved, but then he'd read into it and understood that it had been unrelated.

Jacobs had reeled for months.

What should he do? Why was he doing all this?

Why? Because he couldn't condone it any longer. Innocents were dying. Moloch was taking things constantly to new levels of malevolence. Everything was at stake for Jacobs – his life, his conscience, his belief in good, his new friends. He couldn't even remember where it had all gotten away from him. One minute it was all a game . . . the next it was a very real hell and he was stuck in the middle of it.

The knowledge that he was dying had brought it all to a head. He had nothing more to lose by exposing Moloch and his depraved acolytes. And now, he didn't want to double-cross Mason, but there was the new threat hanging over Sally. Moloch had threatened to hurt his goddaughter. It had been Jacobs' choice to bring her in on all this and now he partially regretted it. There was the very real chance that Moloch would try to kill Sally and her friends.

One way or another, he had to leave the cabal, and he couldn't see it happening whilst Moloch still breathed fresh air. They needed something on him, something entirely incriminating, but he was so careful, and he knew so many influential people that it was proving impossible.

Jacobs regretted ever joining the cabal. But when his wife Margo had died, he had been adrift, at the end of his tether. He had been living in a false world where reality was warped and dreams never came true, pretending that Margo was still alive, cooking their favourite meals for two, pouring two glasses of wine, keeping a seat clear for her on the sofa. That was the world he loved, and the world he wanted to live in, even though, deep down, he knew it wasn't good for him.

Margo died in a car accident, two days before her birthday. Jacobs already had the gifts sorted and wrapped, the flowers ordered. When the flowers turned up two days later, he broke down, unable to deal with it all. Friends had helped, but only during the hours of light. When darkness fell and Jacobs was alone, the terrible hell of it all came rushing back.

Jacobs had been a candle in the wind, wanting to be snuffed out.

And then Moloch had come. An acquaintance only, Moloch had taken Jacobs aside and offered him something new, something wild and fun. At first, Jacobs had been hesitant. He wanted to cling to the new world he'd created. But Moloch had been gently persistent and had persuaded him to take the first step.

Jacobs stepped into Moloch's world, and could never leave. Literally – he could never leave. It was some time before he found out that Moloch secretly filmed all his rituals.

At first, as he'd mentioned to Sally, it had been nothing but a momentary diversion. A bit of chanting as they sat around a table, a few artefacts to hold up, a photo of Old Nick to stare at. The main pull had been the Ouija board, which he suspected Moloch manipulated, but it had at least given him a few hours every week where he wasn't thinking about Margo. As the weeks went on, more people started appearing, and Jacobs saw it as a sort of club.

Moloch called it a cabal. Jacobs thought he was joking.

It was about this time that Moloch started plummeting deeper and deeper into his new obsession. He started to *believe*. The Ouija board vanished, to be replaced by a new altar and fresh chants and hymns, all Satanic. Everyone started wearing black robes and then masks, the masks insisted upon by certain high-profile members. The rituals grew in complexity and soon Jacobs realised he was on the wrong side of the law. He also knew he couldn't leave, and would have to pander to Moloch for the rest of his years.

The only saving grace was that the ceremonies initially happened only once a month.

Jacobs found that every month Moloch added something else, something new. A more macabre touch. The first human sacrifice came after Moloch had softened them all up for months with cats and dogs and other animals. It seemed like a natural progression, and the first few humans they used were already dead, whisked away from the morgue.

But it got worse and worse and, for Jacobs or any of them, there was no way out.

He knew that there were others who felt the same way as he did. He saw it in their eyes, behind their masks, in their body language, the way they cringed when Moloch used his long black knife. Jacobs had considered taking them into his confidence, but had then dismissed the idea, seeing it as a dangerous move. He could name at least two men and one woman who wanted out. But the best course of action seemed to be to take Moloch himself down.

Jacobs stood there now, in the dark, considering his actions. He had betrayed the very people who were trying to help him, had been forced to turn into a double agent and rat on them, to garner their information and deliver it straight to Moloch. He had to speak to them, to encourage them, and then deceive them. The very idea made him sick to his stomach.

He listened hard. Moloch was relating the latest information to Bullion, which meant that the mercenaries had the same information that Sally, Mason and the others did. The problem was that Jacobs couldn't warn them. Not outright. He'd already thrown in a warning about Moloch trying *other ways,* and though that was vague, he didn't dare be any clearer. He just had to hope Sally heeded the warning.

But what else could he do?

It was all a question of information gathering. Maybe, if he listened long and hard enough, he would pick up something that could thwart or even incriminate Moloch. Someone had to locate and kidnap the victims. Someone had to get rid of the bodies, clean up. Someone knew exactly what Moloch was doing and, maybe, would snitch on him.

This was Jacobs' new hope. That he could find another way, even as Sally and her team sought the Hellfire, to stop Moloch. At the moment, Moloch was surrounded by powerful, influential people. They all served the same master.

And speaking of a master, Jacobs pondered for a while on the idea of Satan as he listened to Moloch speak. At the most recent Black Mass, Moloch had invoked several spirits to help with the summoning of Lucifer. This was new, and apparently this was how it was supposed to be done. It had required even more bloodletting, more torture, more sadism. Moloch had been happy to provide all of them. The poor unfortunate soul who died had suffered terribly. Jacobs had been weak at the knees, just one man in the crowd of men and women, all robed, all chanting, their deep voices speaking a dark and deadly mantra that filled the room and curdled the very air. Jacobs spoke it too. He had no choice. He had feared that Moloch might find out, that Moloch's powers were growing.

How ridiculous.

As Jacobs knew, this had all begun with a Ouija board in a basement. There was no such thing as the Devil. It was the image you made for yourself. But there *was* such a thing as highly functioning psychopaths, and a man so charismatic and focused that he could draw others into his circle of madness.

Jacobs wilted as he recalled the plunging of the obsidian knife, saw the jerking of the still-living human on the altar. There had been several strikes, none of them lethal. The sacrifice had been heavily sedated, chained, but he still flinched and mumbled and tried to get away from the terrible blade. Jacobs could see it now. Over it all was the mindless, incessant chanting. It never changed in volume or timbre, it just kept coming. Blood began dripping into the channels at the side of the altar, a *drip, drip* in maddening rhythm with the damn chanting.

Jacobs sank to his knees in the dark.

How is this my life now?

He could no longer hear Moloch speaking to Bullion. He was no longer fully aware of where he was. Blackness filled the spaces in front of and behind his eyes. Pure blackness. The blackness of sin and guilt. How had it come to this?

Yes, he was as guilty as any of them, but at least he was trying to do something about it.

Chanting, chanting.

It was the sound of two dozen cruel, chaotic freaks, all under Moloch's spell. The chanting was a counterpoint to their madness. It pulsed with evil, became something in the room that you could actually cling to, something to centre you. As Moloch performed the rite of murder, the others watched with no emotion.

All focused on one thing.

To raise the master, the thing that couldn't possibly exist.

It was right then that Jacobs' phone rang. It took him half a minute to collect himself, more time to fish the thing out and check the screen. The caller was Moloch.

'Y-yes?' he answered softly.

'Where are you?'

Jacobs winced. 'The, ah, kitchen,' he said.

'I'm glad you stayed. It shows you're more committed to me than ever.'

Jacobs said nothing, not trusting himself to speak.

'I want you to come to my office.'

'Is it important?' Jacobs tried to put a little steel into his voice. He didn't want Moloch walking all over him.

'Of course it's important. I'll see you in five.'

Jacobs put his phone away and tried to slow his heartbeat. His hands were clammy. What could Moloch possibly want?

He killed some time and then knocked on Moloch's office door, heard the summons, and walked straight in.

Moloch gave him a tight smile. 'You'll be glad to know the information you got from your team has been passed on to mine.'

Jacobs grimaced.

'They're on the same playing field now. Going after the next clue.'

'I understand that. You should be careful of them. As good as your team are . . . they may not yet be up to the task.'

Moloch waved him towards a chair. 'And that is one reason I wanted to see you,' he said. 'This team of yours. I want to know everything about them.'

Jacobs thought of young Sally, of her father, and how Pierce Rusk would now hate him for dragging his daughter into the thick of all this. Why the hell had he contacted her? Was it through a weakness of his own?

'I honestly don't know that much about them.'

'But you will tell me everything you know. And especially about your goddaughter Sally.'

Jacobs thought about that. He knew their company name, the people in the team, the name of the man who led them, Joe Mason, and a good deal of Sally's background. It was why he'd contacted her. He knew what she could do, and that she had her father's gift for research.

But none of that information could help Moloch defeat them.

'I'll tell you what I know,' he said.

Chapter 20

It was about seven p.m., cold and windy and growing dark in the city of York. Mason and his team had found a warm, quiet pub in which to ward off the cold and consider their next steps. They had ordered pub meals and drinks and were now sitting back. Outside, the growing darkness pressed against the windows as if seeking entry. Figures passed along the street, heads down.

Sally had just put the phone down after passing on the new information to Jacobs. Now she stared around at her team.

'Any ideas?'

Mason glanced at the table. Between the dirty plates sat the piece of torn map and the scroll. Sally had already read out the new clue. It was different in style from the previous one, just a line of text.

'Find the One True Inverted Cross under the old Duke.'

Was it really as vague as it sounded? Mason didn't think so. It couldn't be. It had to lead them to the next clue.

'The last clue was a page long,' Hassell said. 'Are we missing something?'

Sally shrugged and took a sip of her red wine. 'This came out of the Day Star Altar. There was nothing else.'

'Have you checked the back of the scroll?' Roxy said with a grin.

Sally ignored her. 'It's all we have to go on,' she said.

Around them, it got busier, more people wanting to get off the cold streets and into the brightly lit pub. Loud conversations started up and the bar area became crowded. Mason leaned forward to hear better.

'The Satanic relic is this one true inverted cross,' Quaid said. 'Do we know what that is?'

'Well, the cross of St Peter is an inverted Latin cross,' Sally said, her laptop open but studying her father's Rusk Notes rather than anything on the internet. 'It has been used for non-Christian symbolism. Over time, though, the inverted cross became a powerful occult symbol, one of the best-known symbols of Satanism. It started in the Middle Ages, nobody knows how. I can imagine that the one true cross would be one very powerful relic for these people.'

'So we're talking about a proper cross,' Hassell said, spreading his arms wide. 'Where the hell could they hide that and what kind of condition would it be in?'

'Depends on what they made it from,' Sally shrugged. 'Just look inside any museum. There are plenty of ancient relics in there that have survived the test of time quite admirably.'

Hassell conceded the point with a nod. Mason took up the other part of the clue. 'And the old duke?'

Sally tapped her laptop. 'I've been reading through my father's notes. There is only one duke associated with all this. And you all know his name.'

'The Duke of Adlington,' Roxy said.

'The very same. All we have to do is find out where he's buried.'

'I don't like the sound of that,' Roxy said immediately. 'Sounds like crypt-work to me.'

'Could be.' Sally's attention was solely on her notes. Minutes passed. It was Hassell who took out his smart phone and started looking for the Duke of Adlington's resting place. There was tapping and swiping and silence for quite some time.

Eventually, Sally looked up. 'Any luck?'

Hassell nodded. 'The Duke of Adlington is buried in a mausoleum in Croydon, London.'

'That's close to where his original estate was,' Sally said. 'It makes sense. Croydon has been around for a while. It was mentioned in the Domesday Book.'

Mason drank some of his pint and listened. They were making good headway, he thought, and Jacobs was hanging in there, as evidenced by his phone calls. He felt a certain freedom with this particular quest, a freedom born from the fact that they weren't racing against another team.

'So it's back to the damn train station?' Roxy said gloomily. 'For what I'm sure will be a wonderful trip to the Duke of Adlington's mausoleum. I can hardly wait.'

Mason shared Roxy's reluctance, but didn't show it. The team quickly finished their drinks as Hassell booked the next train to London, which was leaving for King's Cross in about an hour. Then they took a taxi to York station and found a draughty Starbucks in which to wait.

Not long after, they were settled on the train to King's Cross. Two hours later, they were walking through the big station amid a large, highly mobile crowd, heading outside, and turning right towards the underground. It didn't take long to reach Croydon, but by then it was after 10.30 p.m., and the team had a decision to make.

They stood in the lee of an old hotel, the dirty brick building stretching high above them. It was fully dark, and they were lit by the stark light of a streetlamp, huddling together as they chatted. They had their jackets on, and their backpacks, and tried to ignore a brisk chill

119

breeze that tore up and down the road like an out-of-control driver.

'I'm leaning towards a hotel,' Roxy said, shivering. 'A good night's sleep, and we hit the mausoleum tomorrow.'

'It'd be easier in the daylight,' Hassell agreed. 'But it'd be riskier too.'

'It's been a long day,' Quaid said, perhaps feeling his fifty years. 'I'm with Roxy.'

They all looked at Mason. He blinked, still unused to being in charge, probably because he hadn't fully embraced the idea. 'The idea of a bed is appealing,' he said quickly. 'And it's not like we're in a massive rush. But I think we should go now.'

Roxy made a protesting sound.

Mason answered it. 'Purely because it's dark, and I think we stand the best chance of getting in and out unnoticed in the dark.'

Roxy's shoulders slumped in a sign of understanding. They were decided. Mason waited while a group of people walked by, a car rumbled along the road, and Sally brought the route to the mausoleum up on her map app.

'Eighteen-minute walk,' she said after a while. 'Follow me.'

In the dark, passing under streetlamps, they left the hotel behind. Roxy gave it a longing look as they walked away. They passed residential homes with driveways and lots of on-street parking, a small park with swings that creaked, and a badly lit parking area that invited crime. There were a few corner shops still open, a pub throwing its welcoming lights across the pavement, a few people coming from the other direction. Mason walked in silence, wondering what the hell they were about to step into.

Inverted cross . . .

It was, literally, something out of a Satanic ritual, something so alien to him he could barely believe there were people out there involved in it. More people than he could imagine. And it had persisted for centuries. The intellectual and the sensible and the well-to-do were part of it, a big part. Did they really believe Satan gave them the power to fight through another day, to overcome their rivals?

Ahead, Sally slowed. They were following a high stone wall topped by iron railings. The wall ended in a wrought-iron double gate that stood closed, chained and padlocked. Mason cursed their luck – the gate stood on a main street, overlooked by houses on the other side of the road.

He checked his watch. After eleven. They really had no business being here. His eyes flicked to the windows across the street, found most of them covered by curtains and blinds. There were a few bare, but no lights shone in those. He turned to Hassell.

'Go for it.'

'Wait,' Quaid said.

A couple came towards them, drifting along slowly, wrapped in each other's arms. Mason and the team started walking steadily, passed the couple, and waited until they were further down the road before returning to the gate. Now Hassell bent down to it and had the lock picked in just a few seconds. As quietly as they could, they unwrapped the chain, opened the gate, and passed through.

They stood in a cemetery. A large mausoleum stood off to the right, and they moved behind it, out of sight of the street, as fast as they could. The stiff wind blew around the concrete walls and whistled through gaps in the roof, a mournful sound that raised the hairs on the back of Mason's neck.

Sally had her phone in her hands. 'It's a small place,' she said, 'and I have the layout plans. The Duke's mausoleum is towards the back, as you would expect, since it's one of the oldest.'

They started walking between gravestones, following a curving path. Sally led the way. In the dark, Mason couldn't make out much except shapes and lumps, but he saw other mausolea along the way, and a chain-link fence that appeared to run around the far side.

Mason trusted Sally to lead them to the correct tomb. Soon she was slowing and looking up at a rectangular stone building, one storey high, with an arched frontage and two barred windows. The writing above the door was perfectly visible.

Adlington.

Chapter 21

Inside, the Duke of Adlington's mausoleum was dusty, freezing cold and pitch-black. They broke out their flashlights and shone them around the space.

It was a rectangular room with several barred windows in the walls, prompting them to shield their flashlights. They didn't want anyone accidentally spotting the lights. The floor was concrete, the walls tightly packed blocks of stone. The ceiling was pitted and hanging with cobwebs and a few broken spars. Debris littered the floor.

In the centre of the room sat a stone coffin with a stone lid. It too was strewn with debris. Mason remembered a previous mission where they'd been forced to go through the bottom of the coffin, but saw that wouldn't be the case here.

Sally's torch already illuminated the way ahead.

To the right of the coffin, set into the floor, was a square slab. At the centre of the slab was a steel ring.

'Perfect,' Quaid said.

Roxy snorted.

'Actually, it makes sense,' Sally told them. 'The inverted cross is a Satanic relic. They would have wanted easy access to it.' She pointed at the coffin. 'Not having to climb through a coffin or whatever. The slab set in the floor gives them that access.'

'You'd have thought they'd just nail it to a wall.' Hassell looked around.

'Are you kidding?' Sally said. 'Satanists have been hunted through the centuries for good reason. They're paranoid for good reason. They'll hide their relics with a jealous zeal.'

Mason could see the sense in it. If you weren't a Satanist intent on worshipping the inverted cross, why would you enter the Duke of Adlington's mausoleum? There simply was no other reason to be there and, Mason guessed, among Satanists it was a closely guarded secret, passed along from one cabal or sect to another. Did different cabals make contact? Mason did not know.

Hassell moved towards the slab as Sally kept her light on it. He crouched, grabbed hold of the ring and pulled. The slab came up easily and with little sound, revealing a square of darkness beneath.

Roxy moaned, sounding aggrieved.

Sally shone her light into the hole. A set of steps, strewn with leaves and shale, led into darkness. Cobwebs hung down. A dank breeze flew out of the hole, greeting them with a sorrowful wail. Mason shivered.

'Want someone to stay back and stand guard?' Roxy asked hopefully.

Mason looked at her. 'I'm tempted to say no since we have no, um, competition now that Moloch's team is out of the running. But experience has taught me to be wary. Maybe you should stay behind.'

Roxy brightened. Sally started down the steps, treading carefully. Mason went next, letting the clammy cold envelop him. Now he shone his torch without shielding the light and illuminated the way ahead.

A short flight of stairs, perhaps ten feet in length, led down to a narrow passage that disappeared further underground.

The walls were of jagged rock, roughly hewn. The ceiling seemed to be about eight feet high.

One by one, in single file, they started making their way down the passage.

They walked for long minutes. The passage wended its way gently right and left, becoming narrower and shorter as it went, as if the builders had started off with grand designs and then been forced to rein them in. Mason and the others became used to its confines and started making better progress.

Suddenly, Sally flinched and leapt back. Mason got a glimpse of something swinging towards her, flinging off dust as it came. Sally stumbled into him, knocking him backwards. Mason caught hold of her and dragged her away, himself backing into Quaid. As one, they fell and landed on the floor.

Mason could now see over Sally's head. Above them, a strange shape shuddered with tension. Mason looked more closely, breathing hard. Quaid tapped Sally on the shoulder.

'Are you okay?'

Sally nodded. 'Yeah, it barely scraped me. I got out of the way just in time.'

'How did you know?'

'Experience in research. These traps were left behind to catch the unwary in many old tombs. Some need maintaining, others don't. This one probably does. Plus,' she said, 'I felt a depression in the ground as I walked and then heard a click.'

Mason was staring at a frame attached to an arm. To the frame had been fixed several short spikes. The frame had swung out of a niche in the wall and had targeted Sally's chest. Luckily for her, she had remained alert.

Sally inspected her arm. The jacket was torn, but the spikes hadn't touched her skin. She shrugged. 'Wasn't keen on the jacket, anyway.'

'A shame we weren't given the complete story by the scroll,' Quaid said sardonically. 'Maybe the trap came afterwards.'

Mason nodded. 'Sounds probable,' he said. 'Shall we continue?'

They started off again, this time moving with greater care. They checked everything before they moved, studied the floor, the ceiling, and the walls. More tense minutes passed on the harrowing journey, and they'd only moved a few steps forward. Mason felt sweat trickling between his shoulder blades.

It was hard going now, hard and slow. But it was only five minutes later when Sally stepped forward and felt her right boot going straight through the floor.

On purpose, she hadn't fully committed to her step. Now she flung herself backwards as the floor gave way, again striking Mason and bringing him down. He grabbed her arms and held on.

Sally's feet dangled over a hole in the ground. Sitting up and leaning over, she shone her torch through the ragged hole and saw nothing except blackness. 'It's a long way down,' she said.

'Your nerves must be shot,' Mason said.

Sally laughed with a touch of hysteria. The hole in the ground wasn't large, just big enough to admit a person. Cold raced up from below.

'How do we know where to step on the other side?' Quaid asked.

'Good question,' Mason said. 'Give me your backpack.'

'Why my backpack?'

'Is it heavy?'

'Yeah, it's damn heavy.'

Quaid grumbled, but handed it over to him. Mason threw it over the hole in the ground, waited for it to land on the other side. It landed safely, and Mason let out a long breath.

'Looks like we just have to jump,' he said. 'I wonder what they used to cover the hole?'

'Clay hardpan,' Sally said. 'It's another old trick.'

The team leapt over the hole, hearts in their mouths, but all landed safely. Then they continued, still shivering with trepidation, now checking the ground before they committed to a step and looking out for spike traps.

What else would they find down here?

Mason relieved Sally at the front of the pack, guessing correctly that her nerves were shot. It shouldn't all fall on one person to take the risks, so they would share the load. He moved with great care.

Ahead, there came a natural danger. The narrow path turned into an even narrower ledge that ran across a stretch of darkness. They were forced to put one foot in front of the other and cross the void, maintaining their balance as a fusty wind played all around them. Mason did not know how deep the void was – it could be just a few feet – because he didn't have the chance to shine the flashlight into it. He was concentrating on not falling. He inched along the narrow span, arms out, eyes ahead, fully focused. It was a hazardous journey, he mused, just like the one in Whitby. Maybe Satan demanded the harshest of trials for his servants.

They came to the far side. The tunnel reappeared again, as modest as before, and proceeded for another ten minutes of slow, cautious walking. Mason saw symbols adorning the walls. At first they were dark drawings of inverted crosses, of horns, of snarling teeth, of angels with the faces of devils, of broken wings, of a menacing throne and a terrible facemask in the hands of a devil. There were haunting visions of demons feasting on humans, of shapeless things that twisted and roiled and spread hook-lined tentacles. Mason pointed them out to his colleagues.

'We're in the right place,' he said.

As they progressed, the cave drawings became even more elaborate. He saw an entire hellscape, a vision of the Devil and all his demons stalking a shattered landscape, with fires blazing all around. There was an extravagant obsidian throne with spikes, with claws arrayed along the base and a wreath of fire at the head. Next, a drawing of what looked like a million-demon army preparing to march through the gates of Hell and, presumably, invade Earth.

Mason couldn't help but study the drawings. The others were equally fascinated by them. Their progress slowed, but ahead Mason could see an ornate archway. Its sides were encrusted with precious gemstones and shone in the torchlight.

'Heads up,' Mason said on seeing it. 'There's something ahead.'

He stood in the archway – and froze. 'Jesus Christ,' he gasped.

Chapter 22

The macabre sight stopped them in their tracks.

Mason couldn't move, didn't *want* to step forward, to approach the terrible thing that hung on the wall opposite. Sally, at his side, was stunned and immobile. Quaid and Hassell, behind them, peering over their shoulders, were white with shock.

Their flashlights illuminated a round chamber, its rock floor as clean as if it were regularly swept. The walls were rough-cut and dark, almost black. The ceiling somewhere above them was invisible. Something cold hung inside the chamber, plucking at them as if inviting them inside. Mason could feel it in front of him, almost like a wall. Stepping into the chamber would be like stepping into a fridge.

And he knew there would be some natural explanation for it, but right now, standing here with that terrible *thing* hanging across from him, he couldn't imagine what that might be.

The cross hung upside down on the wall opposite them. It was entirely black and made of metal, about eight feet high and six feet wide, and its dark presence took up the whole of the back wall. Its surface bore the same terrible carvings that Mason had almost become used to by now:

demonic faces and beasts and snarling devils. The very sight of the Satanic relic filled him with dread.

'I don't think the words "Jesus Christ" quite fit here,' Quaid whispered.

Could Mason feel evil surging from the cross in palpable waves? It sure felt like it. He was still rooted, unable to move.

It was Quaid who entered the room first. It was only four steps for him, but it looked like a long slog. He did it with his head down, his shoulders straight, but he was determined and moved implacably. Once inside, he stopped and looked back.

'It's not so bad,' he said, shivering.

Mason forced his legs forward, stepping through a band of cold into the room. He kept moving. The closer he got to the cross, the more it loomed over him, the more intimidating it grew. Still shining his light on it, he noticed even more feral carvings – horned goats and demons and things with claws and curled teeth bending over helpless humans, their mouths drooling. Mason made himself walk towards the cross until he stood in its long shadow, looking up.

'You know what we have to do?' Sally was suddenly at his side, her voice startling him.

Mason frowned at her, then looked back at the cross. 'Shit,' he said. 'I do now.'

Soon they had all gathered beneath the cross.

'Y'know,' Hassell said. 'I'm gonna help watch our backs. This chamber is entirely too clean and tidy for it not to be in use. We don't want any Satanic assholes coming up behind us.'

It was a good idea. Mason watched him go, knowing he had an aversion to anything remotely spooky, and not blaming him one bit.

They all looked up at the cross. Steeling herself, Sally stepped forward and reached out a hand. She touched it, then withdrew quickly as if she'd received a bolt of electricity. Mason watched her.

'You okay?'

'It's damn cold.'

Mason stuck his hand out, gritted his teeth, and touched it. The cross was icy to the touch; the carvings made it feel contoured, the shapes jagged beneath his fingers. As he continued to touch it, his brain went into overdrive. Was the cross twisting and turning under his fingers like a decayed black limb?

Mason breathed deeply. They were in a deeply evil place, because of all the Satanic deeds and rituals that had been performed here through the years. Whatever had been done had left some kind of miasma behind, a trace element of wickedness that imbued every inch of stone that formed the chamber, and, especially, the cross itself.

Mason forced himself to touch it again. Sally started feeling around the other side of the inverted cross, her fingers running all over it, searching for a hidden compartment, just as he was.

'Any luck?' Quaid asked after a while.

Mason grunted. 'We're not gonna get that lucky, mate.' He stood back, looked up at the cross. 'Shit.'

He knew what they had to do, and his whole body rebelled against it. But then he couldn't ask anyone else to do it. Sally turned around and looked him in the eyes.

'Boost me up.'

Mason reached out first, grabbing the cross, but Sally slapped his hands away. 'I'll do it,' she said. 'I'm the lightest and, potentially, the fittest.'

Mason knew she was hedging her bets with that one. Sally may once have been a champion fell runner, but she wasn't in that shape anymore. Still, she was determined to climb the cross. Mason dropped to his knees.

Sally gripped the shaft of the cross tightly, and then climbed onto Mason's shoulders, steadying herself. Then she reached up, grabbed the crosspiece and hauled herself up. She stood like that for a while, feeling around for the compartment.

Mason's face was inches from the surface of the cross. Ice surged from it, caressing his face with frigid fingers. In front of him was a twisted carving of a sprite carrying a pitchfork with a human attached to the prongs. He bowed his head. Sally's feet scraped his shoulders.

'Higher,' she said.

He rose, climbing to his feet. Sally rose with him. Again, she reached out, touched and pressed, stroked the cross for hidden compartments. Again, she found nothing.

She looked up at the top of the cross, about two feet above her head. She was hugging the cross now and, to Mason, it almost seemed as if she was worshipping it with her body. Maybe that was the idea. Maybe some twisted mind had engineered all this, so whoever came searching for the clue was forced to perform some act of perverse worship to achieve their goal.

Sally wrapped her legs around the cross and inched her way up, holding on tightly. She was above Mason now, her weight off his shoulders. With one hand and then the other clinging to the cross, she felt around for any kind of anomaly.

And still she moved higher, going all the way to the top. The entire front of her body was pressed against the cross. Mason was below, looking up, ready in case she fell. But Sally clung on tightly, intent on her goal. She reached up now, feeling around on top of the shaft.

And suddenly she froze.

'I can feel something,' she said.

She adjusted her position, steadying her body against the cross, clinging tightly with her legs and her one free arm.

132

Her fingers pressed into the top of the cross. Mason heard a click and stifled a victory cry. It didn't feel right here. The malevolent presence that filled the chamber did so with a heavy hand, oppressing any feelings of hope or courage, promoting despair. Mason looked straight up at Sally, his heart in his mouth.

Sally pulled herself up even higher, now looking down on the top of the cross. She plucked something free, stuffed it in her pocket, and then started climbing down. Mason guided her from below and soon she was back on the ground. Her face was drawn despite her victory, her skin was white, and she was shivering uncontrollably.

'It was . . . horrible,' she gasped. 'Felt like the cross *owned* me. It was pressing into me as I clung to it. Oh, God, I know it's all my imagination, but it's such a *horrible* presence.'

'It's been worshipped for centuries,' Mason said. 'By evil men and women. By murderers. Satanists. Creatures who differ from me and you. I don't doubt that evil has infused it.'

'It's an inanimate object,' Quaid said.

'Then you go climb it.' Sally turned to him.

Quaid stayed quiet, backing down.

'And to be fair,' said Sally, looking at Mason, 'I didn't think the practical, loyal ex-soldier would ever say something like that.'

'There are more things in heaven and earth,' he replied, and then looked down at her hands. 'What have you got there?'

Sally, still shivering, held up her right hand. This time, she had brought the entire cylindrical piece with her. Carefully, she plucked the scroll out of the cylinder along with the new torn page of the map.

Sally held up the scroll. 'Success,' she said.

Mason felt a sense of elation but, to his right, the inverted cross still loomed. Its presence was black and atrocious, the stuff of nightmares. He couldn't wait to get away from it.

'Shall we save the unveiling for later?' he said. 'And get the hell back to normality.'

Hassell was already halfway across the chamber. Mason waited for Sally to get moving and then brought up the rear. He cast a last glance back.

There was movement. The cross shifted slightly. Mason's heart-rate shot up. He knew, he *knew*, it was simply down to Sally's weight. It had marginally repositioned the cross. But the sight of it, the sudden movement, made it all look deliberate and sinuous and twisted.

He didn't turn his back on the thing until he'd left the chamber.

Chapter 23

Outside, in the early hours of the morning, the cemetery lay gripped by swirling shrouds of mist.

Mason emerged into the white fog. There was a deathly silence all around and a feeling as though they were the last people on earth. Mason stopped, surprised to see the white mass. An icy wind still swirled around too, shredding the fog to left and right. Mason could see the misshapen lumps of gravestones and mausolea to left and right and, faintly, the path that would lead them out of here.

'That hotel sounds good about now,' Sally said, still trembling slightly.

Mason agreed. They would get away from the graveyard and then find the nearest hotel that would admit them at such an ungodly hour. Mason's head was still shredded, though, and he couldn't get the image of the inverted cross from his mind. The sight was burned in there, probably for ever.

And the moment it *shifted*.

Now, the team walked wearily away from the Duke of Adlington's mausoleum, cutting through the drifting fog. It had been a long, hard slog, but they had been successful. And still there wasn't another team on their tail. This proved to Mason that all was well. He passed rows and rows of gravestones, walked past the swaying shapes of trees and thick bushes, saw the wrought-iron gates up ahead.

They left the cemetery behind and started walking. Sally found a hotel just a few minutes' walk away. They started towards it, Mason looking forward to a warm room and a comfortable bed. It had been a grind, and it had taken a lot out of him. He looked around now, made sure everyone was with them as they left the worst of the fog behind. They were walking along a street lined with houses on one side, windows overlooking the graveyard and the park next door.

Sally unwrapped the scroll as she walked. 'I deserve this,' she said.

Mason watched her read the next clue, saw a look of bewilderment cross her face.

'What's wrong?' he said.

'The next clue,' she said. 'We're supposed to go to the Church of Santa Maria alla Fontana.'

'Where on earth is that?' Quaid asked.

'I haven't the slightest idea,' Sally said. 'It's the artefact that worries me.'

'And that is?' Hassell asked.

'The Crown of Beelzebub.'

'I've heard of Beelzebub,' Mason said. 'Wasn't he some kind of major demon?'

Sally nodded, pointing out the hotel ahead as they walked. 'Beelzebub's name is derived from a Philistine god and is also associated with the Canaanite god Baal. As you say, he is classified as a major demon, though Christianity has also said it is another name for Satan. But Beelzebub is known in demonology as one of the seven princes of Hell, representing gluttony and envy. His most famous title is Lord of the Flies.'

Mason shuddered anew. 'Can we talk about something else? I'm still reeling from the inverted cross escapade.'

136

Sally shrugged. 'I'll research later,' she said. 'I just hope we can get into this hotel.'

Right then, her phone rang, sounding loud and plaintive in the silent night. Somewhere, a dog started barking, adding to the woeful wail. Sally plucked her phone out and answered it quickly.

'Finally!' a voice cried. 'Where have you been?'

'On the bloody trail of the Hellfire,' Sally retorted. 'Why are you calling at this hour?' She looked at the others, all expectantly waiting. 'It's Jacobs,' she said.

Mason checked the time. It was 2.55 a.m.

'He's keen,' he said. 'But how does he know we've—'

Sally cut him off. 'We grabbed the latest clue from the inverted cross,' she said and quickly told him about it. 'We're heading for a hotel before—'

'Were you safe? No unwanted visitors?' Jacobs sounded strained.

'Nothing like that.'

'I am surprised. I would have thought Moloch would have found another way by now.'

'What other way could he find?'

'Well, that's not why I rang,' Jacobs said in a rushed voice. 'We have a situation here.'

'Has Moloch found you out?' Sally asked.

'Um, nothing like that. But I have an ally here, one that I didn't know of until today. His name is Professor Taylor, and he has just caused quite a stir.'

Sally frowned. 'In what way?'

'Taylor was among a crowd of worshippers who visited today. It wasn't a full Black Mass, those are mostly monthly, but it was a small ceremony, something that Moloch calls his "extras". Everyone's invited, but only about half ever turn up. Anyway, Taylor came today and, mid-ceremony, he called Moloch out. Stood up to him.'

'What do you mean?'

'Taylor denounced the whole cabal. Confronted Moloch. Said it was all a sham, a horrific imitation, and that Moloch was a murderer, a madman. He tore his mask off and ranted right into Moloch's face, then whirled and shouted at all the others gathered there. I wanted to join him, to stand up and agree, but I couldn't.'

'What happened to Taylor?' Mason asked.

'That's why I'm ringing. I know you're here in London because you're following the inverted cross clue. Taylor bulled his way out of the room, stormed out. He's in the wind. And Moloch . . . ' Jacobs swallowed hard. 'Moloch . . . '

'What about him?' Roxy urged.

'He's apoplectic. Ready to do murder. I've now seen what would happen to me if I went against him. I need you to save Taylor's life.'

Mason looked longingly at the hotel in front of them, its light a welcoming golden glow spreading across the pavement. 'Now?'

'I've been trying you for a while. Clearly, you were out of signal. Taylor is out there on his own and Moloch has sent men to look for him.'

Mason felt that familiar tug. A need to protect someone in trouble. He saw the same look on the faces of his friends.

'Are you sure Professor Taylor is okay?' Sally asked.

'Not at all. Moloch's rage wasn't hidden. He didn't clear the room. He called men to him and sent them after Taylor, told them to rip his head off.'

'If Taylor's got any sense, he'll be in hiding,' Hassell said.

'How long ago was this?' Roxy asked.

'Not long. I have Taylor's home address, at great personal risk to myself. Are you ready?'

Mason said that they were. Taylor's address was in Kingston upon Thames, not too far away. Hassell jumped on his phone and ordered an Uber. It was unconventional, but it was the only thing they could do, given the circumstances.

Why do this? Mason wondered. The answers hit him hard. Taylor was under threat from Moloch. Mason couldn't help but want to protect people. Taylor could also be an important ally against Moloch, especially in the evidence-gathering phase. They couldn't let Taylor's life just be snuffed out, leave him as yet another victim of Moloch.

'We can check his home out,' Mason said. 'But beyond that, I don't see there's a lot we can do. If he's in hiding, he could be anywhere. Are you still close to Moloch?'

'He's stormed into his office, but I heard him on the phone. As of twenty minutes ago, Taylor hadn't been found.'

'Maybe he's riding it out somewhere,' Roxy said. 'Or he went to a hotel.'

'There will be people on his house,' Hassell said. 'It's how I'd do it. You have someone watching his home. He's almost certain to show up at some point.'

Mason waited for the Uber to appear, torn. It had already been a long-ass day. And here they were, about to abandon their mission and try to save the life of a Satanist – someone they didn't know – and all at the request of another man they didn't really know. Still, one more person acting against Moloch was a bonus and, later, when it came to evidence-gathering and a trial, Taylor's testimony would prove invaluable.

A minivan pulled up to the kerb. They piled in and the van pulled away. They sat in silence for thirty minutes, their backpacks in their laps, staring out the window. Soon, they were approaching Taylor's address and asked the driver to slow down.

'This will do.' Mason waited for the vehicle to stop and then jumped out.

He looked around. The others glanced left and right. They were on a tree-lined street, cars parked all along the road. Silence hung over the area like a heavy shroud. They stood there for a moment, getting their bearings.

'So, Taylor's home is a few hundred yards that way,' Mason said. 'If we walk past it now, in a group, is that gonna look suspicious?'

'I'd say so,' Hassell said.

'Then it's up to you,' Mason said. 'Stay in touch with your phone. Call us if you need us.'

Hassell nodded. He turned and crept away into the darkness, slipping through front gardens so that he was off the main road. Hassell kept Taylor's home in sight, his focus on all the cars that were parked close by.

He identified the bad guys quickly. They weren't really trying to hide. Two men sat in the front seat of a Ford Focus, the tips of their cigarettes glowing. Hassell was at first surprised to see only two, but then realised others would be deployed elsewhere in the search, maybe waiting close by or on another errand.

Hassell crouched behind a low stone wall, partially hidden by a thorny bush. From here, he could see the men in the car and Taylor's front door. He waited.

But not for long. As he watched, a car came up the street, headlights cutting a swathe through the dark. There was a figure inside. Hassell couldn't see him very well, but he could tell it was a man. The car pulled into a parking space, then sat idling for a few minutes before switching off. Finally, a man emerged, an older man with grey hair and thin cheeks and long legs. He wore a grey suit and carried a briefcase.

And walked straight up to Professor Taylor's door.

Hassell raced back to Mason and the others. 'You see him?'

'What the hell is he doing back here?' Roxy asked. 'Assuming it's him.'

'Put yourself in his shoes,' Sally said. 'He's an older guy, probably unsure what he should do or where he should go. Doesn't know the extent of Moloch's rage or the worst that could happen to him. Probably went somewhere to cool down for a while, and maybe to hide. Assumes anyone following him will have given up by now. The poor guy doesn't know the danger he's in.'

Professor Taylor unlocked his front door and disappeared into his house.

Mason peered as Hassell pointed out the car with the two men inside. Hiding behind parked cars, they crept nearer. The two men were currently on a phone, talking, probably getting orders or calling more men to the scene.

Time was running out.

Mason watched. Once the phone call had ended, there was more movement inside the car and then the click of a door opening.

Both men got out of the car and started walking towards Professor Taylor's home.

Chapter 24

Mason and the others started sprinting.

They ran down the middle of the street in the cold dark, the breath streaming from their mouths. They ran through parked cars and came at the two men from behind. At the last second, both men whirled around to face them.

Mason said nothing. He rushed the first man, and at full pelt, swung an elbow. The elbow hit hard, striking the man across the face, sending him flailing to the right. Roxy was closest to the other man and led with a kick, slamming him in the chest and sending him flying backwards so fast he fell over.

Both men whipped knives from their belts.

Mason circled warily. His opponent's nose was gushing blood, but he ignored it. The man slashed left and right, snarled, tried to cut Mason. Blood flew. Mason danced away from the attacks, waiting for a clear opportunity to attack.

Roxy kicked out again, knocking the knife out of her adversary's hands. The blade flew and hit a parked car with a dull clunk. The man faced her now empty-handed and rushed in. Roxy half-turned and gave a side-kick, striking her oncoming enemy full in the face. The man groaned and slumped, falling to his knees. Roxy stepped in and finished him with a blow to the back of the head.

Mason continued to circle. By now, Quaid and Hassell were ready as backup, inching their way towards the man's blind side, but Mason knew, though they had superior numbers, you didn't take any chances in a knife fight.

Just then, several things happened at once. Two cars flew around a corner and roared up the street. Mason's opponent glanced at them and then smirked at him.

'Now you're in trouble,' he said.

Mason watched the cars pull up to the kerb. There were three men in each car, which now made eight. Not good odds. The men did not appear to be armed apart from the knives they pulled from their waists, and Mason wasn't about to shoot someone in the streets of London and end up in jail.

The guns, if needed, would be a deterrent only.

The newcomers dashed towards the fight. At that moment, Professor Taylor's door opened to reveal the old man standing there, glaring at everyone.

'What the hell is going on here?'

Mason swore to himself. This had quickly gone from bad to worse. Now Taylor was in the thick of it, too. As Mason watched, his knife-wielding opponent turned the weapon in his hand, took aim and flung it at the professor.

The blade whacked into the wooden door frame an inch from Taylor's nose, shuddering in place. The old man looked amazed. Mason's opponent, now weaponless, backed away. His reinforcements were almost here.

Mason took stock. What the hell were they supposed to do next?

'We have to grab a car,' Roxy said.

Mason nodded. He saw Roxy fall to her knees and quickly rummage through the pockets of the man she'd felled, coming up with a set of black and silver keys. Mason was already moving. He ran towards Professor Taylor, grabbed the old man's arm, and hustled him away from the front door.

'What are you doing?'

'Please come with us. They're here to kill you.' Mason pulled the man along.

The professor didn't look surprised, and he didn't remonstrate. Quaid was struggling with the knife thrower and Hassell was facing the newcomers with Sally.

'Move!' Mason yelled.

Roxy shot off first, keys in hand, running for the car. Mason and the others followed with the professor. Mason flung an elbow back into the knife thrower's nose as he tried to stop them and stooped quickly to collect another knife that fell from the guy's pocket.

Roxy jumped into the car, taking the driver's seat. Quickly, she hit a button to start it up, threw the keys in the tray beside her. 'Wrong side of the damn road,' she muttered. 'I'll do my best.'

Mason was stuffing Taylor into the footwell of the front passenger seat. There were too many of them to fit properly inside the car, so they went two-up in the passenger seat and three in the back. They didn't have time to close the doors. As they seated themselves, their attackers were already reaching for them. A man grabbed Mason's arm. Mason threw a punch, fending him off. Another man stooped and reached in. There were arms everywhere.

In the back, Hassell and Quaid, seated on either side of Sally, were fending off outstretched arms, punching the faces of men trying to yank them out or get inside themselves.

'Go!' Mason yelled.

Roxy saw they were all in, engaged gear, and put her foot down. The car lurched and then stopped. The attackers fell away and then came rushing back. Roxy pressed the accelerator pedal again.

The car sped forward, doors flapping. One of them crunched into a parked car. Mason reached out, grabbed a handle, and pulled the door shut. Through the side mirror, he could see their opponents rushing back towards their own cars.

The engine roared as Roxy steered their vehicle down the long street. 'I haven't a clue where I'm going,' she said.

'Just drive,' Mason said. 'They're coming.'

'It's a bit uncomfortable down here,' Taylor said.

Mason pushed his seat back as far as possible. 'It's better than being dead,' he said.

In the side mirror he could see headlights behind them, coming up fast. The three cars shot along the quiet streets, twisting and turning through junctions, their headlights spearing through the semi-darkness. All Mason could see in the rear-view were huge shining lights.

'We could end this right now,' Hassell said.

Mason already knew it. 'If we fire our guns around here, we're gonna end up getting arrested. We're in the middle of bloody London.'

'Only if they find us.'

It was too risky, Mason thought. London was covered by more CCTV cameras than many other cities. The chances of them being seen were pretty high. And it was gone three in the morning with nowhere to go.

'We're not going to shake them,' Quaid said.

Mason struggled for an idea. Parkland shot by to the right, lying in pitch blackness. A row of shops flashed past to the left, then a pub with its lights still on. London was lit chiefly by streetlamps, their stark glares throwing a bleak, impersonal light over everything.

Roxy slowed for a bend. The car behind had had enough by now and didn't bother. It rammed their rear end with a screech of metal. The wheel bucked in Roxy's hands and they went momentarily sideways, but she caught the slide and straightened the wheel. She grumbled about not being able to retaliate, and tried to keep the car straight.

In the back seat, Hassell, Quaid and Sally had been jerked forward by the attack, Quaid smacking his forehead on the back seat. Now they all scrabbled around for their seatbelts as a wash of light came through the back window.

'They're coming again,' Sally said.

Roxy sped up, tried to soften the blow. It worked, to a point. The car still hit them, this time on the left flank, trying to spin them sideways. Roxy was ready for it and compensated, ending up several car lengths ahead of their pursuers. She cheered.

'There are only a few ways this can end,' Hassell said. 'None of them are good.'

'We're not getting away,' Quaid reiterated.

Mason considered the options. If someone called the police, it could get very messy, and eventually that was bound to happen. They had already raced past a few knots of late-night revellers, some of them turning and cheering the speeders on. And there was no way they were going to shake their pursuers.

'Go on the offensive,' he muttered.

'About time.' Hassell reached into his waistband.

'I don't mean get your gun out,' Mason said. 'I mean, we break them before they break us. Roxy, how good are you at driving?'

The raven-haired American looked at him. 'I'm shit, actually.'

'Oh.' He hadn't expected that. 'You think you can do a one-eighty?'

'I might if I knew what the hell it was.'

146

'Turn the car around so it's facing in the other direction. Try to hit them broadside. All we have to do is stop them driving.'

Roxy shook her head. 'You're talking about drifting the back wheels. I can't do that.'

'I can,' Quaid said, leaning forward. 'Slam on your brakes.'

Without a word, Roxy hit the brake pedal.

Chapter 25

Mason jerked forward, head almost hitting the dashboard. Taylor groaned. Roxy, knowing Quaid's intentions, threw open her door and leapt out of the car. By the time the pursuers had caught up, slammed their own brakes on, and started throwing open doors, Roxy and Quaid had switched places.

They shot off again.

Now a little further ahead, Quaid threw the car around a few bends, getting the feel of it. Then, when the other cars vanished from sight for a few seconds around a corner, he half-turned to Mason.

'Ready?'

'Do it.'

Quaid put his foot down and spun the wheel hard. Mason held on, trying to steady Professor Taylor at the same time. The car lurched and then drifted around until it was facing in the other direction.

Now, the pursuit cars were coming right towards them.

Quaid sped up, moving nonchalantly towards them. He drove carefully, trying to look like just another driver. Of course, they wouldn't get away with it . . . but maybe they'd get away with it for long enough.

The cars drew closer. Mason didn't look at them directly, but watched from the corner of his eye. Because the car didn't immediately challenge them, he could tell the driver was unsure.

Maybe they *would* get away with it.

The cars passed each other. Mason saw the faces of the occupants staring at them. He saw the change in their demeanour, when they started to shout and point.

Quaid saw it too. He pressed the accelerator, sped up the road they'd just come down. He drifted around the bend at the top, performed another one-eighty, and then just waited. The engine purred.

The first car appeared, rounding the bend. Quaid shot forward, crashing into its side with a sound of rending metal. The impact sent the other car slewing around. Its rear end crashed into a parked car. Mason heard the engine cut out.

Quaid backed away. Their own car seemed fine. Now the second car was coming around the corner, slowing as it saw what had happened to its companion. Quaid gunned his own engine, sent their car slamming into the other's front. This time it was a stalemate, both cars coming to a sudden stop as, with a whoosh, Quaid's airbag went off. Quaid looked shocked and didn't move, so it was up to Mason to pierce it with his knife and deflate it.

Quaid slammed their car into reverse, backing off.

Taylor moaned in the footwell, but Mason now had powerful arms clasped around him.

By now, men were jumping out of the first car, four of them in total. Quaid was looking ahead, seeing if he could fit around the second car and back down the road they'd just used. The gap wasn't large enough.

He was forced to back up. He did so now, at speed, the transmission whining. The men started running towards the reversing car. The second car was still running. It inched forward carefully, as if testing its roadworthiness.

'Swing it around and we're out of here,' Mason said with a touch of triumph in his voice.

Quaid nodded. He swung the wheel hard. The car wasn't agile enough to spin all the way around, or Quaid wasn't good enough to make it happen. Instead, it turned ninety degrees, now crosswise in the road.

The running men closed the gap.

Quaid flicked the paddle shift, put the car into first gear, went forward. Then he engaged reverse, twisting the wheel hard. Now, the men were very close. Mason stared out the window at them, his face tense.

One man threw his knife. It clanged off the window harmlessly. Another had thought to grab a tyre iron from the back of their car and now threw it end over end. The iron fortunately struck the metal bodywork instead of the window, dented it, and fell to the ground. Quaid shot backwards, and then twisted the wheel again, now flicking the car into first gear.

They were out of here, Mason thought. In the back seat, Roxy swore with pleasure.

And then their car engine died.

Quaid stared in disbelief, pumping the pedals. After a second, he jabbed at the start button. The engine whirred. It didn't take hold. Now their enemy arrived, yanking at the locked doors and banging on the windows. The man who'd hurled the tyre iron reached down to pick it up. It was only a matter of time before they started smashing windows.

Quaid jabbed desperately at the start button. He looked around wildly. 'Shit,' he said. 'We're sitting ducks here.'

Mason still had his arms around Taylor. He hesitated, looking up into the faces of snarling men, many of whom were banging on the windows. They were trapped. There were men on all sides of the car now, eight in total. They were even climbing on the boot and the roof, stamping. There was now no doubt in Mason's mind that the police would have been called.

But they weren't here yet.

He spoke into the stillness inside the car.

'Any ideas?'

'We're fucking trapped,' Roxy said.

'We get out fighting,' Quaid said. 'Try to leave Taylor in the car.'

'I'm done with fighting,' Hassell told them. 'We have our guns. It's time these assholes saw them.'

Mason felt backed into a corner. If they drew their guns, they might be forced to use them. If they didn't, they might be disarmed, and the guns used against them. And the cops couldn't be over ten or fifteen minutes away, if they'd been called.

'We could run,' Sally said. 'Fight our way free and just run.' At least, Mason thought, she had confidence.

'With Professor Taylor though?' Roxy asked.

Quaid was still trying to start the car. Incredibly, on about the fifteenth attempt, the engine fired up. Quaid stared at it in disbelief.

'Well, fu—' he began.

Mason almost jumped out of his skin as the window next to him suddenly shattered. The tyre iron had struck it hard. Glass shards flew in, all over Mason's shoulders and lap and Taylor's head. Grasping hands and arms reached in through the jagged hole.

Mason pulled away from them. Quaid drove them forward, wheel on full lock. They ran over someone's foot, knocked into another man's kneecap, sending him to the ground. They eased their way through their opponents as the car turned, and then they were straight.

The back window shattered. The tyre iron flew inside the car, almost striking Roxy on the back of the head. A man hurled himself through the new gap.

The figure flew over the head restraints and struck everyone's heads and shoulders. It kept rolling, coming down on their laps before it stopped. The heavy rolling body struck Roxy, and she saw stars. Another man was already clambering up the boot.

Roxy punched downwards into the body, aiming for the face and head. The man who'd rolled inside was short, wearing a black jacket and was now curled up, trying to protect himself and probably thinking what a bad idea it had been to jump in over the back seat. Hassell and Sally were also throwing punches at him.

Hassell undid his seatbelt and turned, facing the next man, who was trying to squeeze his way into the car. It was a tight fit, and there wasn't much room to throw a punch, but Hassell managed a few jabs to the face. The man's momentum halted, and he was now blocking the back window rather than coming through it.

Mason had hands grabbing his jacket, hands in his short hair, hands even trying to take hold of his ears. He jabbed at them all, shoving them away, tried to bend wrists and fingers. He took a blow to the side of the face, another to the temple. He couldn't hit back, could barely move. Someone tried to rake his eyeballs.

Quaid pressed the accelerator.

The car started moving. Men were holding on to it as if trying to prevent its forward momentum. They grabbed hold of pillars and bumpers and wing mirrors. They were trying everything in their power to hold on, to get inside, to drag Mason and the others outside. But they couldn't stop the car from moving.

Hassell punched his opponent in the nose. The man blinked in surprise, then fell backwards, rolling right down the boot into another man. Both of them fell away into the road, tumbling.

Roxy had her guy around the throat, choking him. He was flailing around across her lap ineffectually. Sally had hold of his legs to make it harder for him to move. It was just a matter of time before he passed out.

The car was rolling. Hassell threw open his door and, with Roxy's help, threw the man out and into the roadway.

Quaid pressed his foot to the floor. The car sped up and roared away. Behind them, the men stood in harsh silence, watching.

Mason's head and face hurt from the strange beating he'd taken. He reached down now to tap Professor Taylor on the shoulder.

'Are you okay?'

'Never been better,' came the mumbled voice.

Quaid put several junctions and corners between them and their would-be pursuers before slowing to the speed limit. Gradually, Mason began to feel as if they'd escaped. By the skin of their teeth, yes, but they had made it.

He sank back into the seat, elated.

Chapter 26

They drove through London under the stark white lampposts, putting some distance between themselves and their pursuers.

They sat back, relaxed. The car was a mess. They couldn't keep driving it. Some local patrol might spot them. Sally brought up a list of hotels on her phone and they drove carefully to the nearest. As they drove, they spoke briefly with Professor Taylor, though they knew they didn't have any time to waste.

They had to unravel the next clue.

But Professor Taylor was more important for now.

They left the car on a side street, walked twenty minutes to the hotel, and entered the lobby. Mason pondered what the professor had told them, that Moloch was warped, twisted, certifiably mad, and dangerous as hell, that he was escalating, growing more malevolent, that he truly believed in what he was doing, that he wouldn't let anyone leave the cabal on pain of death. Taylor did not know if anyone else felt the same way he did – they didn't mention Jacobs' name to him – but he believed there would be some. They were just too scared to act. On being asked what he thought Moloch would do next, Taylor said, 'He'll just kill. And kill again. This huge Black Mass he's planning – it will be insane.'

Taylor had known nothing about the Hellfire quest, but he knew Moloch was planning something that would put the cabal on the map, so to speak. They could attract even more powerful members and then, who knew where Moloch might end up? Royalty? Part of a shadow government? He really wanted everything.

Sally paid for a room, booking it under her name, and gave the keycard to Professor Taylor. They were standing in the lobby at gone four a.m., amid the plush sofas, the gold wall sconces, and the Persian carpeting. Mason felt the silence that surrounded them like a thick wall. It was the utter deep of night, and there wasn't another soul around. Even the receptionist was sitting with his shoulders slumped, his eyes drooping.

'Lie low,' Sally said to Taylor. 'Low profile, you understand? Stay indoors. Eat in here. Give us time to take down Moloch.'

'And to get this Hellfire?' Taylor looked suspicious.

'Believe me, we're not after the riches. We're in this to save a friend, a friend of my father,' Sally told him. 'And now you. But you must help yourself, too. We will need your witness statement when this is all over.'

'I know that.'

'Don't let anyone find out where you are.'

'I won't. You're guys are really going to take down Moloch?'

Mason answered that one. 'I think we have to. He's a murderer, and he's only getting worse. With you and our other informant, we now have two credible witnesses to everything that's gone on. The trouble is, we have no actual proof.'

'He's a clever guy. Gets everything cleaned up by people he trusts implicitly. Of course, they're very well paid.'

'Maybe we'll catch him in the act,' Roxy said. 'I'd like that.'

'Moloch must be stopped,' Mason said. 'I don't think it's just about the Hellfire now. I mean, look how he turned on you, Professor. Sent those men to kill you.'

Taylor nodded. 'I didn't return home at first, expecting that he might send someone to reason with me, maybe change my mind. That's why I stayed out late. I never expected he would send people to kill me.'

'Is there anything you can tell us?' Hassell asked.

'I don't know what your other informant has told you, but I have Moloch's address in the country. His estate. I can give you that. Unfortunately, I have no photographic or recorded evidence, though. I'm only now beginning to realise what a mistake that was.'

'Don't worry about it,' Mason said. 'If someone had seen you recording on the premises, they might never have let you leave.'

'I was determined to get out of there.'

Mason shrugged. He looked around. Rather than stay at the same hotel as Taylor, they had decided to walk a short distance to the next one, just in case anyone asked about six people checking in late. They probably didn't need to take such a precaution, but it was better to be safe than sorry.

Mason's face and head ached from his battering. He did not know how he looked, but the receptionist hadn't batted an eye, so it couldn't be too bad. It was time to take their leave of Professor Taylor.

'I'm dog tired,' he said. 'Let's get going.'

They said goodbye to the professor, reiterated their warnings, told him they'd be back in touch when Moloch was out of the picture, and stepped out into the street. By now, there were a few early joggers around, a few dog walkers, and maybe still one or two very late revellers. They hastened a block to the next hotel. Once they'd checked in, they quickly parted and agreed to meet for a late breakfast the next day. After that, Mason took an elevator to his room.

Finally, he fell fully clothed on to the bed.

And was asleep in seconds.

Chapter 27

On hearing the bad news, Moloch decided to take the meeting in his dungeons.

He stood there now, looking around, waiting. The rooms themselves weren't real dungeons. He just liked to think of them as such, and had kitted them out to look relatively authentic. There were the naturally dank, dripping walls, with subdued lighting and a damaged floor. There were cells and a room with torture implements that he never used. It was a damp, foreboding place where he rarely ventured.

Moloch checked his watch. His guest was running late. That would be worse for him. Around the room stood four of his guards, all armed with guns and knives, their muscled chests wrapped in tight T-shirts and jackets, their eyes hard and flinty. They had been told to follow Moloch's lead and do whatever he said.

Moloch received a text message. He glanced at his phone, reading that the man had just pulled up to the house. Moloch smiled and shuddered. Though the man was the bearer of bad news, Moloch would enjoy what came after.

He thought about everything he had. A few rooms to the east were where he held his ritualistic Black Masses, where he stuffed in the influential and the powerful, had them wear masks and witness murder. He had come a long way in a short time, and he hoped, soon, to go much further. The Hellfire and its fantastic wealth would facilitate that. The black clouds that accompanied those thoughts currently lay directly above Jonathan Jacobs. Moloch thought himself lucky that he had ousted the old man.

Luck? Or something else?

Moloch was a firm believer. He had seen things. Heard things. He had dreams in which dark souls came to visit. They whispered in his ear, told him what to do. Their voices were legion. The things they predicted always came true. Soon now . . . he *would* summon the Devil himself.

He listened to the voices, carried out their wishes. He felt the presence of a malevolent *greatness*, knew that he had caught something's attention. Moloch preferred to think of that something as Satan.

What had started out as a hobby had developed into something fantastical. These days, Moloch felt guided, steered in the right direction. Satan was his master, his saviour, the glue that held everything together. The voice in his head, directing him, told him where to go and what to do next.

He paced the floor, unable to stand still. He wanted to don a robe and a mask and worship something dark and bloody. Wanted to bring a sacrifice to the master. Well, this time, maybe a dying body would have to do.

There was a knock at the door. Moloch turned towards it, saw it open. A man came through, a tall man with a bald pate, wearing a leather jacket and jeans. He carried a gun and a knife and now looked warily around the room, studying all the guards. Finally, his gaze came to rest on Moloch.

'Sir. I came at your request.'

'Come closer.'

159

'Do you want a report?'

'I said, come closer.'

'Of course. What can I do for you, sir?'

Moloch bristled inside. *What can you do for me?* He maintained a cool outward demeanour. 'What happened out there?'

The man, whose name was Scott Goldwyn, looked a little more confident. 'Of course, sir. I was in charge, but it wasn't our fault at all. We tracked Professor Taylor, left men stationed outside his house, and waited for him to return. I also sent men to his favourite haunts until they closed – the local pub, the coffee shop he frequents – in the hope he might be hanging out there. I got the call that he had returned home very late and I sent the men into action.'

'Action?' Moloch already hated the sound of the man's voice.

'Yes, sir.' Goldwyn looked more at ease now, standing with relaxed shoulders, apparently pleased with himself. 'I ordered the two men at the scene to follow Taylor and apprehend him as soon as possible. They exited their car, came up behind our quarry, and then . . . well, then . . . they were jumped, sir.'

'They were jumped? Just like that?'

'These people appeared from out of nowhere. And they were good, very good. Five of them.'

Moloch got an odd feeling in the pit of his stomach. Five of them? And they were good? He'd already quizzed Jacobs about the team racing and fighting them to get the Hellfire. They were good, too.

'Describe these five to me.'

'A normal guy. Didn't look strong or capable at all, but packed a hell of a punch. One woman with dark hair who really got stuck in and enjoyed the fighting. A younger guy, not as capable but who still stood up to my men. An older guy who gave as good as he got. And a young woman.

Dark hair with blue tips. She kind of hovered around the fight, darting in when she could and getting in a few good shots. They were skilful and worked together well as a team.'

'That's what beat you?'

'Well, I wouldn't say they *beat* us exactly. In the end, they ran away.'

Moloch was still processing the description. Jacobs had told him all about Sally Rusk and her professor father. He knew what she looked like. It appeared that the same team that was hunting for the Hellfire had just rescued Professor Taylor. What did that mean, exactly?

'How did you lose Taylor?' Moloch asked.

'I'd say we didn't really lose him. It was unlucky. They bundled him into a car, took off. We gave chase through the streets. It was a tough balancing act, because we know we're supposed to stay low-profile, but we also didn't want to let them get away. In the end, they caused the big scene, crashed the cars, started the ruckus. We barely made our way out of there before the cops arrived.'

Moloch shuddered to think about what would have happened if they hadn't. At least that was one point in Goldwyn's favour.

'Did you try to track them?'

'Lost their trail completely. We drove around for a while but didn't come across them.'

'You drove around for a while?'

'Yes, sir. Made circuits. Checked car parks, twenty-four-hour restaurants and takeaways. That kind of thing.'

Moloch had heard enough. Goldwyn wasn't totally incompetent, but he had royally fucked up. He had lost Professor Taylor, and Taylor could do them great harm. Taylor had to be killed, wiped out of existence. They also had to find out if the guy had gathered any evidence.

But that wouldn't be Goldwyn's problem.

That would be for the next leader of Goldwyn's team.

Moloch felt a delicious shudder coast through him. The dark master would revel in the next few minutes. This was what he lived for. He nodded at one of the guards. Goldwyn's eyes narrowed briefly before he was shot in the right thigh. At first, unable to believe it, he stared down at the burgeoning wound, but then the pain hit him. He yelled, collapsed to his knees, started foaming at the mouth. He was still a trained guard, and he reached for his own weapons.

Moloch's men were on him in a second. They grabbed his arms, forced them above his head. They disarmed him. Goldwyn groaned and yelled in pain. Blood flowed from the wound in his thigh onto the damp concrete floor.

Moloch walked up to him. This would be no easy death for the man who'd failed. Moloch murmured the words *'Ave Satanus'*, as he approached the squealing man and then kicked him full in the face.

The guards held on tight. Goldwyn's head jerked to the left. His left eye closed. Moloch liked the look. He kicked the man again, this time with the other foot. Goldwyn's head wrenched in the other direction. Several teeth flew from his mouth and there was blood on his chin. Moloch reined himself in. He didn't want to kill Goldwyn too early, and he didn't want to knock the guy unconscious.

'Shoot him again,' he said, bending down to look the man dead in the eyes. 'Take out a knee.'

Goldwyn's eyes flew wide open. He struggled, but could not shake off the grip of the guards. A man came around, aimed his gun at Goldwyn's left knee and then fired. Goldwyn let out a high-pitched whine. The guards let him go. Goldwyn cried and slumped and tried to crawl, then let out a scream of pain as his broken knee dragged on the floor.

'What next?' Moloch said with a tremor of pleasure.

Maybe they should break something. They couldn't keep shooting the guy. He'd either pass out from the pain or die of blood loss. Yes, breaking something sounded good to Moloch.

He trod on Goldwyn's ankle with all his strength. He wasn't sure if he'd broken anything, so did it again. He targeted the man's fingers, dancing around him and laughing. He hadn't felt this good since the last Black Mass. Happiness swam through his head along with a current of blackness, something tinged with madness.

Moloch knew it was his black Satanic master guiding him.

He lashed out again and again at Goldwyn, broke things, cut things, sliced things off. The blood was copious, the screams and cries eventually dying down to murmurs and groans. But, happily, Goldwyn still lived. He hadn't expired too quickly.

The guards were standing around, aghast. Occasionally, they were forced to help. They were all loyal to Moloch and extremely well paid, paid to keep their mouths shut. They were also all ex-military and were used to seeing vile extremes. Still, some of them found it hard not to react as Moloch stomped and chopped and sliced and kneed his way through the misshapen hulk that had once been Scott Goldwyn.

When he was done, Moloch was dripping blood and panting heavily. The blood wasn't his, but it was all over his hands and face. He stepped away from the fresh corpse and told his men to take care of it, then went quickly into the rooms where he performed the Black Masses. He stripped off, now just a supplicant covered in blood, fell to his knees before the black altar. Moloch held up his hands and started chanting a Satanic prayer.

It flowed out of him, flowed from him into the darkness, returned from the darkness as advice and encouragement and acceptance. He rubbed the blood all over his body; he was a vessel, a chalice of Satan. What the dark master wanted, he would get.

And acquiring Hellfire would increase the dark master's hold on the world exponentially. Through Moloch, Satan's influence would magnify.

And Moloch himself would find his holdings increased, his standing untouchable. Maybe . . . just maybe . . . this dark master would finally appear to him.

It was everything Moloch wanted.

Chapter 28

Ed Bullion didn't like killing time.

He was waiting now, pacing the lobby of a hotel, on hold and just waiting for orders. A lot of his job involved waiting, and it was the worst part. In the army, Bullion had been forced to wait and then wait some more. You waited for a mission, waited for the go, then were often told that the mission had been cancelled. And then you were waiting again.

He paced now, watched by the receptionist and a bellboy. He didn't care. The other team members were scattered around the hotel, in their rooms, in the bar, in the restaurant. He didn't care where they were, just so long as they came running when the time came to act.

Bullion had been waiting for a long time. Moloch was supposed to call with the next clue, but that hadn't happened yet. According to Moloch, Jacobs hadn't made the call yet, so they were all forced to wait. Jacobs then told Moloch that he had called, but the phone hadn't been answered. Moloch apparently believed him, telling Bullion that the other team had been busy.

And still Bullion paced.

He was raring to go, eager to find the next clue and earn the big bonus – on top of the half million – Moloch had promised him. The bonus alone could keep him in Vegas for a year. And Bullion liked the sound of that. He was a consummate gambler, but savvy enough to only bet what he had. Bullion never let himself get into debt.

He'd had time now to think about what he was doing, who he was working for. Moloch was an odd creature, perhaps the oddest Bullion had ever known. That meeting in the hotel in London had felt a little surreal. Moloch gave off the most evil vibes.

At the thought, Bullion stopped pacing and reached for the crucifix that hung around his neck. He touched it. Many who saw the crucifix hanging around the neck of the burly ex-army mercenary asked him about it, thinking it out of place. Bullion never told them the truth.

Now it brought him a kind of peace, drove all thoughts of Moloch from his mind. He forced himself to find a seat and sit down. The crucifix helped.

Just then, his second-in-command, the woman Slater, came over and plonked herself in the chair opposite him.

'Did I ask for company?' he said.

'Heard anything yet?' She ignored his question, looking bored out of her mind. Slater was thin and wiry and as fast as anything Bullion had ever seen. She belonged in his team and was good for the second-in-command position. Despite her unruliness.

'As soon as I hear anything, you will be the first to know.'

'What do you make of this Moloch dude?'

Bullion was taken aback. He wondered if she'd got the same bad vibes he did. 'He's the boss.' He shrugged. 'It doesn't matter what we think.'

'Just do the mission?'

'Do the mission. Get paid. Get out. That's it.'

'I heard a few things, that's all.'

Bullion narrowed his eyes at her. 'What is that supposed to mean?'

'Well, you know, soldiers talk. Especially ex-soldiers. Well, we know Moloch's real name, right? He owned that restaurant we went to. I checked him out, found his address, assumed if he wanted our help, then he'd probably have other mercs on his payroll. Turns out I know a few of them.'

'You've been in touch?'

'Wasn't hard. Now, they stayed extremely cagey, but it seems this Moloch is something of a dark horse. Emphasis on the dark.'

Bullion shook his head. 'I don't know what you mean.'

Slater leaned forward. 'Every month, like clockwork, he holds a Black Mass.'

Bullion was momentarily speechless. 'A *what?*'

'You heard right. The guy's a fucking devil worshipper.'

'Well, he is wealthy,' Bullion mused. 'A lot of these wealthy assholes go to extreme lengths to fill their time. Do you have any more details?'

Slater pursed her lips. 'Nah, they wouldn't elaborate. Became standoffish when I pushed. I only thought . . . ' she trailed off.

Bullion engaged her with a look. 'Thought what?'

'It's your crucifix, the one you always wear. I came to you with this in case there's any . . . conflict.'

Bullion was surprised. He hadn't thought any members of his team would care. They were a team, yes, but they were in it for the payoff, and though they worked together, they didn't exactly work *for* each other.

'I'm not religious,' he said briefly. 'This is something else.'

She didn't push. He sat back then, clamming up. Soon Slater got up and walked away, leaving him with his new impressions of Moloch. Devil worshipper? That was different. Bullion guessed it took all sorts, and assumed Moloch and his rich asshole pals were playing at it, chanting and singing and all that crap. Waving their tiny wands about.

He smiled grimly, felt the weight of the crucifix against his neck. He looked down, saw it shining up at him, felt a wave of sadness.

Bullion wore the crucifix in memory. It was the exact one his brother had been wearing when he died. Bullion had been as close to his brother as anyone could be. They'd shared everything together. Both soldiers, stationed together, one working alongside the other. They had shared good days and bad days, hot, hard, dusty days. They had laughed at nights in the mess hall or around campfires. They had shared jokes and stories they knew so well with the other men.

It had been a grand second tour when the 'bad thing' happened.

Bullion saw the 'bad thing' as the turning point in his life. His brother had been walking alongside an armoured vehicle and had caught a sniper's bullet to the brain. It was instant lights out. One second, his brother had been there, solid, secure, Bullion's anchor, and the next he was gone, never to return. Bullion had lost it when he learned what had happened, lost it for days.

Now, he carried the crucifix everywhere, into battle, into the tightest of situations. If there was a heaven, his brother was watching over him. And if there was a Hell . . . well, that just brought the image of Moloch back to Bullion's mind.

Weird.

He shook himself out of his reverie. He'd tell no one what the crucifix really represented. Let them think. Let them talk. He didn't care. The memory of his brother eclipsed everything.

He rose, started pacing once again. Slater's words had unfocused him, but they had at least passed a little time. Here they were, still waiting for some kind of contact from Moloch.

He went to the bar, grabbed a drink, and sat down. Bullion found it hard to relax at the best of times and when he did, it made him think of the worst of times.

It wasn't the best combination.

There was another problem, too.

They had arrived at the London mausoleum of the Duke of Adlington, too late to do anything about it. The other team had already been there, been and gone. Bullion didn't like to lose; he disliked it especially when the losses grew exponentially. They had crawled through the passages, braved the ledges, found the inverted cross in the chamber, and had been forced to touch and feel and climb it just to find out they'd been bested. Bullion now knew the leader of the other team's name – Joe Mason. Well, Mason, he thought, eventually there will come a reckoning.

The inverted cross had formed quite a statement. Bullion had been amazed at the cleanliness all around, as if people visited regularly. He had also been surprised at the declaration it announced, because at that point he hadn't known Moloch was a devil worshipper.

What did the Hellfire represent to a devil worshipper?

It was a mystery to Bullion, and not something he should delve too deeply into. The more he thought about Moloch's proclivities, the more uncomfortable he became.

And right then, as the amber liquid swirled around his glass, as the light caught the diamond-cut tumbler, as Bullion raised it to his lips to take a sip, the phone rang. Bullion checked the screen.

Moloch.

His heart leapt; his mind clicked into gear. He answered almost immediately. 'Yes, Boss?'

'Jacobs has come through. He spoke to them just now, or so he says. I wonder if he got the clue a bit earlier and has been stalling. Anyway, that's not the point. You're headed to Milan.'

Bullion raised an eyebrow. 'Milan?'

'Yes, and looking for the Crown of Beelzebub.'

'Right, Boss. That sounds . . . spooky.'

169

'It should. Beelzebub's a great demon.'

A great demon? Bullion shuddered. 'Anything else?'

'Yeah, I'll text you the name of the church. You should look for the crown inside.'

'Inside a church?'

'Absolutely. But neither I nor you can spare the time for an explanation. You need to hit the road. This other crew is already on it, I'm sure.'

Bullion knew Moloch was right. Quickly, he ended the call and then summoned the men and women on his team.

'We're on,' he said. 'And this time, if we come up against those bastards, we kill them.'

Chapter 29

Joe Mason watched through the windows of the plane as it descended towards Milan's Malpensa airport, which was about twenty-five miles northwest of the city. A crisp-based snack sat before him and a can of soda from which he'd only sipped. Sally had been doing research the whole flight and knew exactly where to go once they landed. She'd also booked them a car.

The plane touched down, allowing them to disembark. They'd decided not to bring their weapons on the flight, though they had permits, so broke them down and discarded them in a rubbish bin. The trouble was, the permits were only valid when they were on a job and could prove it.

They cleared customs and quickly rented a car. Then they were driving towards and into the city of Milan, getting buzzed by young men on scooters and looking absently at the beautiful architecture. There were people everywhere, the roads choked with traffic. Quaid drove, complaining about having to use the wrong side of the road. He didn't like the car either, a Mercedes B-class. It was far too modern.

Sally spoke up from the back seat. 'So, if you remember, the clue points us to the Church of Santa Maria alla Fontana. That's located in the Piazza Santa Maria alla Fontana, which is where we're headed now.' She checked the time. 'It's three p.m. We should have plenty of time to find the crown.'

Mason drew a deep breath, dead tired. They'd only got to bed just before dawn and he hadn't got a great deal of sleep. Even that had been fitful, swimming with images of the inverted cross and how it felt beneath his fingers. When he woke, he was sweating, eyes wide open, breathing heavily.

Now, he tried to shake the memory. It was the bright light of day. There were hundreds of people around and they were headed to a normal, everyday church. How could that possibly go wrong?

'How long?' Hassell asked.

'Maybe twenty minutes.'

They settled back, took in the drive. Soon, they were cutting through the heart of Milan, getting closer to their destination. From the back of the car, Hassell spoke up.

'Is anyone else wondering how a Satanic relic has ended up in a Catholic church?'

'A great question,' Sally said. 'One that I've researched thoroughly. There are many Satanic objects nestling within today's churches, some known, some unknown. There's even one in the Vatican itself, called the Hell Hall. Though not specifically Satanic, it's regarded by many as something bordering on evil.'

'They never showed us that when we were there,' Roxy said with a smile.

'It's not exactly on the to-do list,' Sally said.

'Unlike that guy over there.' Roxy nonchalantly pointed out a well-dressed ice-cream seller.

'Anyway,' Sally went on. 'In many churches you can find drawings of the all-seeing eye of Lucifer. The same worshipped by the Illuminati. This pyramid with Lucifer's eye is evident in chairs, on walls, in cloth. There are also Pagan drawings everywhere. In the seat of the pope of the Roman Catholic Church, there is an inverted cross, and we

172

know what that means. The hall of the pope looks like the head of a serpent. Strange, eh?'

Mason didn't like the sound if it. It went against everything they'd been doing with the Catholic Church during the last few months, everything they'd learned and all the friends they'd made. He said nothing.

'I assume there are reasonable explanations for all that,' Quaid said.

'There always are,' Sally said, shrugging.

Quaid found a place to park, and soon they were out walking the crowded streets. It was a warm day, the sun intermittently peeking through the cloud cover. They stared up at the façade of the Church of Santa Maria alla Fontana, the Renaissance architecture quite striking, especially when the sun came out and struck it at the right angle. Sally led the way to the main door.

'The church is famous not only for its artistic features,' she said, 'but for several legends associated with it. They used it for wakes, and the central characters in them are always ghosts. The church has a haunted past. Other legends arise from the works of art that hang in the church, of which there are many for its relatively small size.'

They pushed open the door and entered, finding themselves immediately in the impressive nave. Mason saw a high vaulted ceiling supported by columns of grey stone, several dozen pews, and an altar at the far end. The church was almost empty, just a few people wandering about and sat in the pews. Sally let out a long sigh and turned around.

'I don't know where to start,' she said. 'But let's get going.'

'Do we have any idea what this Crown of Beelzebub looks like?' Hassell asked.

Sally shook her head. 'I can't remember a time when we were going in *this* blind. We'll just have to get lucky. But listen, this is a sixteenth-century church. The relics, the paintings, the altars, have all been here since those times. Nothing changes much.'

Feeling slightly buoyed, Mason ventured further into the church. There was an air of majesty in here, a sense of gravitas. He walked first to the left, and started checking the walls, the various carvings, even the surface of the vaulted columns that supported the ceiling. He scrutinised the floor and the sides of the pews themselves, trying to miss nothing. All around the church, his colleagues did the same. One break he found was that everything was accessible. There were no fenced-off crypts or displays. Slowly, he moved deeper into the church.

Nothing leapt out at them as they searched. Mason found it incredibly hard. If they had even half an inkling of what to look for, their job would have been much easier. But this was the lofty height of difficulty. How do you find something if you don't know what it looks like or where it might be?

He guessed it could have been worse. The church wasn't huge, and it wasn't packed with visitors. They pretty much had the run of it. He checked the stained-glass windows as he went, taking pictures of them and zooming in, looking for anything that might resemble Beelzebub's crown. So far, he hadn't found anything even remotely likely.

He moved on, noting the others' progress. Sally was inspecting everything minutely as usual and following up after the others, making no secret of always rechecking their work. Hassell was wandering along the pews, staring in all directions. Quaid was in front of him, studying the floor and then the ceiling, ignoring the walls for now. Roxy was walking nonchalantly down the centre aisle, trying to take everything in at once. It wasn't a poor strategy, but Mason thought they might need something a bit more precise.

When he caught sight of a priest, Mason saw no reason not to approach the man. He wore a white robe and was bald, probably in his sixties. He nodded his head as Mason approached.

'We're looking for something in particular,' he said.

The priest shook his head, not understanding. Of course, he wouldn't speak English. That would have been too easy.

Mason spread his arms to indicate the whole church. 'The Crown of Beelzebub?' he said.

The priest blinked rapidly, his expression moving between confusion and disbelief. He backed away and shook his head. Mason shrugged apologetically, realising that the name Beelzebub was the same in most languages and wouldn't go down well if the priest did not know what he was talking about.

The priest walked off, casting a narrow-eyed glance back at him. With no alternative, Mason went back to checking out the depths of the church.

They worked for hours. Fortunately, the priests in attendance were few. Mason didn't see the one he'd approached again. They worked their way from the back of the church to the front and came up empty-handed.

'It's not here,' Roxy said as they gathered near one of the marble side altars, this one depicting a bleeding Christ.

'You could be right,' Sally said. 'But we have to keep trying. Maybe we missed it.'

'We've searched high and low,' Quaid said. 'But you're right. Let's swap positions and try again.'

They went back at it after Sally found out that the church closed at seven. That gave them just under two hours to complete another search. This time, Mason went to the right, decided the pews were too new to hold any interest, and concentrated again on the carvings, the windows, the niches that held marble statues.

Time passed as they bent to their task. Visitors came and went, ambling along the aisles. Mason made sure he kept his phone in view, pretending to take many pictures so that people would assume he was intensely interested in the church.

At six-thirty, they still hadn't found anything and met once again at the side altars.

'No crown,' Roxy said.

'It has to be here,' Sally said.

'But that's just it,' Quaid said. 'It doesn't have to be here. It's been a long time. They could have moved it downstairs, to a different church, even sold it. Who knows? It might have been stolen,' he shrugged. 'Ironically enough, by Satanists.'

Mason had to accept the possibility. He looked back along the nave, gazing left and right. 'Wait,' he blurted. 'The paintings . . . '

Sally stared at him. 'Yes?'

'Well, they're fixed to ceiling along the top of the nave, not on the walls. They're part of a central aisle. Has anyone even checked them?'

Sally frowned. They all looked at each other. Hassell shrugged. 'Not me.'

Sally led the way back down the nave. 'We've been checking the walls, the windows, the floors,' she said. 'No one thought to check the ceiling above the nave.'

There were six paintings, some of them famous. The Maria del Carmine, attributed to Vincenzo Riolo. A late seventeenth-century canvas depicting the Madonna and child. Another showing the martyrdom of Saint Judas Thaddeus. Mason looked up at them, craning his neck. The first four reminded him of something you'd find in the Louvre, classic masterpieces. The other two were different.

One was simple, just a depiction of Christ on the cross at Golgotha. In this picture there were no thieves by his side, no Roman centurions. Just Christ, a skyline, and the cross he died on.

The second painting differed again. It was full of colour, bursting with energy. It portrayed a battle in which Romans fought with slaves, one side in their armour and helmets and wielding great swords, the other in their loincloths, their flesh exposed, wielding clubs and hammers and sticks. One Roman in the foreground was standing with his heavy boot atop a slave's neck, grinning evilly. Dead slaves were piled in the background. The painting seemed to say something wicked about the Roman Empire, and at the same time bemoaned the lot of the slaves.

It was good versus evil.

Mason focused, interested. Beside him, his friends zeroed in on the same painting. It hung above their heads. Mason thought that if he dragged a pew over here, he could easily reach it, but that wasn't about to happen. There were still six or seven visitors scattered about the church, and he could see a priest near the altar, tidying up.

'Do you see it?' Sally asked.

'The crown? No,' Roxy said.

'Really? Because it's right there.'

Mason squinted harder. He studied every inch of the painting and then, quite suddenly, it jumped out at him. The Roman with his foot on the slave's neck wasn't wearing a helmet. He was wearing a *crown*.

Mason's jaw dropped. The crown curved around the Roman's head, thick and black and carved. Mason took a picture and zoomed in. The centre of the crown was a snarling face with slitted eyes and fangs, and curved horns. To him it was the representation of a demon.

'The Crown of Beelzebub,' he said. 'On the head of a Roman soldier. Fitting.'

'And maybe a reason the church put it on show,' Sally said. 'But I'm just guessing. The question is, what the hell do we do now?'

Mason gauged the rest of the church. Yes, they would need to climb on a pew to reach the entire painting. No, there was no chance of doing it now.

Hassell cleared his throat. 'Then I guess we come back after lockup,' he said.

'We'll give them a few hours to get gone,' Mason said.

'And then I'll do my thing,' Hassell said.

Together, the team quietly left the church.

Chapter 30

They returned after dark.

Hassell led the way, first using his lock-picking tools to get them through an outer fence, and then using them on the church's main door. The entire area was dimly lit and heavy with silence. Several hundred yards behind them stood a main road, but it was lined with trees that helped hide them from the traffic.

Hassell unlocked the door to the beeping of an alarm. Quickly, he connected his code reader to the green-flashing device and let it read and spit out the numbers before punching them in. The whole process took less than ten seconds. The alarm stopped beeping, casting the church once again into deep silence.

They took out small torches and turned them on, shielding the glow. Together, and at a rapid pace, they crossed over to the painting. Mason and Roxy lifted a pew and deposited it underneath the painting, and then Sally climbed up, shining her torch on the edges. She didn't waste any time and started testing the sides of the frame.

It got harder the higher she went. She was stretching up to the top when she slipped and came down hard on her side, grunting. Mason caught her before she fell off the pew.

Roxy, standing guard by the closed door, listening, looked over. 'You okay?'

Sally nodded, looking irritated. Mason thought she was probably annoyed at herself rather than anything else. Dusting herself off, she got back to work.

She tapped and pressed and clicked and pushed at the carved frame, trying to find a pressure point. She went all the way around and started again, this time more slowly. From her position by the door, Roxy frowned. She cracked it open a little, reported a couple strolling past and then an old drunk ambling along, resting against the door for a span. Mason's heart was in his mouth as the drunk sat down, thinking that he might fall asleep there, but he soon moved on.

Sally's exclamation was low but succinct. When Mason looked up, she had a cylindrical object in her hand. She brandished it with triumph.

'We have it,' she said.

She jumped down, quickly slid the by now familiar scroll out of the cylinder and then the sheet of thick torn paper. She plucked at the little red ribbon tied around the scroll, saw it come open, and spread it on a pew.

Mason leaned over her shoulder, focusing his torchlight on the writing.

'In fair Florence, between the stars and the church is a door carven with the face of the true Lord. Look for the Crypt of Belial.'

Mason snapped a photo of the scroll and the map. He slid his phone into his pocket. Sally again took out her leather box from her rucksack and placed the scroll and the map inside before tucking it safely away.

'We done?' Hassell asked.

Sally nodded. They made their way back to the entrance to the church. Roxy cracked the door open a little.

'We have company,' she said. 'And it's shit.'

'Bullion?' Mason asked. 'But how?'

Roxy shrugged. 'Doesn't matter,' she said. 'They're here.'

Mason glanced back, saw his colleagues spread out in the dark church behind them. 'We're trapped in here,' he said.

'Then we get out,' Roxy said keenly.

'Rush them?'

'Shock and awe.'

It wasn't the only option, and it might not even be the best, but Mason went for it. The team was ready. He looked to Roxy.

'Do it.'

Roxy flung the door open. Mason, standing before the gap, immediately saw figures on the other side, probably about ten feet away. He set off at a sprint, racing through the door and out into the night. The others were just steps behind. Ahead, he saw Bullion's face and six others, all startled as they suddenly saw people sprinting towards them.

In the next second, Mason crashed into their line, leading with his right shoulder. Bullion's people wore regular clothing to blend in and also carried backpacks. They had clearly been intent on breaking into the church, too, which told Mason that they knew what they were after.

Mason smashed a woman aside, sent her tumbling back so hard she fell over. The others crashed into their enemies, startling them, sending them flying left and right. Roxy grabbed hold of her opponent under the arms, lifted him, and hurled him onto the concrete, spine first. It was Hassell who came up against Bullion, the shock tactic still working as he slammed into the man and flashed by.

Quaid didn't have it so easy.

The woman he attacked reacted more quickly than anyone else. She stepped back, deflected most of Quaid's barging attack, and then reached out, grabbing his jacket. His momentum took him past her, but he stumbled, falling to one knee, before surging back up and continuing to run.

The woman kicked him in the back.

Quaid staggered, flew forward, managed to catch himself before he fell. The team had successfully passed Bullion's people.

Bullion's cry followed them. 'Not again!'

Only six or seven feet separated the two parties. Bullion's people started after them, running hard. It was now that Roxy's shock and awe plan really came into play. They had no intention of running farther than they had to.

Roxy whirled, started running back. The others did the same. They hit their enemies again, this time knocking three of them off their feet. Mason led with an elbow this time, swiping his man across the face and seeing him stumble to the left. Whilst their enemy was regrouping once again, Roxy took off once more, again running away from the church.

They pulled out a sizeable lead.

Bullion was yelling after them, urging his people to their feet. Recklessly, he took off after them alone, leaving his team to pull itself together. Mason knew they couldn't slow down. Now was their chance to get away.

The main road came up and looked to be four lanes wide. Traffic flew from left and right. It was a natural barrier, stopping them. They all pulled up short.

'Shit,' Hassell said.

There was only one thing to do. 'Cross it,' Roxy said.

Mason looked left and right, gauged the oncoming traffic. Bullion was almost upon them. His team was coming too, though raggedly. Mason stepped off the kerb and then ran across the front end of an oncoming car, stopping to let another car zoom past him. Horns blared. Another car slammed its brakes on, adding to the chaos.

Mason waited. A car flashed by. He figured he had enough time to step past the next one that was flying in from the left and ran quickly, stopping now in the road's central reservation.

Around him, his friends made similar manoeuvres.

The night was alive with the sound of car exhausts, rumbling tyres, horns and engines. Mason's heart beat fast. He looked now to the right, saw several vehicles approaching at speed. Looked behind.

Bullion was stuck in the middle of the road, waiting for traffic. His team hadn't stepped out onto the road yet.

Mason sprinted a few steps. A car slammed its brakes on, the front end dipping, and still flashed by at speed. Mason was again in the channel between cars, waiting to run again. Roxy waited close to his right, Sally to his left. Quaid and Hassell were spread further out. Mason stepped out once again.

He'd misjudged it. The car was coming way too fast. When it saw him in its way, it braked hard, tyres skidding slightly, but it couldn't stop in time. As it lost momentum, Mason leapt up onto its bonnet. The car came to a stop with him staring in through the front windscreen.

Cars veered to a stop all around. There was the sound of rending metal as one or more vehicles crashed into each other. Mason jumped down to the ground. In front, another car, ignoring the chaos, simply flew by at speed, just inches away from him. It was quickly followed by another.

Mason checked back. Bullion was still coming. His team was closer.

He had one more lane to cross, a slip road that led to another carriageway. He ignored the owner of the car that he'd leapt on, tuning out the yelling, and tried to concentrate on what was ahead of him.

Cars and trucks barrelled down the slip road as they turned off, a constant stream. Mason would have to risk it. From behind, there was a sudden cry.

He whirled.

Bullion struck him hard.

Chapter 31

Mason staggered as Bullion smashed into him.

Propelled towards the busy lane of traffic, he fought back, pushed the heavyset man away and created some space between them. Bullion didn't stop. He came straight in, fists swinging. Mason was aware of his team closing the gap now, crossing the first road and leaping into the second. Roxy and Hassell were already turning to meet them.

'Where's the fucking clue?' Bullion yelled as he struck out at Mason's face.

Before he could stop himself, Mason glanced at Sally. He blocked a punch. 'No idea.'

'We *want* that clue.'

Bullion forced Mason backwards with his relentless fighting style, landing punches and kicks. Mason was inches from passing cars, only some of which slowed down. Both teams were spread out all along the road now, trading punches, with cars inching or cruising past. It was a wild, chaotic scene, lit starkly by streetlamps and the flash of white headlamps, the glow of red brakelights. Cars thundered by on all sides. Further down, where a few vehicles had come together, people were climbing out of their cars, adding to the confusion.

Mason struck back at Bullion, taking steps towards him. The long mirror of a big truck had just flashed past his skull, mere inches away. If it had hit, it would have at least knocked him out.

Bullion kicked him flat in the chest.

Mason took it, felt the pain shoot through his bones. Ordinarily, he would have cushioned the attack by moving backwards. That wasn't an option. He threw up an elbow as Bullion attacked him with a flurry of blows, tried to step around the man. Bullion, though, was well trained and very capable. He kept Mason on the back foot.

Roxy fought two attackers on the bonnet of the car that had almost run Mason down. She was stretched out along it, head towards the windscreen, trying to fend them off from both sides. She kicked out, caught one in the shins, rolled and landed an elbow on the other. Both of them fell away. Roxy kept rolling, jumped off the side of the car and hit her opponent with a knee, driving him back into another vehicle.

Hassell and Quaid both fought women. They were struggling, driven to their knees and being pounded upon. Sally was in there helping them, darting back and forth, but her blows seemed almost ineffectual. The two women were ex-military, strong, capable. Hassell collapsed on the road and his opponent started kicking him in the ribs.

Some people were rushing towards the fight now, holding mobile phones up as if to say they'd called the cops, or simply filming the action. At a scene like this, the full gamut of human nature was revealed. Other people were actually running away from the scene, returning to their cars.

Mason took a solid punch to the jaw, staggered. It was then that Bullion looked back to check on his team.

'Her!' he yelled, pointing at Sally. 'She has it. Check her out.'

Bullion had a spare man who now turned his attention to Sally. The woman beating on Hassell broke from the fray and also started towards Sally. Flashing lights swept over them as cars came and went, as they continued to cruise past. Sally suddenly saw two enemies coming towards her and cast about, looking for a way out.

There was nowhere to go. Only back the way they'd come, and that meant braving the road again. Instead, she ran towards Roxy, who seemed to be making headway against her own two enemies. Sally thought her best protection was the American.

She ran away from her two attackers, approaching Roxy, but the two were faster than she thought. They grabbed her after a few seconds, wrenched at her arms, pulling her back. Sally hit the floor, kicked out, her blows ineffectual.

The woman fell on her, punching her ribs and kidneys. Sally groaned. The man knelt down close to her head and slipped his hands under her back, took hold of the backpack, and started manoeuvring it around, trying to pull it clear.

Sally fought back, punching the woman atop her, and resting as much weight as she could on the bag. She knew the scroll and the map were safe in the leather box. She kneed the woman in the groin, punched her in the sides.

But the woman appeared to feel none of it. Her hands slipped deep into Sally's pockets even as she took punches and felt around. When they found nothing, they slipped back out and now she was feeling around Sally's waist, still searching for the scroll. Still taking punches, she slipped her hands into Sally's waistband and rolled them from front to back. Of course, she found nothing.

Sally changed tactics. She grabbed hold of the woman's ears, wrenched them up so that her face came up, and then headbutted her. This time, the woman cried out, flinching and trying to pull her head away. Blood spurted from her nose and a red rim appeared around her teeth. Sally hung on tight to her ears even as she tried to wrench her head away.

The man kneeling close to her head had a tight hold on the backpack. He tugged one strap from her right arm now, grabbing her hand and bending the fingers until she let him have the strap. Then he concentrated his efforts on her left arm. He pulled at the strap even as she bore all her weight down on it.

Roxy had seen what was happening to Sally and was doing her best to join the fray. She focused hard on her own enemies, kicked one woman into oblivion and then concentrated on the other. The two stood toe to toe, trading blows. Roxy ducked, stepped in and then came up fast, trying to strike the woman under the chin with the top of her head, but the woman saw it coming and stepped out of the way.

Sally struggled on the floor, trying to pull away from the man.

Mason had just a few seconds to take stock. Bullion was distracted, yelling at his people to grab Sally. Quaid and Hassell were struggling, but still battling away gamely. It was a baffling melee surrounded by vehicles, some still moving. There was a growing group of people watching, many on their phones, and some cars still squeezed by. The other carriageway had also eased in traffic flow now as people slowed down to rubberneck.

Bullion glared at him. *What next?* Mason thought.

Bullion leapt at him. Mason shrugged him off. 'Take a look around,' he said. 'We're all in a no-win situation.'

Bullion's face turned suspicious. He took a step back and appeared to see for the first time all the surrounding activity. Something dawned on him – the knowledge that they would soon have to get the hell out of there.

'Get that clue!' he yelled. 'We can't fail again!'

Sally felt her opponent's efforts redouble. He yanked hard at her rucksack, finally able to get it off her arms. But he was still below her. She twisted on the ground, now atop him, punching down, trying to wrestle the bag back.

The woman she'd been fighting grabbed her by the collar and hauled her off. Sally felt her neck constrict, tugged backwards. She fell at the woman's feet, saw the flash of a boot, felt pain explode in her chest. She was vaguely aware of the man standing with her bag in his hand.

Roxy appeared then, out of nowhere, striking at the woman who was kicking Sally. The pair vanished momentarily from sight. Sally raised herself to her knees.

Looked around.

The man had unfastened the top of her bag and was rummaging inside, his attention on what he was looking for. Sally flew at him.

She caught him by surprise, but he was still strong enough to stay on his feet and hang on to the bag. Sally flinched.

He had the leather box in his hand. At the look on her face, an expression of triumph crossed his.

'This is it,' he said, grinning.

Sally attacked again, desperate to get the clue back. The man fended her off, turned to Bullion and yelled that he had the clue. Roxy still fought to her right, Quaid and Hassell to her left. Mason looked like he and Bullion were exchanging words.

Sally was suddenly paralysed. She didn't know what to do. She couldn't overpower her opponent – he had the clue – and everyone else was busy. She dug deep. What could she do? Her instinct was to keep going, keep fighting until the end. She stepped up to the bigger man and held out her hand.

'Hand that back.'

He laughed at her, but it was all just a distraction tactic. It let her get close. When he laughed, she kicked him directly in the groin. The man folded in surprise, the leather box still in his right hand. As he went down, Sally plucked it free, holding it high in the air.

But as she did so, there came a fast shuffle from behind. The leather box was grabbed from her hand by the fast-running woman. Somehow she had escaped from Roxy and was now sprinting towards Bullion with the box.

'I have it!'

In the chaos, Sally staggered. She had stepped up, won the day, retaken the box, but had then lost it again. Despair flooded her.

Ahead, Bullion made a swift decision. He yelled his orders, shouting for everyone to disengage. They had what they so desperately needed. There was sudden confusion, and then the fighting stopped. It all happened quickly. Bullion waved at his people, ordering them to run.

Mason was left in a quandary. They'd lost the clue. Did they chase after Bullion, back through the traffic, or let him go? Clearly, the two teams were closely matched. Also, the police would have been called. Mason figured he could hear sirens on the horizon.

'Let's get the hell out of here,' he said.

Chapter 32

They bit the bullet and surrendered the clue to Bullion, knowing that they'd already made a copy. But they had to be quick now. Bullion wouldn't take long to crack the clue itself, and then they'd both be chasing the next clue again.

Mason led the charge to the airport. They were aching, bruised, cut and bleeding; they were bone-tired. Everyone wanted to sleep, to take the night off, to find a few creature comforts and just relax, but they all knew it was impossible.

Sally booked them on a fast train to Florence, and they caught the last train out. Any thoughts of sleeping were dashed when they learned the travel time was less than an hour. Instead, Mason contented himself with sandwiches and a couple of vodkas, hoping to numb some of his aches and pains.

When they arrived they quickly left the station and, having learned their lesson previously the hard way, rented a car outside. Already in the heart of Florence, Quaid drove as Sally refreshed their memory of the clue.

'In fair Florence, between the stars and the church is a door carven with the face of the true Lord. Look for the Crypt of Belial.'

Right then, her phone rang. It was Jacobs, keeping up with their progress. They spoke for a few minutes, gave him the clue they'd lost, and explained what had happened. Jacobs assured them he'd try to figure out what was going on.

'As to the clue,' Quaid said a little later, after the man had hung up. 'What have you found out?'

'It's vague,' Sally admitted. 'There are over one hundred churches in Florence.'

'So we concentrate on the Crypt of Belial,' Roxy said.

'Exactly. That's what my attention has been on. I'm cross-referencing any mention of crypts with any churches, trying to narrow it down, especially using the name Belial. I'm looking for Satanic relics in Florence, too.'

'I'm guessing that narrows it down pretty good,' Hassell said.

'Of course. The Crypt of Belial. Now, Belial is a Hebrew word used to characterise the wicked or the worthless. It later became a term for the Devil himself. There is only one Crypt of Belial in Florence and it sits in the Santi Apostoli, one of the oldest church buildings in Florence.'

Mason knew they were on a roll. They hadn't wasted any time getting here. They'd been forced to take the time to rent a car, but even that hadn't wasted more than half an hour. The traffic through Florence was heavy, but surely Bullion and his goons would have to negotiate it, too.

Of course, they weren't about to break into another church in the dead of night. They were forced to find a hotel and bed down for the night, agreeing to meet early in the morning so that they could be on the church steps at opening time.

Mason didn't like to think of it as a race but this time he wanted to get in and out before Bullion turned up. They were all working as fast and hard as they could to make that happen.

He programmed the church into the sat nav. Quaid followed the directions. The church sat in the historic centre of Florence. They were twelve minutes away and, though they were now on a new mission, Mason's wounds still smarted from the last one.

'Get your game faces on,' he said. 'We need to find this clue fast and get the hell out. We don't want another confrontation.'

'On that note,' Quaid said quietly, 'how the hell did Bullion find us in Milan?'

'A good question,' Sally said. 'We thought we'd shaken him. I can only assume there's another way of tracking the clues. Maybe in the Book of Baphomet. Something we haven't seen.'

'Jacobs alluded to another way,' Mason said. He thought for a moment about Jacobs, about the man's intentions, but then dismissed any suspicion. It had been Jacobs who brought them into all this.

'Speculation is useless,' Sally said. 'We just don't know. Maybe we could ask Jacobs to check into it.'

Mason bit his lip. 'It's probably best not risking that. He's endangering himself enough as it is.'

Quaid, wearing a wrist bandage and sporting several bruises, nodded, focused on the drive. Hassell, in the back seat, touched his cuts and bruises. Roxy stared straight ahead, as if relishing another confrontation.

'They won't get off as easily next time,' she said in a hushed voice.

'Ideally, we don't want a next time,' Mason said. 'If we're competing with them for the Hellfire, it's only gonna get harder.'

'I like it hard,' Roxy said grimly.

Mason understood. Hard took your attention from the pain at hand, it refocused so that you had to think about something else rather than the problems that beset you. Sometimes, hard was good.

Quaid piloted the car until the church was just a few minutes away. They found a place to park and were then outside, on the pavement. It was a cool, clear day, with an azure sky. For now, it was cloudless. As in Milan, they were crowded by tourists and locals going about their business.

Mason started to cut through the crowds, following his map app. 'It's up ahead,' he said.

The Church of Santi Apostoli was a Romanesque style church, built in the eleventh century. They crossed into an area of narrow cobblestone streets, archways, brilliant shadows, and small shops that appeared to cater to the locals rather than tourists. The small Piazza del Limbo appeared to be out of time, from historic ages, and, nestled close by, was the neat and tranquil-looking church they were searching for.

Mason stopped outside it to look around. He turned to Sally. 'Do we know what the Crypt of Belial looks like?'

'There are a few images online, all of them different, none of them pointing to this particular church. It's as if no one ever photographs it.'

'Or its identity is kept secret,' Mason said.

'Makes sense.' Sally nodded. 'Shall we?'

As the others started forward, Mason and Roxy hung back. It was instinct for them both. Instinct drilled into them through years of hard training. They scanned the square, all the roads into and out of it, the faces of the passing people. There was no sign of Bullion and his goons.

Mason followed Sally into the church.

Immediately, he saw many beautiful artworks arrayed around the walls. The interior was serene, unruffled. He saw green marble columns, a richly decorated wooden ceiling, a stunning terracotta tabernacle to his left and a masterwork that Sally said was by Vasari on the right. It all stopped him in his tracks.

'Keep going,' Roxy said, oblivious to it all. 'We're on our own in here.'

Mason realised it too. There were no priests, no tourists. This place was a little off the beaten track, he guessed, far from the fashionista shops on Via Tornabuoni. The team spread out, taking in all the sights.

'A Satanic relic should stand out pretty well,' Hassell said.

'Let's hope so,' Quaid replied.

They began their search, hunting high and low. Mason again searched the windows and paintings, the statues and carvings. The Crypt of Belial sounded like something sturdy, something solid rather than a face in a painting or a stained-glass window. Slowly, he made his way from the entrance of the church towards the altar. The church was deceptively long, stretching away into deeper shadows.

Ahead, Quaid and Hassell worked together. The number of artworks inside the church made the going slower. Roxy was turning her attention from the art pieces at the front of the church, and Mason realised she was keeping watch. It was a good call. The last thing they wanted now was for Bullion to come up on them from behind inside this peaceful church.

Sally brought up the rear of the group, looking deeper, still with her phone in her hand and swiping, swiping, trying to find that elusive picture of the Crypt of Belial. Her face was expressionless, her eyes focused.

Mason kept going. The church doors made a grinding sound. Mason was quick to turn, almost swearing in disbelief, but then he saw it was just a couple of tourists entering, guidebook in hand, cameras at the ready. He sighed with relief. This was all entirely too close for comfort.

They kept working, searching for the elusive crypt. The tourists came and went, and still there was no sign of a priest. Mason put his head down and got stuck into the work, trying to see everything and work out if it had any bearing on the crypt. It was frustrating work that required full concentration.

Chapter 33

Ed Bullion was buzzing.

He and his team had hit the little church last night shortly after arriving in Florence. They had considered waiting for it to open the next morning, considered probing and searching and examining every surface, every ridge and ripple. In Bullion's mind, that was what Mason's team would do – search every nook and cranny and hope for the best.

It wasn't what Ed Bullion would do.

Instead, he and his team had immediately hired a car and driven as close to the church as they could get. It was full night, the early morning hours, and there weren't that many people around in Florence's centre. Still, there were enough, and Bullion and his crew, dressed as civilians, looked enough like part of a merry but well-behaved crowd to avoid questions.

They made their way through the cobblestone streets to the church itself and hesitated outside. Jefferson stepped forward. He was their specialist infiltrator and soon had the front door open. There was no alarm set. Bullion assumed it was because at least one priest slept here, and that was his hope.

They made their way inside, into the darkness. Just a couple of low lights were switched on, making little difference, but Bullion still used his torch sparingly. The church was deceptively large inside, stretching back further than Bullion had imagined. Now, where to start? Perhaps the vestry . . .

He doubted that the live-in priest would be in the vestry at night, but the room was close and needed to be checked. Quickly, and silently, he directed his team towards a set of stairs to the right. They crossed over and crept down them. Bullion was aware of the overall silence, the heavy soundless majesty that hung inside the church. He wasn't bothered about breaking that silence – religion meant nothing to him – but he was worried that sounds might carry.

'Steady,' he said.

They moved with a purpose. Again, Jefferson picked the lock. The little room was empty save for a cluttered desk and a few ornaments. It was as Bullion had been expecting. They all backed out now, returned to the church, and looked around.

Slater pointed to the right. Bullion saw it too: a thick, crimson drape that wasn't quite pulled together revealed a wooden door. They walked over to it, tried the handle. It, too, was locked. Jefferson stepped up again, this time nailing the lock in seconds. Soon, they were opening it and stepping through into a narrow corridor. Bullion moved quietly, wishing he had a weapon. Even a knife would feel better at this point. But that was the problem with travel. You just couldn't bring your weapons between many countries, and buying them at each new location took up too much damn time.

Look at them now, he thought. Inside the church, not an hour after leaving the station. If they'd been buying weapons, it would have taken them far longer.

He was third in line. The corridor ended in a narrow set of stairs lined by rough blocks that led up to a wooden door. Bullion started up and soon they were at the top. Jefferson tested the door handle.

Unlocked.

'Could be the bedroom,' Bullion whispered. 'No sound at all now.'

Jefferson turned the handle, pushed the door open. Bullion followed him into the room. It was a small, square area with a single bed. Bullion let his torch wander across the covers.

The light revealed an old head, some grey hair and a set of glasses. The man, sleeping, snored gently. All they could see was the head.

The room was sparsely furnished, just a wooden chair and a small table to the left of the bed. Bullion saw a pair of slippers, sandals, and a walking cane propped up. He let a small smile play about the corners of his lips.

'Wake him,' he said. 'Let's see what he has to say.'

Two men fell on him, giving him a rude awakening. The old man struggled briefly. His arms were then grabbed, and they forcefully sat him upright in the bed, blinking into the torchlight that was directed into his face.

'What is this?' he blurted in Italian.

Bullion blinded the old man with his torch. 'You're gonna tell us everything we need to know. Do you speak English?' It didn't really matter. Slater, he knew, spoke Italian.

'I speak Italian,' Slater reminded him.

Bullion nodded. 'Tell him this,' he said. 'If he doesn't cooperate, we're going to kill him.'

Slater repeated the words in Italian. The priest's face blanched. He stopped struggling and regarded them intently.

'What do you want?' he asked in Italian.

Slater translated and then waited for Bullion to speak. Bullion chose his words carefully, going for clear and succinct.

'Show us the Crypt of Belial.'

Slater spoke in Italian. The priest blinked and then frowned slightly.

'I don't know this,' Slater translated.

Bullion motioned at one of his men, told him to grab one of the priest's hands. He mimed snapping his own fingers back. 'Tell him what will happen,' he said.

Slater spoke a few words of Italian.

The priest started shaking. He cried out when one man took hold of his hand and then started bending a finger back. His liquid eyes stared straight into Bullion's.

'*Please*,' he said in heavily accented English.

'Do it,' Bullion said. 'Slowly.'

The deed was done. The priest's screams rang out until Jefferson planted a hand across his mouth, stifling them. Then the man who'd just broken his finger, Carlisle, took firm hold of the next and watched Bullion.

'Let's try again,' Bullion said. 'Where is the Crypt of Belial?'

Slater spoke. The priest, eyes streaming, nodded. There was no reason for him to take any more punishment.

'I show you,' Slater translated.

They hauled the priest to his feet, threw his dressing gown on, and then shoved him towards the door. He grabbed his cane on the way, hobbling along until he reached the top of the steps. Then there was a very slow journey down, Bullion growing impatient. When they finally reached the curtain covering the door that led into the nave, the priest stopped and turned.

'By the altar,' Slater translated. 'Along the far wall. The Crypt of Belial stands behind the second gate.'

They walked out into the church, crossed to the far side, and proceeded to the indicated place. Bullion saw a wide, gated area paved with marble. There was more than one crypt inside, but it was clear which one was Belial's, even from here.

It was rectangular and obsidian-black. The sides were covered in the by now recognisable symbols: the horned goats, the snarling faces, demons with wings and fangs preying on the innocent and the weak. Bullion saw that and wondered if the priest might view him as a demon. Standing here, right now, Bullion was the priest's personification of evil.

Jefferson again picked the lock. They pushed inside. Immediately, all seven men and women fell to their knees and started testing the crypt, feeling for a secret compartment. They left the priest standing, groaning with pain, staring at them and probably wondering what they could possibly be looking for.

The crypt wasn't large, and soon, they had covered it. Slater found the hidden compartment. The cylinder popped out with a click, bringing a huge smile to Bullion's face. When she held it out to him, he snatched it out of the air triumphantly.

This time, *I* won.

Bullion pocketed the cylinder. Now, he turned to the priest. No doubt the old bastard was hoping they would leave, and then he would raise the alarm. Bullion approached the old man, watching him sway where he stood – not just from pain but because of his advancing age. Bullion didn't care about that. He placed his hands around the man's throat and started to choke him. He watched the eyes, revelled in the feeling of power. The old man's hands came up to grab Bullion's wrists, but they were ineffectual. Bullion squeezed and squeezed, holding the man upright, until he saw the life leave the eyes, until he could let go and watch the man slither, dead, to the floor.

'What do you want us to do with him?' Jefferson asked.

'Carry him back to his room. Leave all the doors locked as we found them. With a bit of luck, they won't find him for a while.'

And then Ed Bullion turned to wait for his orders to be carried out, the cylinder safely in his pocket, an air of triumph and invincibility all around him.

Chapter 34

Mason scoured his side of the church, eyes pinned for anything that might look out of place. There was more activity at the church entrance and he looked over quickly, but saw that Roxy was already on it. She too heard movement and walked straight towards it, ready to act. It turned out to be just two more tourists, though, shedding coats and talking noisily as they entered, ruining the ambience inside the church.

Mason breathed a sigh of relief. He went back to the job at hand, studying a painting that had several subjects. He found nothing suspicious and moved on, now nearing a wide, gated area bordered by railings. Holding them, he peered through.

And saw it right away. A small, pure black crypt on the far side, its sides carved deeply, its lid a mass of sculpture. Mason stepped in. No signage identified the crypts inside the gated area. He had to get closer.

He went to the gate and pulled at it. Maybe it was instinct, maybe he was just being thorough. The gate was unlocked and came open. Mason paused, looked around, saw the tourists inside the church fascinated by the incredible work of Vasari. He slipped through the gate.

He approached the small crypt. As he grew closer, he made out the carved denizens of Hell that he had been expecting, stooped down and looked closer. The crypt lay against a wall where upright carvings complemented it. Mason felt a chill as he took it in.

Staying low, trying to remain covert in case the tourists looked around, he bent over the crypt and started feeling for any compressions that might lead to hidden compartments. As he did so, there came a voice at his back.

'And what do you think you're doing?'

Mason jumped, turned around with a guilty expression. All he saw was Roxy grinning down at him.

'Don't do that. It's not funny.'

'It was a little bit funny,' she said and came through the gate.

Mason wasn't sure about the two of them being in here. It increased their chances of being seen. He was about to mention that when his fingers came across an empty void at the back of the crypt. He felt a sinking feeling as he took out his torch, bent over and inspected the area more closely.

Sure enough, there was a gap where a cylinder had once been.

Mason swore. He looked up at Roxy. 'They've already been here. Or someone's been here. Taken the clue.'

'They've taken it?'

'Cylinder and all.'

Roxy hunkered down beside him. 'You've gotta be kidding me.'

'They must have come in last night, straight from the train. That's what we should have done.'

'In retrospect, yeah. But after that huge fight and all, then getting here, it was barely possible.'

'Well, they found a way,' Mason realised there was no point crouching here and waffling on about it. He had to get the team together. He rose to his feet and left the gated area, walking purposefully through the church. Soon, he had everyone together near the middle of the church, standing by a pew.

'We're knackered,' he said. 'Clue's gone.'

Sally stared from him to the gated area he'd just vacated. 'The crypt is in there?' When he nodded, she made her way over and double-checked. Mason had been expecting it. Soon, she was back beside them, her face white.

'We're knackered,' she said.

'Without the clue, we have no way of knowing where to go next,' Quaid said. 'And Bullion and his team are long gone.'

'That's twice they've bested us now,' Roxy growled.

'But in Milan, we had a photo of the clue,' Mason said. 'Here, we have nothing.'

'There's still a chance,' Sally said.

Mason glanced at her. 'There is?'

'This Bullion. He reports straight to Moloch. Obviously, he'll tell Moloch what the clue is, probably send him a picture of the map.'

'So Moloch will already have the next clue,' Hassell said. 'How does that help us here?'

'Jonathan Jacobs,' Sally said.

Mason saw her logic. 'You think Jacobs can get us the clue?'

'It's the only way I can think of. He's in the right place.'

Mason thought it through. 'Trouble is, he'll have to be quick. Bullion already has a head start on us.'

'Then he's gonna have to take a risk,' Sally said, and took out her phone.

They exited the church, not wanting the tourists to overhear, and found a spot outside that looked relatively quiet. The piazza itself was clear of foot traffic. Sally waited for her phone to connect.

When it did, Jacobs' voice was hushed. 'What is it?'

'Where are you?' Sally asked.

'Moloch's house. We're in the middle of a meeting for the foremost members of the cabal.'

'That's good news.' Sally explained what had happened here in Florence. She told him what they needed.

'Moloch took a call earlier. He left our meeting. Said it was hugely important.'

'Maybe that call was from Bullion.'

'Maybe,' Jacobs said quietly. 'What do you want me to do?'

Sally shook her head. 'Are you kidding? Jonathan, you're going to have to get us that clue. The one we've lost in Florence.'

'I'll be putting my life on the line.'

'Aren't you doing that already?' Hassell asked. 'Aren't we?'

Sally held a hand up, not wanting to overwhelm Jacobs. 'Where did Moloch take the call?'

'His study.'

'Then that's where you need to go. You have to come up with something, Jonathan. Otherwise, we're at a dead end. If you don't, Moloch and Bullion win.'

Jacobs was silent for a while. Finally, he sighed. 'I'll do what I can.'

Sally looked like she wanted to reach down the phone and shake him. 'There are lives on the line here, Jonathan, including yours.'

'I'm very well aware of that.'

'We need to stop this maniac.'

'He's currently regaling us with stories of what he'll do after he gets the Hellfire. The Black Mass, in particular, will be wild. He's going to need a lot of powerful people around him to keep it under wraps.'

Sally tried to keep Jacobs on topic. 'It's up to you now, Jonathan. Get us that clue.'

'I'm on it.'

Chapter 35

Jonathan Jacobs tried to control his accelerating heartbeat. Sally's call had really set the cat among the pigeons. How on earth was he supposed to get that clue? Moloch's study was close by; in fact, he could see the door, a six-panelled oak affair, from this room. But it might as well have been on the other side of the house for all that Jacobs could do to reach it.

He was standing near the room where they were having their meeting. It was late morning, and Moloch had called them all last night to arrange the little get-together. Told them he had important information to impart. He had met them this morning as they arrived with a little ceremony, wearing his dress robes as if to emphasise the importance of the meeting and what it might entail.

They were led to a comfortable room lined with plush black buttoned sofas, wing-back chairs, dark wooden panelling and golden lampshades. A heavy chandelier graced the centre of the room. Moloch bade them all sit down and, despite the hour, poured generous measures of brandy into their crystal-cut glasses, which they immediately sipped. Next, most of them lit up cigars. The air was soon redolent with smoke.

'The Hellfire is within reach,' Moloch had started with. 'My people are just a few days away. As you know, there is a time constriction here. We must conduct the Mass on the correct night.'

Jacobs had sat back and crossed his legs. 'You sound confident.' He had to be careful of what he said to Moloch. He was on brittle ground.

'When *haven't* I been confident? I have the best team at work. They are blazing a trail across Europe. The Hellfire is within our grasp.'

Jacobs studied the faces of the other men and women present carefully, trying to glean from their expressions if he had another ally in the room. It was hard to tell. One man, a prominent banker, leaned forward.

'Can you explain to us how the Hellfire will change things?' He sounded concerned.

'Oh, for the better, for the better. First, I need the sword for the ceremony. Afterwards, our cabal will grow. Our reach will extend around the world. Our—'

'But won't that make us more vulnerable?' the banker said.

Moloch looked annoyed at the interruption. 'Only if we grow too fast,' he said. 'But I have no intention of letting that happen. We influence, we grow, we blackmail if we have to.'

'But where do you start?'

'You start with people you know. For instance, George, who do *you* know who might be interested in joining our group? Only the worthiest, of course.'

George, a white-bearded headteacher of a famous private school, cleared his throat. 'I'd have to put some serious thought into that, Moloch. Some people do come to mind, but it's a great risk when you reveal yourself.'

'There will be new additional levels,' Moloch said. 'Initiates. Intermediates. Advanced, and so on. Newcomers will be invited to earn their way through the ranks. It won't be an easy task. The more they advance, the more they get to know and by the time they've advanced enough to see us in our . . . true form . . . we will own them.'

'And how would they earn their way through the ranks?' the banker asked.

'Depravity,' Moloch laughed. 'We will draw them in deeper and deeper . . . '

'Until they can't get out,' Jacobs finished ironically. 'The more people you have joining the cabal, the less safe it will be.'

'I understand your reluctance, but I am not one for standing still. What stands still withers and dies. It eventually crumbles to dust. We must evolve.'

'I'd say we've already developed hugely from humble beginnings,' Jacobs said.

Now, standing in the adjacent room, Jacobs reflected on that earlier conversation. It was about this time that Moloch had been called out of the room to take a phone call, something he assured them was vitally important.

The door opened. Moloch put his head in the room. 'Everything okay?' He looked a little smug.

Jacobs forced a smile. 'All good, thanks.'

'Nothing you need to tell me?'

Moloch was fishing. He'd probably already guessed who the call had been from and what it had entailed. Jacobs walked towards him, leaving the room. 'Nothing at all,' he said softly.

Back in the main room, he retook his seat and sipped his brandy. Inside, he was churning. Somehow he had to get that information from Moloch's study without the man knowing. How the hell . . .

Moloch sat down and started talking again. Jacobs tuned him out. Here he was, against his will, working for

Moloch against the very people he'd asked for help, and now, *somehow,* he would have to turn the tables and help *them*. Did that make him a triple agent now? Jacobs had lost track.

There was one way.

Jacobs slipped out a cigar and lit it, joining most of the others in the room. He drew on it until the tip glowed. Moloch was otherwise engaged for now, raving on about his cabal and how powerful it would become. Apparently, he already knew politicians and business executives and doctors who would jump at the opportunity to attend a Black Mass. He would offer it on a small scale at first, and gradually reel them in.

Jacobs made the tip glow again. He balanced his half-empty brandy in the other hand. Now, he surreptitiously touched the tip of the cigar to the nearest cushion, waited for it to start burning. When it did, Jacobs rose quickly and 'accidentally' spilled his brandy over it.

The whole cushion went up with a whoosh, flames leaping. The flames quickly took hold of the sofa around it and soon Jacobs was facing a blaze. Moloch was running towards it, shouting for the guards to bring fire extinguishers. The banker and the headteacher and all the others present in the room had jumped to their feet and were backing away.

Jacobs joined them at the back of the room. Moloch was at the front, flapping ineffectually at the blaze. Jacobs could feel the heat, could see how intense it was getting. Moloch was shouting for help at the top of his voice.

Guards rushed in, wondering what was going on. None of them held any fire extinguishers.

'Go get an extinguisher!' Moloch yelled at them. 'Hurry!'

The guards turned tail so fast they ran into each other. It was chaos, and the room was filling with smoke. Now seemed like the perfect time to get out. Two of the guests were already turning towards an exit, probably heading for the front door. Jacobs did the same but, once out in the corridor, went in the other direction.

He ran for Moloch's study, found the closed door and turned the handle. It was unlocked. Quickly, he pushed it open, stepped inside. He was in a square room with a large Persian rug in the middle, an enormous oak desk and dark paintings hanging on the wall. They weren't Satanic, not in here, but they did depict scenes of mayhem and chaos. Ships sinking. The Black Death. A funeral. A fire that seemed to be consuming London.

But Jacobs had no time to waste. Moving fast, he crossed over to the desk and studied the area around the fixed phone. There were several sheets of paper, all of them thick and covered in elegant script. Jacobs turned them slightly so that he could read them.

It jumped out at him immediately. It made sense, since Moloch had recently taken a phone call, that the topmost piece of paper was the most likely.

'This special Satanic bible lies in the archives of the London Library, in the racks between old guide plans and Somerset Maugham.'

Another Satanic relic.

Jacobs memorised the line, wished he could have got a look at the map, but knew that just wasn't possible. Bullion would have found a way to email it or, if Moloch had a smart phone, send it via that. There was a rattle at the door.

He looked up.

The door opened. Jacobs threw himself down behind the desk, trembling. The door was only opened for a few seconds, during which Jacobs smelled the thick stench of smoke. Through the desk, he could see a pair of legs in black trousers. He was sure it was Moloch, checking. Jacobs waited. Soon, the door closed. Jacobs took a deep, ragged breath.

So close.

He rose, legs still trembling. He was far too old for this kind of shit. He went around the desk, willing the door not to open again, crossed the Persian rug and waited at the door. He put his ear to it, listening, heard running feet, the heavy panting of men. He waited a little longer, still running the new clue through his head.

He needed to call Sally back with all haste. Bullion was already ahead of them in the chase.

Jacobs pulled down on the handle, cracked the door open. The corridor reeked of smoke. He waited, heard nothing except distant shouting, and stepped out. The corridor was in darkness, lit only at the far end by the front door.

Jacobs ran down it as fast as he could. As he was passing the meeting room, he cast a quick glance inside, saw the air choked with smoke and foam. There appeared to be no more flames; the fire must have been put out.

Moloch was at the front of the men, wielding a fire extinguisher, sweating. Jacobs ran past without being seen, exited through the front door, and went straight to his chauffeur-driven Bentley. Some of the other guests were already driving away. Jacobs took their cue and told his driver to follow suit.

From his pocket, he withdrew his phone.

Chapter 36

Again Mason found himself on a plane, this time bound for London. Jacobs had not only come through for them, but he had come through with flying colours.

'This special Satanic bible lies in the archives of the London Library, in the racks between old guide plans and Somerset Maugham.'

It was afternoon. That morning they'd searched the Church of Santi Apostoli in Florence. They'd quickly quit the area and headed for the airport, hoping that Jacobs would give them a destination. By the time they reached the airport, he hadn't, and they were forced to sit around and twiddle their thumbs. But then, a little later, the call came through.

'Go to London!'

Before Jacobs had even stopped talking, Hassell had his phone out and was booking them plane tickets. By the time Jacobs had read out the clue and discussed it a little, Hassell had digital boarding passes, a gate, and a time. They didn't hang around. Just went through customs, grabbed provisions from the airport shops, and boarded their plane. They ate and drank in flight, tried to relax. Mason felt uptight. Each passing second beat hard at him. They were behind Bullion;

the guy was at least half a day ahead of them. Hopefully, Mason thought, something would delay him.

Now, he wanted the confrontation, wanted to take Bullion out of the chase. The plane ploughed through the air at 500mph but for him it wasn't fast enough. He wanted to be in London now, ahead of Bullion, searching for the clue. Already, he was planning the route off the plane, through the airport, out of customs.

And soon he was doing it.

The plane landed and not long after, they were crawling through the London traffic on their way to the London Library. Again, they'd hired a car but, Mason thought, using a black cab would have been far quicker. The taxi drivers knew the best roads to take.

It was almost five p.m. They found a car park and left the car behind. There was drizzle in the air and a low grey sky. Mason found the entrance to the library, an unimpressive brown door, and went straight in. At a counter was a receptionist, a grey-haired woman wearing glasses and a flowery dress. They walked right up to her.

'The volumes of Somerset Maugham and the old guide plans, please,' Sally said.

The woman looked up and peered at them through her thick-lensed glasses. 'Wait just a moment,' she said.

They cooled their heels for what felt like an hour. Roxy, as usual, monitored their perimeter, heading back outside the door and watching the approach to the library. Mason paced the floor, trying to quell his frustration.

When the woman returned, they all paid attention. 'The old guide plans are in the archives,' she told them. 'You can book an appointment for seventy-two hours from now.'

Mason's heart sank. 'Seventy-two hours?'

'That's the policy. Would you like to book an appointment?'

'I'm sorry, but we're in a bit of a rush,' Quaid said.

'You won't get any early access to the archives. The request will take seventy-two hours.'

Mason saw they were up against a brick wall. He turned to the others and jerked his head backward, asking them to walk away. They gathered together in a far corner of the room.

'Are we in need of my skills?' Hassell asked.

'It looks that way,' Sally said.

Mason turned to her. 'Do you have a blueprint for this place? It's huge, old, warren-like. We could get lost in here without a proper map.'

'There's snippets online,' she said. 'But they're not great.'

'So we could get in and get lost,' Quaid said. 'Great.'

'There has to be something . . . ' Mason mused.

'Wait,' Quaid said. 'I have an idea.'

He returned to the receptionist. 'Excuse me, do you have an entertainments manager? Someone who oversees events?'

'Of course,' the woman said. 'Mrs Kennedy.'

'Could you call her for me, please? We have an event to arrange.'

'I'll check if she's available.'

Again they waited. Quaid stood off a little by himself, clearly working something through in his mind. Mason didn't bother him. Ten minutes later there was a creak, a door opened, and a short, prim, black-haired woman appeared in the reception room. She wore black jeans and a white blouse. A petite gold watch hung from her wrist.

'Hello,' she said. 'I'm Mrs Kennedy. How may I help you?'

'You are the events manager?'

She nodded.

Quaid introduced himself as ex-British army, retired. He shook the woman's hand and then leaned forward in a conspiratorial manner. He said, 'I am looking at holding a gentleman's evening in your archives. I thought it would be a wonderful venue. Now, I'll only be inviting officers, both current and retired. Perhaps a dozen of us. Does that sound plausible?'

214

'The archives, you say? That's never been done before. You'd need an invigilator down there.'

'I don't mind that. Happy to be supervised.'

The woman actually looked a little excited. Maybe she'd had a dull day. She asked if he had a date in mind.

'Ah, there's the problem,' Quaid said. 'I haven't actually fixed a date yet. I haven't even fixed a venue. You're one of three possibilities. Now, I wonder if I might see the archive room to check if it is suitable?'

The woman blinked up at him. 'Now?'

'That would be fantastic.'

'All of you?' The woman cast a glance at the group.

'Again, fantastic.'

'And who are these other people?'

It was a good question, Mason knew. Quaid took it in his stride.

'My organisers and caterers. They need to see the place to figure out where to place their equipment.'

Mason kept his head down. They all did, hoping their bruises from the previous day's fight weren't too obvious.

Mason thought she'd blow them out of the water. But it was Quaid's manner that was convincing. He was using everything he'd learned as a British army officer, every bit of charm, character, and bearing. He *made* her believe.

'You can't stay long,' she said. 'Although the library stays open until nine p.m., we shut certain sections down earlier. The archives are one of those sections.'

'We will need just ten or fifteen minutes,' Quaid pushed his luck.

If the woman was surprised, she didn't show it. Of course, it was her job to cater to people who wanted to use the library to hold an event. She looked Quaid straight in the eyes.

'Ten or fifteen minutes? All of you?'

Quaid made a pretence of looking over the group. 'Is that a problem?'

'It shouldn't be. Follow me.'

Quaid cast a surreptitious glance at the team before turning around and following her through the door and down a well-lit passageway. They soon came to a room filled with books and crossed it, ignoring the surprised looks of people browsing there. They went through another room, this time down a wide aisle between bookcases, and then stopped by a set of stairs. The woman led them down into the bowels of the library, only stopping at the very bottom, and then through even more doors. Mason was hopelessly lost. He didn't stand a chance of being able to find his way out of here.

'We have over 1800 items down here,' Mrs Kennedy talked as she walked. 'Correspondence, special books, artefacts, manuscripts and much more that constitutes the very heart of the library. Any event would have to be extremely well behaved if it is even allowed.'

'Are you not the person who would allow it?' Quaid tried to sound anxious.

'Along with the library's Archivist, Mrs Jennifer Reid.'

They went through more twists and turns, more doors, followed a winding passage, and eventually came to a stop before a plain oak door. Mason wasn't surprised the blueprints of this place had been a little fuzzy. It was a maze.

'Follow me,' Mrs Kennedy said.

They all pushed through the oak door to find themselves in a vast room that smelled a little fusty. Ranks of bookcases marched away from them down the centre of the room. The edges were full of desks with lights and monitors and leather chairs. Quaid walked alongside Mrs Kennedy, nodding as they went.

'This is excellent,' he said.

Mason already knew they'd have to get extremely lucky to find a shelf full of Somerset Maughams in ten or fifteen minutes, but Sally already had that covered. She walked up to join the two at the front.

'Excuse me,' she said. 'Do you have Somerset Maugham down here? I was told there were some of his in the archives and it would be an absolute honour to see them.'

The woman turned, considering. Then she nodded. 'Two rows over,' she said. 'Section R36. Do not touch.'

Mason's heart leapt. Sally started off. The entire team, apart from Quaid, started in that direction until Sally turned and stared at them.

'We can't all go,' she hissed. 'It looks wrong.'

Mason waved the others after Quaid. He followed Sally. Together, they worked their way up the aisle, looking for R36. Sally counted the minutes, face anxious. Mason was almost running as they swept up the aisle, following the sections from A to R.

They flew past shelves of old manuscripts, building plans stacked in neat rows, correspondence to both sides, property deeds, some of which were yellowed with age and stacks of audio-visual equipment. The aisle was empty apart from them and the sodium lights above shone bright and stark.

Mason raced after Sally, conscious of the passing time. He wondered if Bullion had already been here, but he thought not. Bullion wasn't the kind of man to finesse his way in somewhere. He was a hammer, not a scalpel. If Bullion had received the same brush-off as Mason, then he was probably planning on coming back later after the library closed.

Mason clung to that hope.

Sally arrived at the R section and slowed down. She scanned the shelves for 36, found it and moved towards it, Mason in her wake.

'Finally,' she said.

Chapter 37

The first thing Mason saw was half a row of Somerset Maughams. He looked closer. Sally was balancing on her tiptoes, the shelf in question at head height. To the far right of the Maughams sat two large boxes that might hold old guide plans. But they didn't need to check.

The book in question appeared to be sitting in its rightful place.

'Is that it?' Mason said. 'A Satanic relic right here in the heart of the Library of London?'

Sally worked fast. The minutes ticked away. She reached up to grab the book, which, on first sight, appeared to be a black-bound tome about three inches thick. There was no writing on it and no creases. The book didn't appear to have been handled at all.

Sally plucked it from the shelf and held it in two hands. There was a speculative look on her face.

'A blank cover,' she said. 'I guess it helps something like this hide in plain sight.'

She balanced the book on one arm and prepared to open the cover. She looked nervous. Mason shared her apprehension. He touched the leather cover and was surprised to feel how cold it was. Ice seemed to emanate from it in waves. Maybe it was his imagination.

Sally opened the cover. The first page was also blank. Mason's eyes narrowed slightly. He hoped the entire book wasn't going to be blank, and this turn out to be some wild-goose chase.

But the next page bore a cursive script. The words *Ave Satanus* were written on the page at the very centre. Mason bit his lip.

'What is it exactly?' he asked.

Sally started leafing through it. 'Honestly, I don't know. It's all written in Latin and the writing is ancient. From the chapter and verse arrangement, I'd guess it's a version of the Holy Bible.'

'A Satanic Bible?'

Sally nodded. 'See the way it's set out. I wish we had about a week to study this.'

'Only a week? It's bloody huge.'

'And it's heavy. Here, hold it for me.'

Mason reluctantly took hold of the tome, leaving it wide open across both his hands. Sally had asked him to hold it for a reason, but she was fascinated and couldn't stop leafing through it. Mason reminded her that the clock was ticking.

'Yes, yes,' she said. 'Give me a minute.'

Mason saw pages full of cursive script. He saw crude drawings of the Devil dancing over flames and holding a pitchfork. The Grim Reaper severing heads like so much wheat. Depictions of Hell, of Satan's Throne, of leaping fire and bodies being thrown in. The Devil and an angel standing in judgement, scales full of snakes on the Devil's arm. Demons cowered before Lucifer, who sat on high wearing a robe and a crown upon which the souls of men and women had been spiked.

Mason's mouth had gone dry. Sally's breath caught in her throat as she leafed through the book. Finally, she swallowed heavily.

'Hold on to it.'

Mason took a firm grip. He guessed about five minutes had passed since they parted from the main group. Hopefully, Quaid and the others would keep Mrs Kennedy busy with the cover story.

'Lift it,' Sally said.

Mason raised the book so that it was perpendicular. Sally was feeling around the back pages, and now around the spine. When the book was raised, the cover bulged over the spine, showing a clear gap.

Only it wasn't a gap. Something was stuck in there.

Sally reached in with two fingers and started wiggling the object about. 'It's stuck hard,' she said. 'Keep the book in that position.'

Mason tried to keep it still. The tome was awkward and heavy. Sally worked as fast as she could, probing and pulling until the object finally came free.

She pulled it from the gap between the spine and the cover. It was a small, cylindrical object that brought a smile to her face.

'Got it,' she said.

Mason was pleased. Maybe Bullion had been given the runaround, or maybe just shown the door. Either way, he hadn't breached the library yet and was probably planning on coming in after dark. Maybe his blueprint resources were better than Mason's.

'Open it,' Mason said. 'We learned our lesson last time when we lost the damn clue.'

Sally flicked open the cylinder and drew out the contents. Which consisted of the by now familiar scroll tied with a red ribbon and a small, thick sheet of paper that bore the map. Mason waited for Sally to untie the ribbon, casting glances up and down the aisle as he did so. The place was almost silent. All they could hear were Quaid's dull tones.

Sally unrolled the scroll. Mason didn't even read the clue, just laid down the Satanic bible and took photos of the scroll and the map. It was their failsafe now. He watched as Sally, having lost her leather box, put the scroll and the map carefully in her jacket pocket.

Mason replaced the book, thankful to get the thing out of his hands. As he pushed it back into place, he fancied the cover squirmed under his hands. He shuddered. Yes, it was all just creeping him out, but this mission was immersed in evil. There was no wonder he was feeling a little uneasy.

'Let's get out of here,' he said.

He turned. They made their way back down the aisle and saw the others standing just a few yards away. Quaid saw them and nodded as they came up.

'Everything okay?' he asked.

'Did you find what you were looking for?' Mrs Kennedy said.

'The books are . . . fascinating, thank you.'

'And you, Mr Quaid?' The woman turned to him. 'Have you found what you are looking for?'

Quaid smiled pleasantly. 'Yes, I believe that I have. Thanks for your hospitality.'

They were ushered out of the room and back through the underground warren. Soon, they were climbing the stairs and heading towards the front doors. Mason was elated. Maybe, just maybe, they had once again neutralised Bullion and Moloch's presence on this mission. Maybe they had won. He didn't fully believe it, of course. Bullion and Moloch had an uncanny knack of popping up where they were not wanted.

They reached the exit doors and said their goodbyes to Mrs Kennedy. The receptionist eyed them dourly. Roxy turned to him.

'Did you get the clue?'

'Let's talk about it outside.'

They left the reception room and pushed through the doors, back out into the approaching night. According to Mason's watch, it was just past six-thirty and the dark clouds were leaching the light from the sky. The pavements and roads were slick with drizzle, though the rain had stopped now. The sound of car tyres rumbling wetly along the nearby road overpowered everything else. Mason and the others stood near the flow of people in the street for a while, chatting about the discovery of the book, occasionally shouting to make themselves heard.

The crowds pushed past, men and women going about their business, leaving work or just window shopping or meeting friends. It was a dense hubbub and, occasionally, one of them brushed past Mason or Roxy or Sally. It wasn't surprising then when a tall man wearing a knee-length, fawn-coloured coat bumped into Sally, knocking her to the left. The man apologised and moved on, quickly disappearing. Sally frowned and watched him go.

And then thought to check her pockets.

'Shit,' she said. '*Shit*. He stole the clue and the map.'

Roxy gawped at her. 'Who? That guy who just bumped into you?' She started off in pursuit before realising she had no idea where the man had gone.

Mason was scanning the fast-moving crowd. The guy had blended in perfectly. He was gone. Mason raised his eyes, scanned the street, half expecting to see Ed Bullion standing on the other side, a small smirk on his face.

This was his ploy? To *steal* the clue?

'How did he even know I had it?' Sally muttered.

'You had it last time,' Quaid said. 'They stole your box. You don't have your backpack. It's a logical deduction to think it would be in your pocket. If they'd failed, they'd have lost nothing and might have returned and tried Mason or me.'

Sally cursed, blaming herself. Mason pointed out that they still had a copy of the scroll and the map.

'But so now does Moloch,' Sally said.

They started moving, heading back to the car. Sally followed the usual routine and rang Jacobs, giving him the next clue and informing him of their progress. It was a brief call. She didn't tell him they'd lost the original copies of the scroll and the map.

And, having scanned for Bullion just a few moments ago, it was a major surprise for Mason to suddenly find himself facing the man in the busy street.

Chapter 38

'You again,' Mason blurted out.

'I'll give you one warning,' Bullion growled. 'Stop hunting for the Hellfire right now.'

The two men stood facing each other, faces impassive, as the sea of humanity parted around them. It was like a face-off in the middle of a stampede. Neither man flinched.

Roxy joined Mason, the two of them standing shoulder to shoulder. 'Or what? You aren't exactly measuring up so far.'

'Really? We just took the latest clue right out of your pocket. How's that for measuring up?'

'Not even close.'

'We have the clue,' Bullion insisted. 'You did all the legwork. Quite satisfying.'

'How about you go satisfy yourself, asshole?'

'We will kill you if you don't stop,' Bullion said.

'You've already tried,' Mason said. 'Didn't get you anywhere.'

Bullion had to raise his voice over the ambient noise. 'The opportunity to snuff you out hasn't really arisen yet. But believe me, it will happen.'

Mason couldn't see any sign of the man's cronies. 'You gonna try right here? Now?'

Bullion smiled. 'No time like the present.' He eased his jacket aside to show Mason the butt of a gun. 'We're in our home country, after all.'

'You stopped to pick up guns.' Mason shrugged. 'Won't do you any good.'

'And why is that?' The man's striking blue eyes were staring, his hook of a nose thrust out at them. He stood easily, confidently, the golden crucifix still hanging around his neck.

'You won't use them in a place like this.'

Bullion shrugged. He placed one hand easily on the butt of his gun. Mason felt a moment's uneasiness. The thing that concerned him was how easily the pickpocket had melted away, but then what was Bullion going to do? Shoot them all and try to hide?

'We're coming for you,' the man hissed.

'You'll never be—' Roxy began.

There was a sudden movement from Bullion. It all happened so quickly, it took both Mason and Roxy by surprise. The burly man slapped her in the face, rocked her head sideways. The sudden slap turned a few heads, but none of the general public paused in their comings and goings.

Roxy's mouth fell open. Mason recovered from his shock and stepped forward. Bullion delivered a hard strike to his solar plexus. Maybe he should have been ready for it, but Mason wasn't. He hadn't expected Bullion to attack here, alone.

Except he wasn't alone.

They came rushing across the street now, his six mercenary backups. They threaded between the cars, a lethal group, rushing to the scene. Mason faced Bullion, breathing heavily.

'You can't be serious.'

'As a fucking blade.'

Bullion came at them, swiping out. His team struck from the left. Mason's team had seen what was about to happen and came rushing in from the right. There was suddenly a tight knot of people tussling in the middle of the rushing crowd.

The pedestrians flowed around it, looking askance, walking faster, trying to pull away from the trouble. Most of them wanted no part of it. Mason blocked a low blow from Bullion, brought an elbow up, but found that deflected. Bullion was now in his face. Mason grabbed him by the ears and forced his head back.

Exposed the throat.

He headbutted that. Bullion choked and fell backwards. Around him, both teams were fighting close up, using short punches that sought the most vulnerable spots. For long seconds, the fight continued.

Mason had created some space between him and Bullion. When the man stepped in again, he kicked out at his knee, missed. Bullion punched him in the forehead. Mason saw dark motes spinning before his eyes. To left and right, people surged past them, many of them still oblivious to the skirmish.

Mason knew this couldn't go on. They were in the middle of the bloody street. What the hell was Bullion trying to pull? He backed away, almost tripped up a passerby and was grumbled at. He stepped to one side and nearly bumped into a woman. This was madness.

They had to de-escalate. 'Let's go,' he shouted.

His team heard and understood. They broke away from their tiny melees, turned and joined the human flow, walking quickly. Mason did the same, dragging Roxy along, predicting that the American would want to stay and fight. She didn't protest much, but gave him a glare.

They hurried up the street amidst the flow of humanity. Heels clicked and boots thudded all around them. People brushed up against them, skipped past. They passed the entrance to an underground station and hit a cross-flow of people, all scurrying by.

They threaded through it, still walking fast.

Mason looked back. Bullion and his team were following far behind. They must have started off slowly, surprised. Mason and his team had put a bit of a gap between them. He looked ahead for possibilities.

'There,' he shouted.

The team saw it. There was a street leading off this major thoroughfare, a wide one that had to lead somewhere. They took it, and then ran, their feet pounding the pavement. By the time Bullion had struggled clear of the crowds, Mason and his team were already halfway down the new street.

They flew past shops and eateries, their boots splashing through shallow puddles. Mason glanced back. Bullion and his goons were running now too, but there was still a substantial gap between them.

In front, Sally switched quickly to the right, chasing down another street. Mason's worry was that they would hit a dead end, but they had to risk it. They didn't know this part of London. Hassell had his phone out and was trying to find them on a map app, hoping to guide them, but the jogging about and jerking was making it almost impossible.

Roxy was at their rear, perhaps hoping she could get stuck back into the fight. Mason met her eyes and shook his head grimly. She nodded, seeing sense. They had forsaken the busy streets to get away. Conversely, the quieter streets meant Bullion and his team could potentially use their guns.

Mason increased the speed, trying to establish a decent lead. Ahead, Sally, the champion fell runner, swerved once to the left, took another street, and then flew to the right, taking another. If they could lose Bullion, they could make a clean getaway.

The team ran swiftly, heads down. More twists and turns came hard and fast, and Sally took them at random. When he glanced back now, Mason could see no sign of Bullion.

'Keep it up,' he hissed. 'We're losing them.'

They kept going, running as fast as they could, the streets of London dark and wet all around them, the night sky pressing in. There were shouts from behind – Bullion and his people yelling in frustration. Sally twisted left and right a few more times and then came to a major street.

It might even have been the one they'd recently left.

Mason was hopelessly lost, but they were free and clear. Hassell had given up trying to use his phone at the same time as running hard. Sally jogged on the spot, attracting a few odd looks from passersby.

Mason looked back down the street. It was empty save for a lone dog walker.

'Move,' he said. 'Blend with the crowd.'

'Shouldn't we head back towards the car?' Quaid said, panting.

'That can wait. First, we need to make sure we've escaped our pursuers and their guns.'

Together, they blended with the flow of pedestrian traffic, walked for a few blocks, passed several brightly lit pubs and a steak restaurant. Five minutes passed and then ten. They were clear, he was sure.

Mason waited for Hassell to bring up their position on his map app and plot a route back to the London Library and their car. It didn't take long. They had escaped Bullion. Was the guy getting desperate? Was that why he wanted to fight in the middle of the street? Or was he just a little baffling?

Desperate and dangerous. Mason thought it might be a good idea to get off the streets for a while, give Bullion and his team a chance to disperse before they headed back to the car. He took them into a nearby pub, made his way to the bar, and ordered a drink. They could afford to waste twenty minutes in here.

Mason didn't think Bullion knew where their car was parked. It was in a quiet side street, a better place for a confrontation. He had attacked them outside the library because that was where he'd been waiting for them.

'All right,' he said, sipping his drink. 'Let's take a proper look at the next clue.'

Chapter 39

'To the Great Altar of Pergamon, Satan's Throne.'

Sally's voice cut through the general hubbub. Mason frowned. 'That means nothing to me.'

'Luckily, Pergamon is of great archaeological significance,' Sally said. 'My father studied the place at length and there's a lot of information in the Rusk Notes. It's now just ruins, but it was once a major hub of prosperity, perched along the Turkish coastline and watching over the Aegean Sea. It was a centre of commerce and medicine. Once, its buildings, all of the finest white marble, presided over the entire area. Its library rivalled that of Alexandria.'

'And the altar?' Quaid said gently.

Sally went on. 'The oldest section of Pergamon is its acropolis, towering over the ruins of the city below. One of the most studied structures of the acropolis was the Temple of Zeus, the immense foundations of which remain, on the southern side of the site. Now, we get to the altar.' Sally took a long swallow of her drink and looked around. The noise level within the pub had risen several notches.

Mason noticed several people leaving a far corner and herded them all in that direction. He took a seat and leaned back against a wall. It was noticeably quieter over here, and it was good, after the long run, to get off their feet.

Sally spoke from memory. 'The altar, known as the Great Altar of Pergamon, is also known to be associated with the great Temple of Zeus.'

'How is it known as Satan's Throne?' Hassell asked.

'It's a common story, but I don't know it well enough to explain properly. Give me a few minutes.'

Mason sat back as Sally slipped out her smart phone to do some research. On it, she would have access to the internet, the Rusk Notes – as she called them – faithfully copied from her father's work years ago, and her own scribblings. Her father, especially, had left behind a wealth of information. He had been a professor of archaeology and a teacher for decades.

Mason waited for Sally to get up to speed. He didn't see it as time lost but as time in the bank. Whatever Sally learned would do them good in the long run and it was better to be informed than running off as if your tail were on fire. He studied his team. These last few days had been a whirlwind. In fact, every moment since Jacobs had contacted them had been a tense jumble of action and adventure. The team had barely had time to think, and no time for themselves.

Sally spoke up. 'It seems that the prophet John of Patmos referred to the altar in the Book of Revelation. After a vision of Christ, he went to the Pergamon people and said, *"I know where you dwell, where the throne of Satan is, and you hold fast to my name, and you did not deny my faith even in the days of Antipas, my witness, my faithful one, who was killed among you, where Satan dwells."* Scholars have always believed it is a reference to the Great Altar of Pergamon.'

'So the Throne of Satan is the altar,' Quaid nodded. 'And we're headed for Turkey?'

'Sadly, no,' Sally said. 'The altar, believed to be one of the greatest monuments enduring from antiquity, now resides in Berlin's Pergamon Museum. It is a magnificent structure.'

'Not Turkey?' Roxy asked sadly, as if miserable at the loss of all that sunshine.

'Berlin,' Sally reiterated.

'If it's been moved, lock, stock and barrel,' Mason said, 'wouldn't they have found the scroll?'

Sally shook her head. 'Unlikely,' she said. 'They wouldn't have been looking for anything. And they transport these things in relatively large pieces. Finding anything would have been a stroke of luck. And they'd have put everything back just the way they found it. The scholars and archaeologists of the time would have insisted on it.'

'Still . . . ' Mason said.

Sally shrugged. 'Anything's possible,' she said.

'Just how big is this altar?' Quaid asked.

'Oh, it's bloody huge,' Sally said, consulting her notes. 'Thirty-five metres wide, thirty-three metres deep. The front stairway alone is twenty metres wide.'

Quaid's jaw dropped. 'How the hell are we gonna search all that?'

'That's quite the question,' Sally said. 'And one we're going to have to put a lot of thought into. We're talking about a structure that had been considered one of the wonders of the world.'

Mason drank up, his mind awhirl. Quaid was absolutely right. They were talking about inspecting an extensive structure regularly visited by tourists that was no doubt standing proudly out in the open. This was an entirely new dilemma.

Armed with knowledge, they finished their drinks and left the pub, walking warily at first as they made their way back to their car. They approached it surreptitiously, testing the shadows, didn't find anything suspicious, and left the area. Bullion and his goons had to be long gone by now.

Hassell drove them towards the airport.

Sally looked at booking the flights, but there were none to Berlin available until the next morning. It forced them to stay overnight at an airport hotel and board a plane the next morning, bound for Berlin.

Mason tried to calm his active mind. This was no simple task. Add to that the problem of Bullion, and who knew what might happen in Berlin? How long would it take to search the altar? Surely, both parties would be present at the same time.

The plane landed, and soon they were driving through Berlin. The Pergamon Museum was a UNESCO site on Bodestrasse, a forty-five minute drive from the airport. Mason stared out the drizzle-coated windows at drab, grey office buildings, rows and rows of parked cars, and unappealing shop fronts. Those pedestrians he could see trudged along with their heads down, their jackets and coats pulled tightly around their shoulders, umbrellas waving like fields of multi-coloured flags on a battlefield.

It was a little after 11 a.m. when they entered the museum, passing beneath its high stone entrance into an airy interior. Since they had left the car, they had all been on high alert, watching out for their enemies, but, so far, there had been no sign of them.

They headed to their right, past the entrance to the Sanctuary of Athena, on their way to the altar. The crowds were minimal, this being a midweek morning. There was plenty of room to walk. The corridors were wide and spacious, punctuated here and there by elaborate statues and carvings mounted on pedestals. Mason saw only one guard, who had his head in a guidebook, directing a group of tourists to some destination.

They followed the signs to the altar, taking their time. When they approached the room, they slowed, looked around. Deliberately they stopped, made sure they weren't being followed.

Finally, they entered the room where the Great Altar of Pergamon, Satan's Throne, stood in grand repose.

Mason whistled softly. It was an incredible sight, a monumental construction. A twenty-metre-wide staircase led up to rows of marble columns, and similar rows of columns held up the wings to left and right. Mason saw an eye-catching frieze – a marble high-relief – running across the base and on the inner court walls and wrapping around the entire exterior. On the roof were four statues, none of which he recognised. There were a few people sitting on the wide steps, and others climbing them to the actual fire altar on the upper level at the top of the stairs.

Sally stared at it wide-eyed, a smile on her face. 'This,' she said, 'is what makes archaeologists want to be archaeologists. Pieces like this are the motherlode.'

Mason took it in slowly, not only because of its vast size but also because of the almost impossible mission it represented. To his inexperienced eyes it looked well preserved, almost pristine, but Sally had mentioned earlier that parts of it had fallen into disrepair and there were scanty remnants of some of the dedicatory inscriptions, which made it difficult to know which friezes were dedicated to who.

Mason looked around the room. The one good thing he could see was that people were allowed *onto* the altar; it wasn't roped off. There were other ancient items scattered around the room that captured people's attention, but nothing like this. Mason saw no museum staff of any kind.

They approached the altar, trying to take it all in. Sally reasoned aloud that the secret compartment would be accessible, rather than way above head height. It was just a theory, but it was a plausible one.

'Shall we?' Sally said.

'Now?' Hassell looked around, taking in the people milling around.

'No time like the present.'

'I agree,' Mason said. 'We need to get this done before our enemies turn up.'

They took front, back and sides and started pressing and prodding and sliding their hands into recesses. They felt both low and high and ignored the odd looks they got from several passersby. Mason took the left front at first and found himself feeling along a blank marble wall with the massive frieze above his head. He looked up when a woman tapped him on the shoulder.

'*Was machst du?*'

Mason shook his head. 'English,' he said.

The woman frowned at him. She was in her forties with dark hair and a severe expression. 'What are you doing?' she said.

'Preparation for cleaning,' he said off the top of his head, leaving it at that, remembering the less you embellished when you lied, the more believable you were.

The woman continued to frown, then shook her head and walked off. Mason was certain she'd seek out a guard or a staff member. He berated himself for not being able to conjure up a better cover story.

Sure enough, ten minutes later, a guard appeared at the entrance to the room. Mason saw him immediately, straightened, and backed away from the altar. But the guard had already spotted Sally and Hassell on their knees, working their way around to the right. He stared for a moment and then made his way across the floor. Mason noticed he had a radio mic on his shoulder, but hadn't used it yet.

Quickly, he went to Sally's side. 'Heads up,' he said.

She looked up just as the guard arrived. He started speaking to them in German until Sally shook her head.

'English,' she said.

The guard was forced to call one of his colleagues over. Now there were two of them. The second man addressed them politely.

'What are you doing to the altar, please?'

'We're looking for something,' Hassell said truthfully. 'Maybe you can help us.'

The second guard looked doubtful. 'This is museum property, obviously. We have been told nothing about this. Show me your permits.'

Sally made a point of patting her pockets and then checking in Hassell's backpack. She took her time before turning back to the guards, holding her hands out, and shrugging.

'What is that?' the guard asked.

Sally waved a wad of cash. 'It's money,' she said. 'For looking the other way.'

The two guards looked at each other as the first one explained the situation to the second. Both men looked uncomfortable and stared around as if seeking help. Mason kept his mouth closed with difficulty. He hadn't been expecting that from Sally.

'Give us a couple of hours,' she said. 'We have a lot of space to cover.'

'This is our job,' the guard said, torn. 'You won't harm the altar?'

'You have my word,' Sally said. 'The thing we're looking for is small and can be replaced. We'll upset nothing. It's also important that you stand by the door and ward any other guards off for us.'

Both men eyed the cash hungrily. Mason watched out in case the frowning woman returned, or indeed Bullion or any of his people. The vast room remained serene, quiet, with little knots of people entering and wandering about.

The two men conversed in German. A minute passed. In the end, the second man plucked the money from Sally's hand and turned around before exiting the room.

'Keep a watch out for us,' Sally called after him.

'Wow,' Mason said. 'What made you think of that?'

'Desperation,' Sally said. 'What else could I do?'

'Let's make good on it,' Hassell said.

They got back to work, toiling just as precisely. Long minutes passed and then an hour. Mason was asked twice more what he was doing and told the questioners that they had permission to search the altar. The presence of a guard just outside the door helped assuage any fears the guests might have had.

They had been at it far longer than two hours. When they'd checked the wings, they all started on the central unit, finally closing in on the fire altar, which stood at the centre of the marching columns. Mason and Sally reached it first and started crawling around before Hassell and Quaid came up and started along the top. Roxy stood at the top of the stairs, looking back out across the hall.

'Still no sign of Bullion,' she said dubiously. 'I don't like it.'

Chapter 40

A Black Mass was not Bullion's idea of fun, but Moloch took his Masses more seriously than life itself. They were the centre of his universe. In his madness he probably thought he was doing Bullion a favour, but all Bullion was conscious of was the lost time.

Come attend, Moloch had said.

We don't have the time . . .

Nothing halts a Mass. Do you understand? Nothing. The way he'd said it sent a lance of anxiety through Bullion, despite himself. In the end, Bullion knew he had no choice.

The atmosphere was loaded. He didn't want to look too closely, but it still fascinated him. There were countless men and women crammed into this room, all wearing robes and hoods and chanting softly. There was the smell of sweat, of nervous tension, of unwashed bodies. They were crowded in close enough to be touching, and Bullion felt the bump of an elbow, the brush of a shoulder, as the people around him started swaying. It was surreal, and it put him completely out of his comfort zone. Bullion was a soldier, a fighter, not a voyeur at a den of iniquitous murder.

And unfortunately, he had a good view. He stood at the head of a slope and could see exactly what Moloch was doing.

The man was insisting on taking his time. Bullion knew instinctively that part of why Moloch had embraced this whole concept was that he loved torture. The man was a sadist, and it was those proclivities that were even now messing everything up. Moloch put his own needs above everything, which was why the Mass came first and everything else was overlooked. The man was sick.

Even now, as he watched, Bullion saw Moloch grasp the hand of the trussed-up figure on the altar, spread the fingers, and steadily cut into the thumb. Blood welled. The figure groaned, tried to squirm, but it was too firmly tied. Moloch watched the spread of blood, savouring it. The crowd groaned. Moloch licked his lips, eyes aflame. These were the pinnacle moments of his life. And something he was desperate for Bullion to see.

Bullion watched the slow execution. It sickened him. Yes, in his life, both personal and professional, he'd done bad things; he'd killed many people. But it had all been done in the name of a country or a cause. It hadn't been this . . . this wanton slaying.

Bullion realised he felt intimidated. The almost tangible mood in the room was growing; it was thickening into something ugly. He could well imagine how these fools might think they could conjure something, because *something* was rising. It was their own inner ugliness, their hatred, their diseased minds, their vile infection, twisting and mounting and budding like poisonous flowers. It was something solid all right, he thought. It was their own manifested *evil*.

Bullion watched Moloch split the victim's thumbs and then fingers. He watched the victim suffer in the name of some dark master. Eventually, he made his eyes stare into the middle distance, so that he saw nothing, unwilling or unable to watch. Moloch knew just what to do by now; he had been doing it long enough. How much pressure to exert, how deep to cut. With every stroke of his blade, his eyes shone, and he looked to the shadows, exultant. It was then that the chanting started in earnest, the dull monotone rising all around Bullion and sweeping up to the concrete dome of the roof. It was earnest and gratified and self-assured, the grunting of men and women happy to be where they were.

Bullion gritted his teeth and watched. The ritual went on and on. The chanting deepened. In the end, as the victim finally, mercifully, died, it became crazy. The assembled people started falling to their knees, crying out as if possessed. They swooned, fell to the floor. Some of them fell atop each other in carnal abandon. Bullion didn't know where to put himself, and saw it as more time lost. What would his team be thinking, twiddling their thumbs whilst he was being exposed to all this? He'd never breathe a word of it. What he was seeing today would remain with him for ever, but it would remain a secret.

There were men and women of every size and shape copulating all around him, their bodies squirming. The sound of them filled the air, made Bullion want to cringe. A woman reached for him, and then a man. Bullion threw them both off forcefully. He could see Moloch standing above it all, his hands drenched in blood, his face aflame with some perverse kind of religious fervour. The man's eyes were like hellish fire, blazing. Bullion understood perfectly why the Mass had overcome the importance of the mission, at least in Moloch's eyes. It was absolutely everything to him.

How long would it take to get Moloch back on track?

The thought sent his mind racing. It evoked images of Joe Mason and his friends. In his twisted way, Moloch had already told Bullion that he would like to torture Mason, to get him *under the blade*. Bullion saw Mason as a capable enemy to sweep aside in any way possible; he didn't share Moloch's fantasy of torture.

So Moloch wanted Mason, and Mason's friends. If possible, he wanted them alive so that he could do his very worst to them. These darkest desires had been revealed to Bullion just before the onset of the Mass.

'I can't promise,' Bullion had said. 'The only thing you can be sure of in battle is that you can't be sure of anything. It's . . . just arbitrary. Doesn't matter how good you are, everything's got chance stamped on its ass.'

'Ideally,' Moloch had said, 'even if it's just Mason. I want one of them.'

'Understood.' Bullion had seen no point arguing with the madman.

'In fact, the more I entertain the idea, the more I like it. I'm paying you very well. Make sure it happens.'

Bullion had said nothing. He wouldn't risk his own safety, nor the safety of his team, just to bring Mason or one of the others back alive, but Moloch didn't need to know that. Out in the field, *he* was in charge.

'Do you hear me?' Moloch spoke imperiously, as if he thought himself a king.

'I hear you,' Bullion answered and didn't elaborate.

'Perhaps the sacrifice of a great adversary is what will ultimately make the dark master appear,' Moloch said with verve. 'Perhaps that is what we need. It could be the last piece of the puzzle. How apt that would be. Success right before we enlarge the circle. How close are you to finding the Hellfire?'

Bullion could hardly believe his ears. His retort, *'We'd be a damn sight closer if I hadn't been summoned here,'* died on his lips, though. Moloch wouldn't understand, and it might jeopardise their relationship. One thing Moloch was right about – he was paying them good money to do

241

their jobs and Bullion loved a good payday. As evidenced by today, he would do anything for it.

'And don't worry about any time you may have lost by being here,' Moloch said, as if reading his mind. 'We still have Jacobs.'

'Close,' Bullion had said finally. 'The team is close.'

But they weren't. He wouldn't let them loose without his guidance. He didn't trust them enough, hadn't worked with them long enough. They were in stasis, waiting for Moloch's all-important Black Mass to end and for Bullion to make his way back.

And so the man stood before Bullion, covered in blood. He raised his hands in the air, and he spoke several lines. The room went quiet as they all listened. Moloch's voice rang through the stillness like a blade.

And it went on and on. Bullion had no choice but to listen as Moloch praised the darkness and some dark master and all the men and women who grovelled in his wake. And they did grovel. They got down on their bellies; they stripped naked; they did unspeakable things. Bullion closed himself off to it. He could see Moloch's eyes on him, since he was the only one standing, but he had had enough. If Moloch expected any more from him, he was going to be disappointed. This wasn't Bullion's game, and he saw no reason to take part in it. He was here by invitation, as an observer, nothing else. Perhaps Moloch had hoped to gain a new initiate.

It wasn't going to happen.

Bullion watched the final proceedings. He got the impression some of these old fossils might come here just for the debauchery, but then dismissed that idea. Watching someone murdered in order to get your rocks off was beyond his understanding.

But all these people were sick. There was no getting around that point. The entire room was a lair of gruesome, revolting souls, all soaked through with darkness.

Bullion felt crushed by evil, encompassed by it. There were the writhing bodies, the dripping altar, the low flickering lights, the crawling shadows that inhabited every corner, the low susurration that seemed to come from dozens of throats. It was all around, overpowering. He had to find a way out of here.

He turned, but there was no way between the bodies. He couldn't pick a route through them. The door was locked anyway, preventing anyone from leaving. Bullion was just going to have to wait it out.

All round him, the ritual went on.

Chapter 41

Joe Mason stood back as his team continued their search of the enormous structure known as Satan's Throne.

Roxy had climbed the stairs to investigate an inner sanctum. Sally was still making her way around the edges. Quaid and Hassell were engrossed in the stairs themselves, wondering if some mechanism might be present. Mason had just finished pushing and prodding along one of the friezes.

It was a long, hard, sweaty job. The guards were still watching out and had had to be paid off once again. Neither were happy even then. Their window of opportunity was rapidly closing.

Mason trod the steps to Roxy's side. The raven-haired American was feeling around a small altar, her tongue between her teeth.

'Need a hand?'

'This is hopeless, Joe. It's just too big.'

'Not something I ever thought I'd hear you say.'

She looked archly at him. 'You know what I mean.'

'I do. And I think we're all doing a great job. We've almost been over this whole thing.'

'And found exactly zilch.'

'Don't lose heart.'

He was the team leader, and had to encourage his friends, even if he felt the same way they did. The task in front of them was mountainous.

'One step at a time,' he said. 'Just like you approach any seemingly insurmountable problem.'

'Oh, I have a few of those.' Roxy continued to test the altar.

'Don't we all.' Mason joined her, moving around the other side.

Roxy looked up for a moment, meeting his eyes. 'But we're doing better, yes?'

Mason raised an eyebrow at her. His own burden was lighter now than it ever had been, and it was all because of the new team and the jobs they were doing. 'I believe so,' he said, and asked hopefully, 'Do you?'

Roxy breathed deeply, still looking into his eyes. 'I've broken through a load of barriers.'

'You found her?'

'The woman I wanted to be? Not yet, but I'm trying my best.'

Mason nodded and continued the search. Roxy had always opened up to him quite easily because, he thought, she saw a fellow wounded soul. They had gelled from the very beginning and had worked together well ever since. He watched her now as she worked.

Time marched on. They went from small altar to small altar, checked around the columns as far up as they could reach. Sally came to see them once, stating that she was starting her search again. Mason's heart dropped.

Had they reached a dead end?

Perhaps the clue had been found and discarded. Perhaps it had been broken or lost. Maybe it was just too well hidden. But no, he thought. The people who secreted the clue wouldn't make it impossible to find. It had to be . . .

Roxy gave a sudden sharp intake of breath. She was kneeling, head down, at the foot of an altar, feeling around its base. Something had come off in her hand.

Mason shuffled over to her.

'Got something?'

She held up a cylindrical piece of stone. 'Just clicked out from the altar when I pressed the seam,' she said. 'I think it's what we're looking for.'

Mason thought she was right. He looked around. For now, they were alone, though he could hear someone approaching up the steps. He rose and helped pull Roxy to her feet, and then the two of them turned their attention to the cylinder.

'We should take this to Sally,' Roxy said.

Mason agreed. By now, two other people had entered the great altar's inner sanctum and were happily nosing around. They gave Mason and Roxy amiable smiles. Mason led the way back down the steps and to Sally's side, waving at Quaid and Hassell as he went. Soon, the team had assembled at the foot of the steps.

Mason noticed one of the guards regarding them suspiciously. He waved, gave the guy a big thumbs-up. What else could he do?

Roxy handed the stone cylinder to Sally, who took it gratefully and turned eager eyes on it. Tentatively, she reached inside.

Mason watched, still keeping his eyes on their perimeter, just in case Bullion showed. Something was wrong there, he knew. Bullion had been right on their tail. What had happened? Of course, he was grateful for the reprieve. Bullion was proving to be a powerful adversary and working for some warped masters.

Sally plucked something from the cylinder. 'Part of the map,' she said with relief. 'We've found exactly what we were looking for.'

'And the next clue?' Quaid asked.

'It's here. Just stuck inside the cylinder. Hang on.'

No one had to tell her to be careful. Sally knew what she was doing. It was right then, as she was trying to finesse the scroll out, that the English-speaking guards came up to them.

'What are you doing?'

Mason stepped in front of Sally, covering her. 'Thanks for your help. We're almost done here.'

'If you find something, you will put it back.'

Mason fully intended to slot the empty stone cylinder back into its home. 'That's a given,' he said and to the suspicious expression. 'Definitely.'

'We won't be long now,' Quaid added.

The guard looked them over once more, then turned on his heel and walked away. Sally let out a deep breath. 'That was close,' she said.

'Did you extract the clue?' Hassell asked.

'Not yet. It's well and truly stuck.'

Sally worked for a while, becoming increasingly agitated, but eventually she managed to coax the small scroll out of the cylinder. She then gave the empty vessel to Roxy, who quickly returned it to its rightful place. Sally had secreted the map and the scroll about her person and now turned to the others.

'We should get out of here,' she said.

Mason agreed. There was no point hanging around to study the new objects, risking the appearance of Bullion or whatever other machinations Moloch might have in place. They made their way out of the museum and back into the day. It was getting on for evening by now and a grey overcast sky hung overhead. Mason grew aware of the fact that he was extremely hungry. Soon, the team had found a place where they could eat and drink at a table in a far corner and take a look at their new acquisitions.

The map was similar to the others they'd already found, just an outline of a geographical region somewhere in the world. Mason already had a good idea how they would fit all the maps together to find a final location.

The scroll, when smoothed out, yielded up a new clue.

'In the Hell Hall of the Vatican, there is a visage unlike any other, the face of the Lord.'

Mason frowned at it, not understanding. 'The Hell Hall of the Vatican?' he said. 'You mentioned it before. What's it all about?'

Sally's mouth fell open. 'You have got to be kidding me.'

'What is it?'

'Don't you see? This shows . . . that the Satanists infiltrated the very Vatican itself. It's blasphemous, profane. A way of instilling their filth into even the most godly of places.'

'Not only that,' Quaid said, 'but their "filth" has been there for a long time.'

'Luckily,' Mason said, 'we have some sway with the Vatican.'

Sally let out a long breath. 'First, we need to decide if we're gonna tell them or not. I mean, the ramifications of this could be huge.'

'We need a friendly face to help us,' Mason said.

His thoughts immediately went to Cardinal Vallini, and his heart went cold. Vallini had been murdered by the terrible killer known as Cassadaga not so long ago.

'Premo Conte, the leader of the Cavaliere,' Quaid said. 'Also, Cardinal Gambetti, the young man who was Vallini's replacement.'

These were both good contacts, Mason knew. People whom they'd done business with before and who would immediately take their calls and listen. It was a way in. He waited as their food arrived, and then tucked in, famished.

It was Roxy who suggested they call Jacobs with the good news.

Feeling secure, Mason waited until he'd finished his food and then did just that, managing to get through to Jacobs and furnish him with the new clue.

'The Vatican? Are you kidding?' Jacobs gasped.

'I wish we were,' Mason said. 'I didn't even know the Vatican had something called a Hell Hall.'

'Neither do many,' Sally said. 'Though it is a spectacular sight.'

'You've seen it?'

Sally nodded. 'Unfortunately.'

As the team ate, Sally made the necessary preparations to head for Rome at their earliest convenience. They couldn't be sure Bullion wouldn't eventually make it to Germany, but they did know he wouldn't find the next clue. The knowledge gave them an extra layer of security. In flight, she would make the calls to Conte and Gambetti.

It had taken some time, Mason thought, but finally they seemed to be getting on top of this mission.

Chapter 42

Considering the delicacy of the discussion, Sally waited until they'd landed in Rome and were firmly ensconced in a hotel coffee shop before making the call to Premo Conte.

Conte was their best contact within the Vatican, but he was a hard-ass – leader of the Cavalieré, a group of soldiers within the Swiss Guard. Their only other contact was Cardinal Gambetti, but they hadn't known him long enough to consider him a genuine friend.

Not that Conte was in any way to be considered a friend, Mason thought. They were close, and they had been through some extreme action together, but he was still the Inspector General of a small army.

'The *what?*' he said in answer to Sally's request. 'There is no such thing.'

Sally, luckily, was well aware of the controversies surrounding the so-called Hell Hall. She had encountered them numerous times whilst working alongside her father. 'We both know I'm talking about the Hall of Pontifical Audiences,' she said. 'It sits partly in Vatican City, mostly in Rome, and is treated as an extraterritorial area of the Holy See.'

Conte exhaled sharply. 'I was actually pleased to take your call,' he said, as if berating himself. 'I hadn't heard from you in a while. And then you tell me you're on a job.' His voice dropped. 'I should have known.'

'What do you mean by that?' Roxy asked with a bit of prickle in her voice.

'You bring danger to my home whenever you're here,' Conte said.

Sally frowned. 'That's a bit unfair.'

Conte sighed loudly. 'Yes, I suppose it is. But unfortunately it's also true. Why do you want access to the Hall of Pontifical Audiences, and what *kind* of access do you require?'

Sally sipped at her dark-coloured coffee. 'We want to inspect the bronze sculpture.'

Conte went quiet for several minutes. At this point, Mason was glad that Sally had explained what she meant prior to calling the Inspector General.

The so-called Hell Hall was a title bestowed on the Hall of Pontifical Audiences by the press, by enemies and, most likely, by Satanists. First, it had to do with the shape of the hall, which had the head of a viper when viewed externally, although the Vatican refuted this. Inside, at the top of the far wall, there were two round holes that might be eyes and one that could be a mouth, also giving the impression of a venomous snake. Once seen, it couldn't be unseen. Sally knew that from experience. Any resemblance to an actual viper was said to be coincidental, but the reality was there for all to see.

Second, and most controversial, she thought, was the bronze sculpture. It was supposed to be a study of Christ's resurrection. It stood two enormous storeys high and, in the artist's own words, depicted Jesus Christ emerging from toxic smoke and human skulls after a nuclear Armageddon. It had been described as everything from 'Satanic-looking' to 'horrific' and worse, but there were also certain circles that adored it. In any case, Sally knew, it was controversial at

251

best. Everything from blasphemous to pious, a real talking point.

'What business do you have with the "Resurrection"?' Conte asked finally.

Sally hesitated. They had discussed just how much they should reveal to Conte, and what access they might be able to squeeze out of him. In a way, he owed them. They had fought hard only a month ago to protect the Vatican from Marduk and his terrorists. They had put their lives on the line.

'We want to inspect it,' Sally said. 'Closely.'

'Closely?'

Clearly, he didn't like the sound of that. Sally bit her lip and tried to be judicious. 'We believe it holds the key to a puzzle,' she said. 'Now don't worry. We won't harm your sculpture. After we're gone, you won't even know we've been there.'

Conte sighed once more. 'It's a big ask,' he said.

'But one you would immediately grant my father.'

'Cardinal Vallini might have,' Conte reminded her. 'They were good friends. I will have to discuss with Gambetti and some others and get back to you. These things take time.'

'Time is what we don't have,' Sally said. 'We're here now. In Rome.'

'*Now?*' Conte blurted. 'I cannot admit you now. Is this a joke?'

Sally assured him it was no joke, that it was of utmost importance, and that they were calling in all favours. Conte moaned and complained and went quiet some more. In the end, he had to go away and think about how best to proceed, but promised them he'd call them back shortly.

Mason took the opportunity to relax. 'Is this sculpture that bad?' he asked.

Sally turned to him. 'I wouldn't say bad. It's all about definition,' she said. 'A devious eye can make a mockery of anything, stir up all kinds of fervour. Everyone sees it differently, I guess.'

'But how do you see it?'

'I'd rather you see it for yourself without my opinions colouring your views,' Sally told them.

'If we gain access,' Quaid said morosely.

Mason sipped his hot drink. They had come so far, only to be potentially thwarted by a place they had become intimately familiar with during the last six or seven months. Had it really only been that long since they chased down the Vatican Book of Secrets?

Mason looked around the group. The team looked relaxed, the opposite of how they normally looked at this stage of a mission. Of course, they were under no real duress. Their enemies didn't have access to the last clue and thus would not be here in Rome. Mason luxuriated in that fact for a few minutes, smiling.

And then Sally's phone rang.

'Conte?' she said.

'Yes. I have spoken with Cardinal Gambetti. The sculpture is popular, as you probably know. Special researchers are often allowed access. What do they say – all publicity is good?'

'Something like that,' Sally said.

'Well, you can come see me whenever you like. I will print out your temporary passes and have you escorted over to the Hall. You understand, this is a little irregular. It is only our personal history that gets you fast access.'

Sally thanked him. They all knew Conte was taking a chance for them. They quickly drank up and headed out of the hotel to make the short walk to Vatican City. It had felt strange to Mason, discussing meeting Conte over the phone when the man was so close in person, but they had his personal mobile number and could get hold of him far easier that way than approaching the Vatican officially, in person. Now, they had access.

It was a warm August morning. A bright sun filled their vision, and the skies were blue with just a few errant clouds. The crowds were thick on the pavements, the sound of conversation loud. Mason and the others found they were forced to nudge their way through to gain access to St Peter's Square, which opened out before them.

Immediately, they saw the aftermath of the battle they had been involved in just a short month ago.

When terrorists had attacked the Vatican last month, they had done considerable damage to the façade and the main doors. Those areas were now covered in scaffolding and there were workers' vans parked close by. Mason could see people working to repair the damage.

It was a sad sight. Mason saw the others regarding it with melancholy and tried to stay upbeat.

'Hey,' he said. 'It's raw, but we still won the day. We helped stop the attack. It could have been much worse.'

They all nodded and proceeded to the right of the Basilica, where Conte had his offices. Soon, they were standing in front of the man himself.

Conte was an imposing figure, broad-shouldered, tall, wearing the usual wraparound sunglasses and a tailored suit. He approached them just outside the main doors to his offices. At first, he smiled, but then his face dissolved into a frown.

'Care to tell me more?' he asked.

'Great to see you too.' Roxy leaned forward and clasped his hand, shaking it. 'We've fought together,' she breathed. 'That means something.'

Conte's face broke out into a smile, signalling that he felt the same way. He didn't ask them again to expand any further. He just took them at their word. Mason was grateful for Roxy's well-worded insight.

They spent a few minutes with Conte, passing small talk and learning what was happening with the repair works.

They shaded their eyes and looked over at the damaged façade. Conte called a man over and asked him to take them to the Hall, but remain with them. Sally balked a little at that.

'We don't need a babysitter,' she said.

Conte hesitated. 'Then I won't give you one,' he said. 'But know this. You will not be alone inside the hall, and you must treat everything with respect.'

Sally nodded easily, as if that went without saying. Soon, they were following the guard in the direction of the Hall of Pontifical Audiences. Mason couldn't help but keep an eye out for their enemies, just in case. It came naturally to him, and it was a habit he didn't want to break. It had saved him many times through the years.

He saw nothing, no one.

Mason didn't let the absence of an enemy take the edge off. He preferred to keep sharp, as, he was sure, Roxy did too. He looked at her now, saw her casing the perimeter just as he was.

Soon, they arrived at the hall and went inside. Mason found himself in a vast, partly lit auditorium with a stage at the far end. There were a few people wandering about the enormous floor space, most clad in robes. The first thing Mason found his eyes drawn to was the shape of the viper's head which, once Sally had pointed it out, was unmistakable. The ceiling at the far end definitely looked like it had two eyes and a snake's mouth. Maybe if Sally hadn't mentioned it . . .

But then Mason's eyes were drawn to something else.

The bronze sculpture towering over the stage made his jaw drop. At the centre, there was a rising Christ. To left and right, the toxic smoke spread out, looking like random bronze tentacles waving back and forth, dotted with skulls. It stood high and proud, like a sinister presence, commanding the entire room.

Although it was a vision of Christ's resurrection, if Mason hadn't known, he could just as easily have likened it to a Lovecraftian nightmare or a scene from *Aliens*. He stayed silent, not wanting to voice his thoughts, especially inside here. He noticed that the rest of his team kept quiet, too.

Sally started towards the magnificent sculpture, her footsteps echoing in the relative silence. The team followed, ignoring the surprised looks they got from a few priests, and made their way steadily towards the stage.

Once there, they climbed the steps and regarded the sculpture. Up close, in Mason's view, it was harder to look at. The delicate, precise sculpting that had gone into forming the human skulls was exquisite. Scarily so. Mason stared at the vision of Jesus Christ rising from the ashes of a nuclear holocaust and wondered why it sent tremors of fear through him, even in here, amid all the devoutness and godliness of the Vatican.

'Are you ready?' Sally said.

'Do we actually have to touch that thing?' Roxy breathed.

'Remember the clue,' Sally said. '"In the Hell Hall of the Vatican there is a visage unlike any other, the face of the Lord."'

'The Lord,' Mason repeated. '*Their* Lord?'

Sally nodded, regarding the entire sculpture. 'On here somewhere,' she said softly, 'is the face of a devil.'

Chapter 43

There were dozens of eerie, shrieking, skull-like faces. Mason studied the massive artwork, intimidated. Each sculpted face was slightly different, nightmarish, disturbing. He took a look back towards the vast 6300-seat hall, saw the priests going about their business, and turned back to the sculpture. The others were already leaning close to it, studying the faces.

This had become an ominous, unsettling business, he mused as he worked. Recently, during their missions, they had fought evil individuals, yes, individuals like Marduk, for instance. But this was an entirely different kind of evil, something he had never imagined encountering. He wasn't sure he had ever believed in Satanists, not in the proper sense of the word. He supposed all sorts existed; there were many religions out there – but chanting, sacrificing, murderers bent on conjuring up a beast known as Satan?

Mason tried to force it out of his head, but each twisted face slotted it right back in there. They were dealing with mad, sick men and women and, at some point, there had to be a reckoning. Their evil machinations needed to come to an end.

Mason checked face after face, getting far closer than he liked. The others did the same. At one point, a priest came up to them, speaking first in Italian and then in English, asking what they were doing. Sally gave him Premo Conte's name and showed him a form signed by the Inspector General that gave them access to the hall. The priest smiled and walked away, seemingly content.

Mason continued his work. To his right, Roxy moaned about each screaming face. Hassell and Quaid worked in silence, and Sally checked all along the bottom row, guessing that the face of the Devil might be the lowest. In truth, none of them knew exactly what they were looking for, but they hoped they'd recognise something when the time came. Mason was certain he'd notice the terrible visage they'd seen so much of already.

It happened sooner than he'd imagined. It was Quaid, searching around the far left of the sculpture, who quietly caught their attention.

'Hey,' he said. 'I think I have something.'

Quickly, they crowded around him.

Quaid pointed out a shrieking face to the bottom left, but this one appeared to have a goat-like quality to it. Also, the way the 'smoke' twisted away from it seemed to form two horns. It was subtle, Mason thought, but if you looked long enough at it, you certainly could see the face of the Devil.

'I see it,' Hassell said.

Sally was already on her knees. Mason moved to block her from the view of the hall. Roxy helped. Together, they shielded her as she started feeling all around the face and pressing the hard bronze. She worked fast.

'I think I feel something,' she said.

Mason stood nonchalantly, Roxy at his side. Below them, Sally worked. In seconds, she was rising to her feet with a cylindrical object in her hand.

'Got it,' she said. 'Nice work, Quaid.'

As they stood there, Sally reached into the cylinder and extracted a torn piece of paper. The map. She reached in again, scooping her hand around.

'There's nothing else in here,' she said.

Mason frowned hard. 'You're kidding?'

'No, it's empty. Why would it be empty?'

'A good question considering the map was there,' Quaid said.

'If anyone had found this before us,' Hassell said. 'Surely they'd have taken both the scroll and the map.'

Mason nodded his agreement. 'They wouldn't leave the map.'

'I can think of only one explanation,' Sally said. 'We've reached the end of the clues. This is the last piece of the map.'

Mason felt a jolt of elation. Surely Sally was right. Nobody would take the clue and leave the map.

'Eight clues,' Quaid said. 'Eight pieces of the map.'

'We didn't get them all,' Roxy reminded him.

'I know.'

'We have a plan for that,' Mason said.

'Care to elaborate?'

'It's pretty straightforward, but let's get the hell out of here first.'

Sally pocketed the map and then replaced the cylinder so that nothing appeared out of place. The team backed away from the sculpture, gave it a few more cursory glances for show, and then started walking across the great hall, heading for the exit.

'This brings us closer than ever to the Hellfire,' Mason said as they walked. 'Way ahead of Bullion and his friends.'

'A long way to go yet,' Sally said. 'Somehow, we have to join the pieces of the map together.'

Mason slowed as they neared the door, put out a hand to push it open. 'Maybe we should talk about that,' he said.

And Bullion's voice answered, 'Yeah, let's all talk about it right now.'

Chapter 44

Mason's heart thudded and his eyes grew wide in disbelief.

How . . . ?

There was no time to think, not even time to breathe. Bullion was surrounded by his comrades, blocking out any light that might have entered through the door. Mason glanced down but saw no weapons in the hands of Bullion or his crew.

Bullion lashed out. Mason stepped back into the hall. The blow flew by ineffectually, but Bullion was driving forward, pushing them back.

Roxy smashed her way in from the side, pile-driving a fist into a man's ribcage so he grunted loudly and folded. The others were pushing through the door by now, two of them tripping over the falling man.

Around the hall, priests were looking up to see what the commotion was all about.

Mason stood his ground as Bullion came at him, blocking a left and then a right. He looked the man dead in the eyes.

'How did you find us?'

'Oh, we have our ways. Didn't you know? We converse with the Devil.'

He laughed and struck out again. Mason blocked the blows easily, but saw several men and women with Bullion; once again, they were outnumbered. This wouldn't go well. He backed further into the hall.

'We want that clue,' Bullion said.

'That's gonna be difficult,' Roxy said. 'There wasn't one.'

Mason winced slightly. The less information they imparted, the better.

Bullion frowned at her. 'What the hell do you mean?'

'How did you find us?' Mason decided that since Bullion was in a talkative mood he might offer up some information.

'I'm just that good,' Bullion scoffed.

Maybe not.

Mason backed away slowly. Bullion's team crowded into the hall, spreading out, their faces menacing.

'The map?' Bullion said next.

'And if we give it to you? Are you just going to turn and walk away?'

Bullion grinned, looked at Sally. 'I bet you have the map, don't you?'

It was an educated guess, an oversight they'd have to correct in the future. Mason moved instinctively closer to her.

'We've bested you before,' Hassell said.

'You got lucky, you ran away.' Bullion shrugged. 'Now, there's nowhere to run.'

With that, Bullion sprang into action. He leapt at Mason, threw a couple of punches. Mason caught one on the temple that made him see stars. He staggered back. All around Bullion, his team attacked.

Roxy waded in hard, kicking one man in the knee and another in the groin. Both collapsed immediately, temporarily taken out of the fight. A woman engaged with Roxy and tried to grab her around the throat, but Roxy danced to the side.

Sally stood her ground, dodging from side to side as a man attacked her. She'd learned a lot during the last few months of teaching, and it was now time to put all that learning into practice. She was quick, hardy from years of fell running, and she knew how to deliver a punch properly. The rucksack slung across her shoulders was tight-fitting and didn't hamper her too much.

Hassell and Quaid threw themselves into the fight. They ran at the approaching group like a pair of bowling balls, scattering their opponents left and right. They were grabbed, caught around their waists and throat, and struggled in place as men and women staggered all around them.

Mason knew he couldn't let Bullion distract him. This was not a one-on-one battle. His team needed his help. He blocked, twisted and delivered three solid punches that Bullion managed to counter. The punches hit hard, making Bullion grunt and wince. Mason grabbed hold of the guy by the shoulders and tried to throw him aside.

It wasn't to be. Bullion was solid, strong, and trained. He stepped in to Mason and managed a cheap shot to the abdomen. Mason gasped, backed up some more. They were well into the main hall by now, almost among the chairs. The priests were standing, staring, unsure what to do, no doubt flabbergasted at what they were seeing.

Mason deflected another punch. Around Bullion, he got a quick glimpse of his own team. Apart from Roxy, who was taking on two at once, they were floundering. It wasn't going well. What was Bullion going to do? Beat them all up and search them right here? It appeared that that was exactly what he was going to do.

'Boss wants you dead,' Bullion whispered vehemently. 'Well . . . ' he amended. 'Not right away.' He grinned.

Mason wondered if he had a van, or something bigger, parked outside. Was this a kidnapping?

'Your boss is crazier than batshit,' he said.

263

Bullion nodded. 'Oh, I know. But he pays the wages. Now, how about you all come quietly and accept your fate?'

Mason didn't want to think about that. He felt the back of a chair pressed up against him, reached around and picked it up. With a vicious swing, he smashed Bullion across the shoulders with it, sent the man to his knees. Next, seeing an opportunity, he threw the chair at Sally's attacker. The metal legs struck him in the side, made him stagger away so that Sally could rain blows down on his exposed neck. The man collapsed in a heap.

Mason picked up another chair.

'What are you doing?' A priest was running towards them, robes flapping. 'Please, please, stop.'

Mason raised the chair above Bullion, saw the priest in his eyeline, and hesitated. Immediately, he knew he'd just made a mistake. He should have pushed his advantage. Bullion saw the hesitation, levered himself to his feet and was suddenly back on level terms, panting, rolling his injured shoulder.

'Cheap shot,' he said.

'Here's another,' Mason said.

He swung the chair, this time aiming for Bullion's face. Closer to the door, Roxy had one hand around a woman's throat, the other wrapped in a man's hair. She squeezed with one hand, pulled with the other, sent them both to the floor. As they fell, she kicked out, caught one on the chin and the other across the cheek. The man flew into the wall, cracking his head. The woman collapsed into a groaning heap. Roxy, momentarily free, whirled to take stock of the fight.

A man filled her vision, a big brute with steroid-enhanced muscles. She knew just where to hit. She felt a hand fall across her shoulders and saw that it was Sally taking a momentary reprieve.

'You okay?' she yelled.

'No,' Sally yelled back.

'All right then.' Roxy had expected nothing less, and turned back to her opponent.

Mason lashed out with another chair, driving Bullion back. His team was with him now, stumbling amongst the wide rows of chairs. They fought back and forth, striking out, ducking, dodging from side to side. Chairs flew left and right. Mason knew they couldn't overcome their enemy and had to get away.

There was no other option. 'Run!' he yelled. 'Run!'

He threw chairs, making Bullion and his team cover up. Roxy and Hassell did the same. They squeezed out a moment of opportunity, looked to the exit doors, and started running. Roxy hung back a little, deterring those who would try to come straight after them. Mason did the same. He threw a chair at a man who leapt after Sally, struck his legs and tangled him up so that he hit the floor face first. Blood exploded from a broken nose. The woman directly behind him tripped over him. Another man got caught in a rolling chair.

Mason saw his chance. He yelled at Roxy, turned tail and ran for the exit. Their enemies were hopelessly snarled up in the crazy, upturned rows of chairs. Mason was a step behind Roxy.

Outside, the sudden brightness stung his eyes. The street was busy, packed with pedestrians. Mason's team ran among the civilians, the flow of people parting and curving around them.

'Just go!' Mason yelled.

He slammed the door behind him and the team took off. They flew among the crowds, leaping from side to side, somehow managing to avoid collisions. They darted between men and women and children, following no path but trying not to get hopelessly lost. Mason chanced a glance back at the door.

Nothing.

They turned corners, flew across junctions. Rome spread out all around them. Mason had no idea where he was, but he *did* know that they'd evaded Bullion. He pulled up under a wide, grey, anonymous porte cochère, gathered the team around him.

'Anyone take a bad hit?' he asked.

They shook their heads. They were all bruised, battered, but in good spirits. Sally had a minor cut across her forehead that had already stopped bleeding. As Mason looked at her, she broke out into a grin.

'We've done it,' she said. 'Succeeded. We got all the clues and the maps.'

'Not all of them,' Quaid reminded her.

'Fair point, but we have enough.' She faltered with the last word, her voice changing from certainty to hope.

'It's time to find out,' Mason said. 'We should look for somewhere quiet.' He knew they needed to get off the streets, find a safe, obscure place so they could attend to the next step of their mission.

He looked around. 'Thousands of hotels in Rome,' he said, thinking of Premo Conte and how he would react when he learned what had happened at the Hall of Pontifical Audiences. He tried to put the thought firmly out of his mind.

'You have the maps?' he asked softly.

Sally nodded. 'Safe and sound.'

He turned to Hassell. 'Find us a random, quiet hotel.'

Hassell fished out his phone, found their location, and entered a few words. Five minutes later, he was leading them once more through the streets.

On the way, Mason hoped, to the culmination of their mission.

Chapter 45

As he walked, Mason considered the thorny question raised by Bullion's appearance.

How the hell had he found them?

Having complete and utter trust in his team, Mason decided there could only be one option. The phone connection. Somehow, Bullion or his boss Moloch had to be monitoring the phone lines. Bugging them. That meant every time they talked to Jacobs, they talked to Moloch, too.

It was the only thing that made sense to Mason. And something they would have to be wary of from now on. In one way, he thought, the knowledge might even help them send Bullion on a wild-goose chase.

They found the hotel, walked into the dimly lit lobby, and booked rooms. They were all worn out and decided to take a few hours for themselves. Mason walked to his room, took a shower, and then collapsed on the bed. He set an alarm after telling the others they should meet downstairs in three hours and then promptly fell asleep. He slept dreamlessly. When he woke, he had no idea where he was and just lay there, trawling through his memory for a few minutes. Slowly, it all started coming back to him. He sat up, breathed deeply, looked over at the grimy window that overlooked the street. The brightness had left the skies by now as early evening took over. He could hear traffic noise, the sounds of many people passing by. He considered showering again, then decided it might be overkill. Mason checked his watch. Still forty minutes to go before they all were due to meet up.

He made a hotel-room coffee, tasted it, and instantly regretted it. He left the room, heading down to the lobby. Mason expected to find Roxy propping up the bar and wasn't disappointed.

'Hey,' he said, sliding on to the seat next to her. 'Been here long?'

She sipped at her neat rum. 'Not long enough.'

'You still soak your sheets in it?' He couldn't help but repeat their standing joke.

'You know me. Every damn day.'

He sensed she didn't really want to talk, sensed that perhaps she'd suffered a setback on her personal journey. Instead, he supported her by being there, ordered a drink, and sat alongside her in silence. Soon, the others started making their way downstairs.

Sally came last, her laptop in its case slung across her shoulders.

'We ready?' She was grinning expectantly.

The team found a quiet corner of the room and sat down. The bar area was extensive and dark, all oak panelling and dim wall sconces. At this time of the day, it was practically empty. Mason watched Sally pull her laptop out of its bag and lay it on the table.

Two minutes later, she reached into her rucksack and brought out a file. Inside, slotted between plastic sheets, were all the pieces of the map they'd accrued. Carefully now, Sally slipped the pieces out and laid them on the table.

'Six pieces of the eight,' Quaid said. 'It's not a bad haul.'

Mason looked closely at the maps for the first time. Until now, he'd been intent on just finding them. Now he studied them. The paper was thick, torn at the edges. Sally was trying to piece them together like a jigsaw, sliding them round and round each other. Quaid leaned across to help her.

'They fit,' Sally said finally.

The two missing pieces made the piecing together harder, but Sally and Quaid had succeeded as far as was possible. Mason saw it was a crude fit. The lines of the map didn't quite meet in some places, but they were all distinct. He sat back.

'What next?' Roxy asked, studying the black contours. 'I mean . . . it could be anywhere in the world. Couldn't it?'

If Mason had been expecting a revelation when the map was pieced together, he was sorely disappointed. He blinked now, looked down at the table, and then up at Sally.

'She has a point,' he said.

'I see a coastline,' Quaid said.

Sally nodded. 'But as Roxy says, it could be anywhere in the world. We need a bit of professional help.' She tapped her laptop.

Quaid looked nonplussed. 'You want me to search my contacts for a cartographer?'

Sally looked up at him. 'Not yet,' she said. 'I have another idea.'

'I suppose it involves the bloody internet,' Quaid muttered.

'There are map programs,' Sally said. 'Where you can let the computer do the heavy lifting. You simply scan in the various pieces – or sketches – and let the program do its work. The program has the most definitive maps of the world already preset and matches any drawing to the right set of contours. I'm hoping it can do that for us.'

'Depends how accurate the drawing is,' Hassell said.

'Whilst that's true, the results should still be pretty accurate. As you know, the shapes and contours of the world's ridges and forests and coastlines, hills and mountains, are unique to themselves. One coastline does not look exactly like another. One set of mountain ranges will not match the next. A river, a road, a tributary. They're all distinct.'

Mason watched as Sally scanned the pieces of the map using her smart phone and then sent the pictures to herself. Next, on the computer, she opened the pictures and inserted them into the program she already had open. It took some time.

Mason sat back, looked around. A few of the tables were filling now, people coming in after work for a quick drink or an early dinner. There were people seated at the bar, the bartender doing a brisk trade. A waitress came over to them and took their order. Mason saw no reason not to eat and drink and do their business at the same time.

Sally, unfamiliar with the program, took her time, carefully reading instructions and following a tutorial. Her fingers flew across the keys.

First, their drinks appeared, and then their food, and Sally still worked. Mason felt a little guilty about cutting into his medium steak but then, mouth watering, remembered how hungry he was and dug in. Sally picked at her food as she worked.

More than an hour passed. Sally pressed a few final buttons with a flourish and then sat back. She nodded in relief.

'That should just about do it.'

'Now what?' Quaid asked.

'Now we wait for the computer program to do its thing,' she said.

'And how long should that take?' Quaid said.

Sally shrugged. 'Honestly, I have no idea. First time I've ever used anything like this. I even had to buy the whole bloody program online to use it properly.'

They finished their meals. Mason wondered just how long they would have to wait. Sally stared intermittently at the computer screen. They ordered more drinks. The bar grew noisier and noisier as early evening became seven and then eight o'clock. People came and went.

Finally, there was a beep from the computer. Sally blinked rapidly and then turned her attention towards it.

'It's found something,' she said.

Mason leaned in. 'Is it definitive?' he asked.

'Hang on. I really don't know how to read this.'

They waited until Sally got her head around the software, chatting among themselves. Mason was on edge, prepared to move even now. He was ready to end this, to find the Hellfire and uncover the Satanists, to take Bullion down and stop Moloch. The mission was only part of this op. They couldn't let people like Moloch continue to operate.

'You think Bullion's gonna do the same thing?' Roxy nodded at the open laptop.

Mason shrugged. 'I think his boss will. He has to. They've come up short, but as Sally said, the contours of the world are unique.'

'You think he has enough map pieces?'

'I think it's possible.'

Roxy shook her head. 'Not fair.'

Mason smiled, liking the innocence of the remark, reminded that Roxy was still a vast work in progress. He looked around at the other members of his team, grateful for their presence.

'This Moloch,' Mason said. 'I'm starting to think he may be too big for us to handle alone. His network may be too vast. Quaid . . . I want you to think about contacts. Valid contacts. Someone we can reach out to when we need to, a person we can trust.'

'That's always the problem,' Quaid murmured.

Mason said nothing, confident that he'd started the wheels in Quaid's head turning. That would be enough. By the time they found the Hellfire, he knew Quaid would have at least one candidate in mind.

'I have it,' Sally breathed suddenly. 'My God, I have it.'

Mason switched his attention to her. 'The resting place of the Hellfire?'

'The place the map leads us,' Sally nodded. 'It . . . it's in England.'

'Where?' Roxy asked.

'My God . . . ' Sally said. 'My God . . . '

Chapter 46

Moloch was livid. He balled his fists, wanted to throw the phone across his office, but refrained. He felt like wrapping his hands around someone's scrawny neck and squeezing, squeezing until the life in some random, beautiful blue eyes went out.

Bullion had failed again. The useless bastard and his team of useless bastards had gone all the way to Rome and fucked it all up. Mason had escaped with the map and, apparently, no clue. What the hell did that mean? Was Mason lying? Had they come to the end of the clues?

That meant . . .

Yes, they were at the end of their quest. Moloch made himself lay the phone carefully back down on the polished oak table. He took several deep breaths. Bullion was already on his way back with his tail between his legs, a tail that Moloch would just love to cut off.

He paced his office now, walking from the desk to the floor-to-ceiling window and back again. Outside, there was a good view of his estate, the grounds and the driveway, a few guards patrolling. Moloch was reminded of how busy those grounds had been just a few nights ago when he'd performed the most recent Black Mass. What a night that had been. The ceremony dedicated to Lucifer, and all the delicious rituals it contained, always came first. The dark master would never be ignored, no matter what. He was the essence of Moloch's life.

As he walked, he tried to calm himself. He knew what to do. He'd known what to do since the very beginning but had become obsessed with the search, with the clues and the maps. The more they gathered the better.

Already, he had someone feeding the maps they had into a certain program, trying to come up with a location. It was the most obvious thing to do. Apparently – Moloch hadn't known this until recently – the contours of the earth were unique. If the map was good enough, they'd find out what part of the world it represented. From that point, Moloch would be guessing, since he only had two parts of the map to work with, but it was better than nothing.

Right now, he itched for another Black Mass. He walked over to a cupboard where his robes were kept and slipped them on. They smelled of the abyss, he thought, of death and darkness and all things wonderfully vile. He stroked them, loved the feel of them against his skin. He would live in them if he could.

Moloch walked over to the window, an apparition dressed in a hooded black robe. If they located the Hellfire's ultimate resting place . . . if they found the sword . . .

Moloch's heart beat faster at the idea. Did he have enough people to see the job through? Bullion and his crew were seven, though Moloch no longer trusted them to get any job done. How many guards did he have, and could he pay all of them off sufficiently to keep quiet? He'd been doing a pretty good job of it so far.

Moloch had over twenty guards. He could draft more in if required, but with the addition of more guards came more risk. You couldn't trust them all. There was always a rotten apple. Moloch knew all about rotten apples. Look at Jacobs, look at the other traitor whom Mason had saved.

Moloch felt sorry for himself. Fools and traitors beset him left and right. He was the best of them, trying his hardest to succeed against the odds, to serve his master well.

The phone rang. Moloch blinked at it, then, still clad in the robes, walked away from the window to the desk.

'Yes?' he answered, anger in his voice.

'This is Anna.'

Moloch blinked. This would either be very good or terrible, world-destroying news. Anna was the tech assigned to studying the two pieces of the map.

'What is it?' he tried to keep his voice neutral.

'I've extrapolated the data. The program we're using feeds off relevant information and then searches for the right shapes, reliefs, curves.'

'I understand.'

'Also as you know, it is a time-consuming process. We have the most powerful computers we've got working on the task. Three of them running on separate cycles. The processing power is tremendous.'

Moloch started to feel as if she was setting him up for bad news. 'And have you succeeded . . . ' He left the sentence unfinished, not wanting to add the 'or . . . '

Anna went quiet. Eventually, she said, 'Not yet.'

'Then why are you calling me?'

'You asked for constant updates, sir.'

Moloch bit his tongue. She was right. In his apprehension, he'd forgotten. He checked his watch, stroked his robes, put the phone down. He was struggling.

Mason had to die. That part was obvious. Mason and his crew had plagued them every step of the way, almost as if it was a personal vendetta. Moloch thought about that for a while. Could it *be* a personal vendetta? According to Jacobs, it was Sally's late father who had initially started up the investigation. What did Moloch know about Professor Rusk?

And what did Rusk know about him?

Nothing. Not a damn thing. Moloch knew it was all just bad luck. He tried to turn his thoughts in other, more pleasant directions. Mostly, towards Satanism. For instance, he thought, who could he attract to the fold next, and how much power and influence would they wield?

He needed that Hellfire.

As if in reaction to his desperate thought, the phone rang again.

Moloch stared at it, nonplussed. When you dabbled in the occult, coincidences like that were suspicious at best.

'Hello?' he answered tentatively.

'Sir? It's Anna again.'

Moloch frowned, unsure whether he was happy to hear her voice. 'What is it this time? I don't need updates every—'

'We've found something,' she said.

Moloch drew in a sharp breath. 'What?'

'A location. Even better, it's not far away.'

Moloch gripped the edges of the table with his free hand. 'Are you sure? There can be no mistakes.'

'I follow the data. That's what I do. It leads us to a single spot along a rugged coastline. The contours are precise, exact. There can be no mistake. I guess we're lucky that it's such a chiselled, jagged coastline.'

Moloch doubted there was any luck in it. The Hellfire would have been hidden where it could be found. Of that, he had no doubt. He suddenly found that he couldn't speak, couldn't summon up the next words.

'Do you want to know where?' Anna asked finally.

'Of . . . course.'

'Cornwall's north coast,' Anna said a little vaguely.

'Is that . . . it?'

'I have only two pieces of the map,' Anna reminded him. 'But common sense dictates a more precise location. And in the area suggested by the two pieces, there is only one significant place.'

'Which is?'

'Tintagel Castle.'

Moloch blinked. 'Isn't that a tourist destination?'

'I believe so. Yes. Whatever you're looking for must be hidden in the caves beneath.'

Hellfire, Moloch thought.

It's at Tintagel.

It was quite fitting, actually. The castle was surrounded, surfeited with legend. That it might hold the Hellfire itself, the dark fruits of Satanism, was comforting to Moloch. It pleased him. The thought of it sitting down there, perverting history in its own way, made him smile. That smile broadened when he thought of the sword and the coming deadline for the great Mass. If he moved fast, he would make the date.

'Why do you think it's hidden in the caves beneath?' he asked.

'I don't see any other places where it might be kept secret. And Tintagel is known for its tunnels, its sea caves. It wouldn't have been hard to make a journey there, to hide something beneath. And, of course, it wouldn't have been too long a journey.'

Moloch thought about it. Anna was right. The Satanists' house, the one they'd taken from the old Duke of Adlington, had been situated around here. The journey to Tintagel wasn't too arduous.

He put the phone down. It all hit him at once. He was here . . . now . . . with the ultimate knowledge. He had the men and women, the firepower. Bullion would be here soon. All they had to do was mobilise and go get the Hellfire.

And if Mason got in the way, so much the better.

Chapter 47

Mason and his team wasted no time returning from Rome. From running out of the Hall of Pontifical Audiences, to losing Bullion in the street, to their long conversation in the hotel bar, they moved as quickly and efficiently as they could.

Sally had discovered the location of the Hellfire – Tintagel – and they had decided very quickly to haul ass. They had no time to waste, no time to recover in their rooms, not even time to stay for a few more drinks – which both Mason and Roxy thought they needed. Sally booked them on the next flight out of Rome that landed anywhere near London, and they rushed to the airport.

Bad luck struck. Their flight was cancelled, and they had to hang around for hours, waiting for the next one. Mason found himself trying to eat the time away, pacing the carpets in front of stark floor-to-ceiling windows that overlooked a dark and windswept airport and several runways. Every second that passed hurt them. Every lost moment was like a nail driven into a coffin. They knew well that Moloch had access to the same technology that they did.

It didn't matter that they had more pieces of the map. Throughout the mission, all they had been doing was gathering more pieces of the map, hoping they would get enough to complete a picture. Also, they hadn't known what to expect or what other revelations each clue might raise.

Eventually, the plane took off and winged its way back to England. They tried to rest on the flight but were too het up, raring to go. They knew they had to reach Tintagel before Moloch but were also aware of the man's advantage.

He was far closer than they were.

On landing, they rushed out of the plane, got hung up at border control, and then quickly exited the airport. They found a taxi and immediately asked the driver to take them back to Sally's house – for an excellent reason.

This time, they were going in armed.

Mason moved fast when the taxi dropped them off at their home. He jumped out, ran up to the front door, and unlocked it. The others followed on his heels. He raced to the weapons lockbox and opened it, pulling out and feeling the cool metal of the semi-automatic Glock 17 polymer-framed, seventeen-round handgun. He handed the others their weapons and then stood up.

Checked the time.

It was early afternoon. They'd lost a lot of time on the journey home. Now, though, they were ready to move.

They collected rucksacks and filled them with flashlights, helmet cams, provisions, and other items they thought they would need for a journey under Tintagel. Quaid stayed in contact with his friends in authority, not giving them the full lowdown on Moloch yet but whetting their appetite. They had no absolute proof about Moloch's wrongdoing up to now, only the testimonies of two men who might or might not be telling the truth. Professor Taylor's testimony would be crucial. But to get that absolute proof, they needed to catch Moloch in the act.

For which Jacobs would work nicely.

But first they had to stop the Satanist from obtaining the Hellfire. He would become a very different animal if he got to it first.

They left the house, jumped into a car, and started out for Tintagel. It would take several hours. The roads were crammed with traffic, making it harder. Quaid drove, letting the journey take his mind off things. Mason was sitting in the back, fighting motion sickness, listening as Sally talked.

'Any ideas what we're gonna do when we get there?' she asked.

'Hope that Moloch hasn't beaten us to it,' Roxy murmured.

'Do we have any idea where to look?' Mason asked.

'Well, yes,' Sally said. 'Obviously, Tintagel is a well-known tourist spot. The Hellfire won't be up top, or anywhere near the bridge, or along the bluffs. It has to be underneath.'

'There are sea caves,' Hassell said, holding up his phone.

'Then that's where we start,' Sally said.

'Will we need a boat?' Roxy asked.

'Accessible from above,' Hassell said. 'And extremely dangerous.'

Roxy snorted. 'Of course they are. Wouldn't expect anything less.'

They thought about calling Jacobs, decided against it. Mason remembered the phone lines might be bugged and didn't want to give away their location just yet. Every passing moment brought them speeding closer to Tintagel.

The roads towards Cornwall's rugged northern coastline were twisty, hedge-lined and hard to negotiate. Mason had to transfer to the front seat, unable to take the constant twisting and turning. The narrow, winding roads slowed them down even more, and now the light was gradually beginning to leach from the sky.

'Gonna be dark when we get there,' Quaid pointed out.

'Ah, good, that'll make things easier,' Roxy grumbled.

Another hour passed. They began to see signs for Tintagel and followed them all the way to a remote parking area that had no major barrier, just a short metal arm. Maybe someone had stolen the barrier or removed it. A mystery. Still, it made things slightly easier.

Mason wasn't sure what he'd expected to see here at Tintagel. What he *had* found was a lonely, windswept car park situated up on a bluff. Harsh gusts blasted at the car. The skies were grey now, and full of scudding clouds. It was getting dark, but the weather was turning too – a storm was coming. The team sat for a few moments in the car, regarding the area.

'Staring at it ain't gonna make it any better,' Roxy said finally. 'Let's get out there.'

Mason exited the car into the weather. It was just wind for now, but a wind that plucked at him and made him brace himself. On two sides, he could see a roiling darkness far below. In another direction lay Tintagel Castle, and the last was the way they had come. The bluff was high up, well above any sea caves.

Sally had done her own research. There were ways down to the sea caves from the cliffs, but none of them were well documented. Obviously, the authorities didn't want people risking their lives at the tourist spot, so it had taken Sally's persistence to seek out local groups dedicated to climbing and hiking to discover the right places from which to start. If it wasn't for social media and blogging, she wouldn't have been able to do it.

She stood for a while, getting her bearings, then started marching off to the left. Mason followed, bending his head against the wind. Soon, the team came to the edge of the cliff and looked down. Mason caught his breath. It was a long way, and the path twisted along the face of the cliff, disappearing down into darkness.

It wasn't sheer though, he noted. The cliff jutted out, making the path seem less treacherous. Mason shrugged his backpack tighter around his shoulders and took a deep breath.

'Let's get down there before the rain starts,' Sally said.

It was a good shout. She led the way, jumping down to the path and grabbing hold of a nearby rock to steady herself. Mason followed, next in line. The wind tugged at his clothing as he jumped, unsettling him, but his boots hit the rocky surface soundly and he started down. The path ran straight for a while at an incline, rocks on both sides. The wind funnelled along the path, striking them hard in their faces. Mason was forced to squint. They reached the first switchback and turned, the sea now on their other side. At the switchback, the rocks disappeared, treating Mason to a proper view of the area.

It was a view he didn't want. Now he could see out across the cliff to the rocks far below, to the pounding waves. The noise of the heavy surf rolled up the rocks, assaulted Mason's ears and then thudded up towards the skies. To the right, he saw shadows and shapes that could only be Tintagel Castle itself, on a piece of land that looked remote and barren. He turned away from it, feeling practically seasick. He focused on Sally's back, looking at nothing else in particular. As they walked down this next switchback, the rocks on the seaward side disappeared, leaving the path exposed and a deadly drop to their right. Mason hugged the cliff face, stepping carefully. This far up, the salt spray didn't reach, something he was grateful for.

They descended switchback after switchback, turning on themselves again and again. Some of the path was nicely sheltered, offering a little comfort, but a lot of it was scarily exposed, leaving them breathing deeply in fear. The path was narrow, only about three and four feet wide in some places.

They kept descending, minute after minute, for perhaps half an hour. Once, Mason looked up and saw the cliff stretching above and the perilous way back. He didn't look up again. The wind still tugged at him and he dreaded any stronger gusts. It would be so easy to be plucked off this path.

Sally finally raised a hand and pointed ahead. Mason squinted, making out an outcropping around which the path ran, becoming a ledge that hung out over a steep drop.

'The cave is around there,' she shouted.

They proceeded carefully. Mason hugged the cliff face. They ventured out over the drop, acres of space below them, and came around the rocky outcropping. Halfway along they spied a darker space to their left.

A cave entrance.

Sally went in first, reaching around for her flashlight and turning it on. She shone it on the floor, then on the walls, revealing black, craggy, damp surfaces and a tunnel that led farther back. Mason breathed a sigh of relief when he stepped in after her. Soon, they were all inside the cave, shining their torches around, revealing their surroundings.

They also revealed something else.

'We're not alone in here,' Sally said.

Chapter 48

The team immediately hooded their flashlights.

There were noises ahead, the sounds of many people. Mason crouched low and stayed absolutely still, listening. Around them, the cave echoed softly to footfalls, to whispered conversation, to the odd bray of laughter. Whoever was in front of them wasn't trying to stay especially quiet.

In the dark, it was hard to tell exactly how far away the noises were. Mason remained in place for a while, then started to creep forward, heading for the tunnel in the back, the only way forward. He considered pulling out his gun, but a gunshot down here would totally expose them and probably get them captured, or worse. The last thing he wanted was to be hightailing it at speed back up that cliff.

The tunnel was wide, jagged. It led deeper into the mountain, winding, and there were no junctions, no parallel routes. Mason led the way now, using his hooded flashlight sparingly, confident they were well behind the other infiltrators because he could see no light. The others followed in silence, at least for a while.

It was Roxy who tugged at his arm. 'Why are we still down here?'

'We have to confirm who it is.'

'We know who it is.'

Mason leaned in so that his lips were an inch from her ear. 'But we have to be sure. And we have to know how many people he has down here.'

'In case we can overpower them?' She liked that idea.

Mason went on in silence. Minutes passed. The tunnel wound left and right, smooth in some areas, rough in others. The passage had been hewn out of the rock over centuries, he thought, entire areas at a time and probably for many different purposes. In some areas, it was so narrow they had to turn sideways and brush up against the sides; in others, they could almost stretch both arms out and not touch rock.

They proceeded slowly. Mason glanced back, making sure everyone was with him, and stayed low. Then the noise level increased. Ahead, he could discern a faint light and started to see the shapes of many legs and torsos.

Mason slowed to a crawl. He turned back to the others.

'From here on,' he said, 'just me and Roxy.'

The others all crouched down or found a place to perch. Mason tapped Roxy on the shoulder. 'Absolute silence,' he said.

She nodded. They inched their way forward, closing in on the bodies ahead of them. Mason saw at least three men, with others standing in front of them. As they continued forward, those ahead moved forward, too. Mason now saw that the people ahead were standing on a downward slope. He moved faster.

A voice came from the side. 'You'd best hurry. You know what a bastard he can be.'

Mason stiffened. His teeth clenched, but he said nothing. From out of the shadows, a burly man appeared, zipping up his fly and giving his whole body a shake. He grinned at Roxy and held out a hand.

'Jake. Wanna shake?'

She ignored him. Mason nodded at the man and stood aside to let him lead the way. Jake stared at him curiously, and then went ahead, looking back.

'Like I said, don't linger for too long, no matter what you're planning to do.'

He gave them a lascivious leer and then moved away. Mason and Roxy followed him, staying close. They went up a slight slope and then topped it and, suddenly, the way ahead opened out. The first thing Mason saw was the standing crowd of people. There were many men and women, all decked out in camo and leather and utility vests. Mercenaries all, too many to count. Mason saw that most of them carried guns, some knives, others all kinds of weapons. Even though he couldn't get a proper headcount, Mason knew there were well over thirty people gathered below.

The ground ran away into a vast chamber littered with rocks. Dozens of powerful flashlights illuminated the chamber.

Most of them were shining on one man.

But it wasn't the man that was the centre of attention. It was the incredible sight at his back.

Mason stood at the top of the slope, Roxy at his side. Together, they witnessed Moloch claiming the Hellfire.

It was a gleaming, glimmering, shining, slithering heap of gemstones and gold bars. It was a pile of sturdy old chests with their lids thrown open, revealing even more things glowing in the torchlight. It was treasure and lustre and glitter and flare that stretched dozens of feet up from the ground, the mass so large it dwarfed the man standing in front of it. Mason found that when the light fell on some gems in a certain way, he couldn't look at it. The glare was too strong. And everything shimmered and dazzled, taking his breath away. For long moments, everyone stared in shock, in wonder.

Roxy was the first to find her voice. 'It's fucking incredible.'

Her words drew attention but, in the crowd, they appeared just like all the other mercenaries. Nobody looked twice at them. Except Jake, of course. Jake found it hard to keep his eyes off Roxy, even with the Hellfire glistening in front of him.

'My legacy . . . ' the man standing in front of the magnificent pile started saying. 'This is the day I have been waiting for. The day of judgement. The dark master will be so pleased with me.' He picked up a large, gleaming sword and held it high above his head, its sharp edges glinting. 'Now I have everything I need.'

There were no murmurings among the mercs, no sounds at all. They were no doubt being well paid and were just waiting for fresh orders.

Mason looked at Moloch. He was a tall man, clean-shaven, and wore a well-tailored suit. A fanatical light shone in his eyes, and his face was twisted with emotion. He held his arms in the air, sword extended, and looked up at the roof.

'Bless me, O master. Bless me so that I might honour you even more. Soon . . . we shall feast on their flesh.'

Mason saw a couple of mercs turn to look at each other with raised eyebrows. Then they just shrugged.

'The Hellfire is mine,' Moloch said.

Mason made out the figures of Bullion and his six colleagues, standing in the front row of mercs. Moloch had brought them along despite their failures, probably to beef up the number of mercs he had on site. Mason was glad Bullion kept his eyes firmly on Moloch. Maybe he was the guy's bodyguard.

'What's next, Boss?' someone shouted. The mercs were getting antsy.

Moloch blinked at the crowd as if suddenly realising he wasn't preaching at a Black Mass but standing in front of a bunch of paid soldiers. He lowered his arms, took a breath to steady himself, and then started speaking.

'Everything,' he said. 'Pack it all up and transport it back to the house. I want it all. This is my legacy and I will use it to do good.'

Mason winced a little at that. He was in a quandary. He looked at Roxy, knew he couldn't discuss it right here, and looked away. Moloch had the Hellfire. He'd brought a bloody army with him, and Mason had arrived a little late. Thinking about it, he was glad he'd arrived late. It wouldn't have done to get stuck in here with all these mercs.

You are *stuck in here with all these mercs.*

He backed away, stopped himself. Roxy was looking at him. So was Jake. Mason decided they were going to have a problem with good old Jake.

Carefully, he looked left and right. The entire crowd of mercs were minding their own business, either staring at Moloch and listening to instructions or talking quietly among themselves. Mason backed up even more, now half inside the passage. Roxy was at his side.

Jake came towards them. 'I knew it,' he said, grinning. 'You two going somewhere?'

'Yeah,' Mason said softly. 'Wanna join us?'

Jake puffed his chest out and winked at Roxy. 'Damn right I do.'

Mason took a last look at the Hellfire, at Moloch and Bullion, and at the crowd of mercs that were already starting forward towards the gleaming pile. He turned to walk back along the tunnel. Roxy came behind with Jake and slipped an arm around the man's shoulders.

'Oh, that's real friendly,' Jake said. 'I think I really hit the jackpot here.'

Mason smiled in the dark. Roxy's looping arm tightened harder and harder around Jake's neck. Mason walked on, knowing she wouldn't need his help. There was the sound of a brief scuffle, of Jake trying desperately to breathe, and then the noise of him being dragged carefully into a shallow niche. Mason waited for Roxy to rejoin him.

'Sorted,' she said.

They made their way back to the others. Mason figured they had about twenty minutes before Jake awoke and even then, he wouldn't really know they were impostors. The merc might even just feel embarrassed and say nothing, taking what had happened in his stride.

Quaid met them first. 'What happened?'

Mason spoke fast, explaining everything he'd seen. Roxy waited back down the tunnel a little way, just in case someone had in fact followed them.

'Moloch has the Hellfire?' Sally breathed. 'That's the worst thing that could have happened. How did we let him beat us here?' She cursed.

'He also has an army with him,' Mason said. 'We'd stand no chance against them.'

'So our best bet is to get out of here?' Hassell queried.

'We can't fight them,' Mason reiterated.

'And there's no way we can get our hands on the Hellfire,' Sally said.

'We could pretend to be mercs,' Quaid said. 'Infiltrate his organisation.'

'Even if we could,' Mason said. 'Bullion's here. Sooner or later, he would recognise us.'

'What's next?' Sally pushed. 'We can't just let Moloch win. Don't forget, he has Jacobs under his thrall, too. We can't let Jacobs die. And—'

Mason held up a hand. He knew all the options, all the risks. They were flooding his mind too, like a great storm, flashing past so fast he could barely think. They had to decide, and they had to do it fast.

'We can't affect any of this,' he said. 'Not right now. Not here. We're gonna have to fight another day.'

Sally's lips went tight. She knew he was right, but didn't want to face the fact. 'Then he beat us,' she said. 'After this damn mission, everything we've done, all the times we bested him, he beat us.'

Mason didn't like it either. He spread his arms. 'We're outnumbered,' he said. 'If we don't leave, we'll be captured, and then what?'

Sally nodded, eyes flashing. Together, the team turned and walked away, leaving the tunnel behind, leaving the cave behind, and leaving Moloch to his grand prize.

Chapter 49

Mason crouched in the dark of the night, ready for action. His team was all around him.

And not just his team. There were dozens of other men and women, all toting weapons and wearing body armour, all ready for a fight.

Four days had passed since Mason and his team had walked empty-handed out of the Tintagel caves. During that time, they had wasted not an hour. First, they had used the contact Quaid had already spoken to, explained the situation, the terrible significance of Moloch gaining the Hellfire. They had waited for that man, a respected retired police chief, to speak to others with influence, to raise interest in the chain of command. At the same time, Mason had contacted Jacobs and, despite realising the phone lines might be bugged, by speaking carefully had learned a little of what Moloch was up to.

The Hellfire had been transported from the Tintagel caves back to Moloch's house using trucks. Moloch had been forward-thinking and had already had those arrangements in place. The treasure now sat in a large room inside his house, waiting for him to act on it. Jacobs had been one of the prized few allowed to see it; he didn't know why.

Perhaps Moloch just wanted to gloat in the face of the man he considered a traitor.

During their conversation, one piece of interesting information came up.

Moloch was planning a special celebratory Black Mass in honour of finding the Hellfire. He had sent out a rash of invites, urging everyone to attend. The house that night would be crazy busy . . . and vulnerable.

Mason concentrated on getting the right backup in place. Using Quaid's contacts wasn't enough. In addition, he went to the Vatican, to Premo Conte, and explained what these Satanists were up to and what their ultimate goal was. Of course, the Vatican couldn't directly intervene, but they could use their own extremely powerful contacts to grease some wheels. It took a day or so, but soon Mason was being offered the help of members of the British SCO19, highly trained armed police who acted as London's SWAT units. Besides this, the powers that be sent other skilled units, capable men and women, to join the effort. It was a mishmash of talent and, at least at the start, nobody seemed to know who was in charge.

They met in London, inside a big, dusty, empty warehouse, and thrashed it out. The meeting had been planned for early afternoon with a view to hitting the house that night, just as Moloch's Black Mass kicked off, when his attention would be firmly elsewhere.

Mason stood at the front of the gathering. He counted fifty heads, searched their faces, saw grim determination and utmost seriousness. They had all been told of Moloch's crimes, of his murders in the name of Satan, of his mission to find the Hellfire and then use its vast wealth to pull even more influential followers to his cause, to create a terrible, murderous entity. And of his intention to perform a murderous Black Mass.

Mason spoke before them all, going through the details. He said he had no interest in leading the group and asked for volunteers. In the end, one of the senior SCO19 officers stepped up, saying he would take charge. The teams had all brought their own equipment, and were still answerable to their bosses, but were all known to be on this special assignment. Mason's chief hope was that the information wouldn't leak to Moloch through his already influential contacts, but Quaid had made sure he used his own network. They couldn't do any more than that.

The new officer in charge, a man named Keeling, detailed the forthcoming operation and what he expected to happen. They would move from London to a staging area and then consider approaching Moloch's house after darkness fell. They expected stiff resistance. Nobody knew what to expect when they reached the Black Mass. They also had no idea of the number of people likely to attend, nor who they might be. Shocks were expected, but they would have to take that in their stride.

The entire afternoon passed in discussion. Keeling organised the fifty-strong group into teams, most of them within their own units. Looking at them, Mason saw a ragtag but capable crew, and was reminded of his own team.

'You didn't want to lead, then?' Roxy asked him during the afternoon.

'No,' he said shortly.

'I understand why. I actually thought you'd got past that reluctance, but I do understand.'

'Past it?' Mason knew what she meant. After Mosul, and the deaths of his friends, he'd never wanted to lead a team again. As it happened, and reluctantly, he had become the leader of their little team. But that didn't mean Mason was ready for full leadership. He wasn't in that zone yet and was pretty sure he never would be. The thought made him anxious inside.

Eventually, they were ready to move out. They climbed aboard a fleet of big vans and made their way out of London into the country. The trip to the staging area, which was close to Moloch's house, would take about fifty minutes. Mason sat with his team in the back of one of the vans, being shaken and rolled this way and that, clinging to a strap all the way. They arrived at the staging area under the cover of darkness. It was a large picnic site set amid acres of forest and would easily conceal their vehicles from sight. Moloch's home lay about a twenty-minute hike away through the trees.

They'd had surveillance on it all day.

Now, that surveillance called in to report that Moloch's house had been peaceful for most of the day but, as evening fell, a bevy of vehicles started to arrive, disgorging figure after figure, all dressed to the nines, all eager to get into the house. The vehicles then drove around the back of the house where the chauffeurs congregated in a single building in which, surveillance assumed, they had been told to remain.

'How many guests?' Keeling asked.

'Thirty-two.'

Several of the assembled cops whistled. Mason, too, was surprised by the large number.

'For a Black Mass?' one of them shook his head incredulously.

'For murder,' Sally reminded them.

'How many guards?' Keeling asked.

'We've been counting all day. Not too many outside. You're looking at about nine. We think there are more on the inside, though. At least another nine or ten. So maybe twenty, twenty-five total.'

'That's still plenty,' Keeling said. 'How are they looking?'

'They're well drilled, competent. Keeping a sharp eye out. Of course, they never spotted us, but we haven't got close.'

Keeling asked several more searching questions. Mason sat in the van alongside his friends, ready to act. They wore tactical body armour and carried the guns they were licensed for. They had been told to hang back, let the authorities do their work, but Mason knew none of them would do that. He had a beef with Moloch, a big one, and wouldn't mind meeting up with Bullion one more time. They still had a score to settle.

But the action, when it started, would be quick and fluid. Mason knew they could count on nothing. He had been in enough battles to know that.

They sat in the back of the van for a while. Eventually, the back doors opened, and they all climbed out and gathered at the centre of a clearing. Mason breathed the night air deeply. It was fully dark, about eight in the evening, and surveillance reported that no more cars were arriving. They had to time this just right. Moloch's focus would be at its keenest during the Mass and, they assumed, so would the guards'.

If the cars had stopped arriving at eight, Mason guessed the Mass would probably start around nine. It made sense. Surveillance could see inside the house quite well since all the lights were blazing, and reported seeing the guests standing around with drinks in their hands, being served canapes and generally chatting. Laughing.

As if this was some fancy soirée.

Mason gritted his teeth as he waited. The guests would get what was coming to them. They were all complicit. He waited for the order, ready to go. Besides their guns, they wore Bluetooth earplugs, carried tasers, and wore tactical helmets. If they didn't want Bullion to recognise them, they were set.

Keeling started a countdown. They were ready to go. Mason looked to his team, glancing from one face to the other. They all looked nervous and ready. A good sign. A few butterflies were expected. They kept you on the edge where you needed to be.

As one, the team set off through the trees. As they walked, they parted, as planned, into smaller groups. They would approach the house through the trees and assault it from several directions at the same time. The response they would receive was unknown. Would paid mercenaries fire at law enforcement after they identified themselves? Would they risk death or jail to guard their boss?

Nobody knew with mercenaries. Mason figured if one opened fire, they all would. It was how he thought of them, how they acted.

They paced through the trees. There was a breeze tonight, a cool wind that played around his face. It whistled through the tops of the trees and stirred the branches but, apart from that, all was quiet.

The mass of men and women moved silently through the forest. Mason concentrated on the here and now, the physical exertion, the trees and bushes all around them. They closed in on the house.

Apart from his team, he did not know who he was working with. Yes, he knew their reputations; he could tell they were capable. But still . . . Mason liked to know his team. Around him were Roxy, Quaid, Hassell and Sally, all carrying their handguns and wrapped up in some kind of Kevlar. He hoped it wouldn't be required.

They neared the house. It was a blazing shape in the distance, surrounded by lawns. Mason saw it intermittently through the trees. He could see the shapes of the guards too as they wandered between their stations, with no idea of the force that was heading towards them.

The force kept in contact through their state-of-the-art comms system. Each group slowed as they came to the treeline, crouched down and waited.

Mason noticed the guests had all vanished; they were getting ready for their Black Mass, or maybe it had already begun.

From three sides of the house, men and women rose and walked out into the open.

'Police officers!' they yelled. 'Don't move. Stand down. Put your weapons on the ground!'

Mason watched from cover. This was the moment of truth. This next few seconds would determine whether they were going to be in one hell of a firefight. From where he was standing, he could see three guards. He watched them closely, waiting.

The guards were shadowed by the light that blazed behind them. The first guard raised his hands in the air. A good sign.

'Put your weapons on the ground!' one cop yelled out.

Mason saw a guard pluck his gun from his belt and lay it at his feet. He saw the man with his hands in the air unhook a rifle from his shoulder and throw it to the ground.

So far, so good.

Mason started walking forward, weapon drawn. He strode easily between the trees, exiting the treeline and heading across the lawns that led up to the house. Tension filled him. His eyes were on the third guard.

And now, at the window, Mason could see a figure looking out. This figure held a sub-machine gun and was staring out in shock and consternation. Mason saw the man shout into a handheld radio.

Instantly, a voice crackled across all the guards' radios.

'Fight! Attack! Safeguard the house! That's your damn job!'

Mason acted instantly. He burst into a run, dashing forward and heading for the cover of three nearby parked cars. The guards on the lawn ahead hesitated. The one who hadn't thrown down his weapon yet drew it and levelled it.

Guards burst from the house, weapons drawn. Nobody had fired a shot yet. They came out of three doors, running hard, flying towards the intruders.

'They're cops,' someone said through the radio.

'You don't know that! Now do your job and guard the house!'

'Hey,' a guard yelled out. 'We need to see some kind of—'

Right then, a shot was fired. Mason didn't know where it came from. He was running headlong toward the shelter offered by one of the cars. The shot echoed through the dark night for a moment, severe, harsh, deadly.

And then it was joined by hundreds more.

Chapter 50

Mason rolled behind the first car. His team were a step behind, diving headlong. Bullets flew across the grounds of the house, sweeping the lawns. Guards exited the house at speed, already firing, most of them not knowing who they were firing at, just following orders. The force of cops scattered, some diving forward and rolling, others jumping behind trees or into ditches.

Mason peered from around the back of the car. A bullet whined past. Quickly, he drew his head back and let out a deep breath. The guards were acting on orders. He didn't want to shoot them, but it was a case of kill or be killed.

He looked out around the car's left side; Roxy around the right. Together, they fired several shots into the oncoming guards. Cops were returning fire too now. The sound of gunfire exploded in the countryside. Mason saw two guards twist and fall.

They were still rushing out of the house, over a dozen of them. And they were fighting all around the house. Mason could hear it through the comms system. He winced as a bullet slammed into the front of the car, then ducked as another smashed through both front and rear windows, scattering glass over his shoulders.

Roxy muttered a curse, shooting blindly around the side of the car. A guard yelled out, hit the floor hard. Sally, Quaid and Hassell were crouching a few feet away, looking nervous.

The guards continued to pour into the grounds. The house blazed behind them. The men were mere silhouettes, racing from point to point, firing their weapons. Some cops, those who had been stranded on the lawn, rose to meet them now.

Mason saw at least three guards approaching his position. He rose fast, aimed at them, and yelled at them to stop. When the first levelled his weapon, Mason shot him. The others were too quick. One got off a shot that flew past Mason's right ear. The other just ran at him, barged into him, and knocked him off his feet.

Mason hit the floor with his spine and felt a bolt of pain run the length of his body. A figure fell on top of him. Mason looked immediately for the gun, grabbed the man's wrist and broke it. The guard grunted, drew a knife with his good hand, and thrust it at Mason's vitals.

Mason blocked the knife, but got a nasty cut on the wrist. Blood poured out of the wound, making his grip slick. Still he grappled for the knife. He rolled out from under the man, whirled, threw a punch that connected solidly, and sent blood flying in all directions. The man fell back.

Mason reached down to pick up his gun.

'Stop,' he said.

But the guard ignored him, raised the knife and lunged. Mason shot him in the chest, sent him hurtling back against the rear of the car.

Roxy shot a guard as he came around the car. He was quickly followed by another, the man's face stretched in a

301

roar of anger. She buried her fist in his stomach, saw him literally fold in half. As his head fell toward the floor, she smashed her gun down on top of it, knocking him out.

Behind her, Quaid, Hassell and Sally had their guns up. They fired into the mass of guards who ran before the house. It was a melee. They fired when they could because, soon, in the shadows away from the house, they wouldn't be able to tell friend from foe.

Mason checked his perimeter. He was momentarily free. Roxy was ducking as a man raised his sub-machine gun in her direction. Mason yelled out a warning.

Just in time. The gun started chattering. Bullets riddled the car, some of them piercing the metal. Mason flung himself prostrate on the ground. Roxy crawled under the car, aimed, and took the shooter's legs out. When he fell, she shot him in the head.

Mason then heard a Bluetooth conversation.

'Dammit, the chauffeurs are coming out of their house.'

'Get a couple of people over there,' Keeling shouted back. 'Herd them back inside. Arrest them if you have to.'

Mason knew it was all hypothesis. You never knew how anyone would react to a situation until they were actually in it. A normal person wouldn't venture out of a house into a gunfight. But maybe the chauffeurs were worried about their bosses, their bosses' wives, their own jobs, if they did nothing. It was an impossible, unguessable situation.

There was a mass of fighting men and women to Mason's left. Bullets still strafed the ground between the forest and where some of the guards had dug in. The guards had stopped coming out of the house by now and were thinning out. A group of cops came up behind Mason and crouched down.

'How we doing?' one asked.

'I see a straight shot to the house,' Roxy said.

'Why haven't the guests come running out too?' someone asked.

Mason had actually mentioned that to Jacobs a few days ago, anticipating what would happen. 'The room where they conduct the Black Mass is totally soundproofed,' he said. 'No contact allowed whilst they're in session. Makes sense, really. They don't want outsiders knowing what goes on in there.'

'So they're at it now,' a cop said. 'Worshipping the fucking Devil whilst these guards fight for their lives?'

Mason nodded. 'I'd say so, yes.'

Roxy smiled. 'Then how about we go ruin their day?'

Mason looked left and right, studied the terrain. The guards were all focused on the cops. He started creeping around the three cars, saw about twenty feet between him and the entrance of the house.

He turned. 'Let's end this,' he said.

They streamed towards the house, twelve of them in total. They kept their heads down, running quickly and efficiently. Mason was the first to reach the open doorway and slip inside. He found himself in a large study with a desk, a comfortable chair and pictures on the wall. A quick scan told him it was empty.

Everyone crowded in through the door, spreading out. Mason thought about his conversations with Jacobs. The man had described where Moloch's Black Mass room was located. Now he just had to find it.

He spoke into the comms. 'Twelve of us are in the house,' he said. 'And going for the room.'

'We're pinned down to the east,' a voice returned.

'Similar,' another man said. 'To the west.'

Keeling's voice came next. 'Subdue them and subdue this Moloch. Once he's in custody, this whole shitshow should end.'

Mason led the way, running off through a hallway and finding a library. Through that he ran, boots slamming the floor. Beyond the library, he raced through a drawing room and then a living room, heading for the back of the house. Once in the extensive kitchen, he found a door, opened it and stared down a row of concrete steps. They were well lit. He started down, two at a time, hand close to his holstered gun. He didn't expect to find any guards down here, but you never knew.

There was a noise from behind, the sound of people fighting. Mason paused and looked back up the stairs. Quaid was on the top step.

'Guards have entered the kitchen,' he said.

As he spoke, there was a gunshot, then another. Quaid dived headlong, hit the ground and rolled. Mason couldn't get back up the steps for the press of people above him. Agonised by his impotence, he just had to wait whilst the cops up top fought with the guards. Quaid rose to one knee and opened fire. There was the sound of men falling, of a table crashing and wood splintering. A window shattered. Boots slammed across the tiled floor. Mason was about to start clambering up through the herd of people when there came a sudden silence.

Quaid rose to his feet. 'It's over,' he said, subdued. 'Three guards down. We lost a man.'

Mason cursed silently. His inability to help wasn't his fault, but he took it hard. After a moment, people started crowding at the top of the stairs, forcing him to carry on. He walked down the rest of the flight, found himself in a wide passageway, and followed it for about two more minutes. It ran straight. The whole area was empty. The stark passageway ended in a door.

Nothing special. It was a double, white, six-panel door with a silver handle. Mason took out his gun and opened the door.

It led to a brightly lit, dusty antechamber. The ceiling was arched and carved in flowery shapes. A moulded cornice ran around the walls. The floor was dirty and covered in footprints. Now Mason stopped in shock.

Before him stood another door, and it took his breath away.

This one was over fifteen feet high. It was grand, double, carved, and colourful, made up of golds and yellows and reds and greens. Ordinarily, Mason would have been impressed, but this was no normal door.

The surface was covered in hellish carvings, each a terrible, twisted, demonic face. The eyes were slanted, the tongues were forked, the skulls all had horns curling out of them. Multicoloured gems encrusted the insides of the eye sockets, making them gleam. Twisted claws were raised as if to attack. Mason saw taloned feet and spear-like ribcages, teeth that glistened with red rubies like blood, and hung dripping from misshapen mouths. The door handles were two spines of a four-footed creature that curled sinuously around the doorway.

There was silence in the antechamber as everyone stared in shock. From beyond the door there was no sound, but then they hadn't expected to hear anything. For the first time, Mason wondered if Bullion was inside, or if the man had been guarding the grounds and was now engaged in the firefight. One thing was for sure . . . Moloch was in here.

'Only one way forward,' Roxy said.

Mason nodded. He felt like he was facing the gates of hell.

'Evil bastards,' someone spat.

'There are at least thirty people beyond this door,' Mason said. 'Most of them are civilians and non-combative. But it's going to be a high-stress situation. Keep your wits about you and stay calm.'

'If someone looks at me wrong, they're gonna regret it,' a woman said.

'We should put an end to this,' Sally said.

Mason agreed. He readied his gun, strode forward, and placed a hand on the horrific-looking door. It felt cold under his grip and for one second, he almost expected it to squirm as he had imagined the inverted cross did. He grabbed a handle, turned around, stared at the assembled group.

'Be ready for anything,' he said.

Chapter 51

Mason grabbed both door handles and pulled.

The door opened easily. The room's interior was vast, the ceiling out of sight, no walls to be seen. In front of him, though, Mason saw a mass of people.

They all had their backs to him and, since the doors opened silently, nobody turned to look. Any change in light that might be shed by an opening door was masked by a row of thick columns that marched across the entrance. The assembled people were all facing a stage of some sort.

But it wasn't a stage, Mason realised. It was a terrible altar. On a raised dais stood an ornate stone table. On the table, a figure lay, its arms and legs bound. It squirmed and struggled weakly as Mason watched.

And now he saw Moloch. The man was standing next to the altar, a huge sword held in his hand. Mason became aware of a low chanting. It filled the room. Something hushed and monotonous, at the edge of sound. Something creepy and disturbing. And, as Mason listened, it rose in volume.

The gathered crowd started shaking.

Mason saw them raise their hands in supplication. The noise increased some more. The dull litany set his teeth on edge. The figures all wore robes. Most wore masks, some were bare-faced.

Mason walked into the room. Around him, his team and the other cops spread out. Still they hadn't been noticed.

Moloch nodded his head in time to the chanting, staring down at the altar. The gleaming blade in his hand stayed by his side for now, though he looked at it often and reverently. The chanting rose again, and now it was pitched at a normal level, repeated again and again, endless repetitions of *'Ave Satanus'* and other Satanic murmurings. Mason looked up, saw churning shadows that hid the roofline. Smoke roiled and curled up there, and gave the impression of boiling shapes that twisted and turned and leapt upon one another.

The crowd grew agitated. Some started shouting. Others tore at their robes, trying to rip them off. A strange sense of abandon ran through the room, of barely subdued rage. It was infectious. Mason saw several people clench their fists and start pumping the air.

The sound level rose again. Now the people were chanting at the tops of their voices. Some were screaming for a kill.

Mason raised his gun and aimed it at the roof.

'Everyone stop!' he yelled. 'Stop this madness!'

Either they didn't hear him, or they didn't care. Mason realised they'd entered the room just a few minutes too late. The fever – whatever it was – had already gripped these people. They were lost in it, lost in mad passion, lost in vehement agitation. They heard only the chanting and the assumed whispered promises of demons.

Moloch, by the altar, looked over and frowned. He'd heard Mason, and now he saw him. The man's eyes went wide. Swiftly, he raised the sword and poised it over the struggling figure. 'It is now,' he screamed. 'It has to be now!'

Mason's heart leapt. He fired the gun into the ceiling, fired again when he heard no sound of a ricochet. The sharp cracks of the gunshots overwhelmed the chanting and sent dozens of heads turning in his direction.

Mason was shocked, despite himself. Those countless eyes turning towards him . . . the eyes were terrible . . .

In each face that turned, Mason saw a blank, malevolent leer. Eyes that glittered with evil, mouths twisted in hatred. It was as though the entire assemblage was under some kind of horrific spell. Humanity appeared to have deserted them.

Mason shuddered, momentarily freezing. The sight of so many soulless faces turning towards him was unprecedented. For a moment, he didn't know how to deal with it. Some Satanists stared blankly, others snarled, lost in their own private hellish moment.

Near the altar, Moloch kept the chant going. The sword was poised.

And, as Mason watched, mouths started to open and close. The chant kept going as the dead eyes stared at him. The moment was a snapshot of horror, something he'd never forget for the rest of his life.

It was Roxy who broke the spell. She walked up beside Mason, raised her gun in the air, and fired again – three shots. By the time the third went off, the civilians were shaking themselves, blinking rapidly, bringing their hands up to their faces to rub them vigorously. They stared at the newcomers as if they were ghosts.

'Who are you?' someone asked.

'Get out of here,' another snarled.

A shudder of violence swept through the room. The crowd was hostile; it hated the fact that their ceremony was being interrupted, their chant halted. Moloch was still doing his best to keep it going. Mason was shocked by him. He had to know the game was up, had to know he'd been discovered, found out, but he was too far gone in his madness to care. Too much the Satanist.

Perhaps he was hoping something far more sinister would intervene.

The crowd began to whisper, to shake. Aggressive eyes turned on Mason and his colleagues. People hissed at them, cursed at them, raised their fists. Mason made sure they could see his gun. This was ridiculous. These people were citizens – politicians, accountants, solicitors, doctors. They didn't act this way.

And then everything pivoted. There was a collective growl of hatred that passed through the room and the crowd started towards them. Mason saw fists clenched. He saw snarling lips, eyes that glowed like death. As the crowd moved, the people reached deep into their robes and brought out dozens of knives.

Mason's heart skipped a beat. His own team started moving. The knives were raised above the heads of the crowd, many blades catching the light and flashing as they twisted and turned, a deadly field of glinting, gleaming sharp edges that filled the air. In another terrible moment, the crowd rushed forward.

Mason struck out, hitting a man in the chest, another in the gut. A knife flashed past his skull. Gunshots rang out as the cops opened fire. It was a melee, a horrific glimpse of hellish chaos. Roxy was bodily shoved away from him. Someone flung themselves on Sally, bearing her to the ground. A knife flashed, its blade striking the floorboards.

Mason ducked aside as another knife thrust at him. It nicked his arm, another war wound. Blood poured freely. He fired into the aggressor, smashed his gun across the face of another, shot a man who was preparing to stab him.

The man went down, robes flying. In front of Mason was a surreal field of flashing knives and flapping, roiling black robes. It was a nightmare vision from hell. The attackers were screaming and shrieking, drowning in their madness. Mason hadn't expected this. He fell to one knee, looked up, saw a blade arcing down at his face, knew he couldn't stop it.

Roxy was there, slapping the blade away, breaking the arm that wielded it. Then she was gone, knocked bodily aside by a big man wearing a goat's mask. Another mask-wearer came up to Mason, swung a knife in a wide, inexperienced arc. Mason caught the wrist easily and broke it, smashed the man in the groin and saw him fold like a wet towel. The next attacker wasn't so lucky. If Mason hadn't shot him point blank, the guy would have stabbed him in the heart.

A high-pitched, keening noise filled the entire room, some kind of ceremonial ululation. It took Mason some time to realise it was coming from the throats of their attackers. He'd heard of crowd mentality, where rational people just gave in to their base feelings because they felt part of the herd. This had to be what was taking over.

The cops were making a difference. The crowd was thinning. Mason shoved an unarmed woman aside, sending her towards Hassell and Quaid. A knife flashed. Mason let it pass between his arm and his ribcage, trapped the arm and twisted. There was a loud cracking noise, a yelp, and then he was free.

A gap opened up ahead.

But then something terrible happened. Sally, several metres to his right, was struggling with a heavyset blond woman, bowing under her relentless attack. The woman had a large knife and looked like she knew how to use it. Sally was backing away, but there was nowhere to go. Bodies crammed the space all around her. She was in trouble, and Mason couldn't get to her.

The blond woman only hit harder, forcing Sally to her knees. Mason could see what was coming. He struggled to get close, to force a path to her side. He failed. Screamed at himself in silence. There was no saving Sally.

The blonde stood over her, knife raised. Sally's own gun had already been knocked from her hands and had skidded away across the floor, lost between a tangle of legs. All Sally could do was raise her arms to ward off the killing blow.

It came almost immediately.

Mason saw the blade flash, saw the deadly edge striking down. Sally's upturned face was incredibly vulnerable. Mason could only scream, thrust a hand out.

And then, incredibly, at the very last second, a body intervened, launching itself between the battling pair. Mason gasped. By all accounts, this was Jonathan Jacobs, Sally's godfather, coming to her aid, the dying man punching through the crowd and trying to save Sally's life. He managed to get himself between the two adversaries just as the knife came down.

The blade sank into the man's ribcage. Both he and the blond woman screamed. Jacobs slumped, blood pouring from the wound as the woman tried to wrench the knife free. Sally attacked the woman when her guard was down, jabbing her three times in the face and knocking her unconscious, and then whirled to the dying Jacobs. She fell to her knees beside him and cradled his head. Her lips moved, but Mason couldn't hear what she was saying. All he knew was that the older man had saved her life at the cost of his own.

He tore his gaze away towards the front of the room, saw Moloch still hovering close to the altar, a self-confident smile on his face. He still chanted in some obscure and terrible ritual, arms raised above his head. The sword still glinted; the body squirmed on the altar. Smoke and shadows curdled the air above the man, thick and roiling. In the next moment, Moloch was looking up, searching, eyes wide.

Did he think he'd conjured something?

Mason put the idiocy and the madness of it out of his mind. He had to rescue the figure strapped to the altar. He started running forward, shrugging attackers off. One tripped him, but he caught himself, landed on one knee, and was up in less than a second. He ran on.

A figure close to the stage was staring up at Moloch as if listening to orders. That figure turned when Mason came closer.

Bullion.

This time, the killer was alone. His features twisted when they saw Mason, his eyes flashing with hatred.

'I've been waiting for you,' he said.

Mason saw Moloch staring from the churning smoke above to the figure on the altar. Then his eyes strayed to his blade. Mason knew what he was going to do. In his craziness, he thought that the smoke was thickening shadow, the precursor of some terrible entity, and he was also thinking that the sacrifice would finish the job.

Mason appealed to Bullion. 'You can't let him kill that woman on the altar.'

'Time to die, Mason. I've been looking forward to this.'

Bullion pulled a KA-BAR knife from his waistband and lunged. Mason almost wasn't fast enough. Most of his attention had been on Moloch. The knife sliced his cheek, opened up a flap of skin. Bullion, despite himself, looked surprised and stood back.

'Nice,' he said.

Mason backed away, giving himself time to glance around. The others were fully engaged; they couldn't help. He was on his own, facing Bullion and the mad Moloch with an innocent victim tied to the altar.

He hunkered down, let the violence gather in him. This would have to be done swiftly and precisely and with no mercy.

Bullion lunged once again. Mason stepped into the man, let the knife pass by, then delivered a stunning uppercut. Bullion's head snapped back. Mason didn't let up. He treated Bullion like a punchbag, smashing a combination of punches to his neck and face. First the uppercut, then a left jab and a rolling right, which immediately became a sharp jab to the throat that left Bullion gasping, and a roundhouse to the right ear. It didn't end there. Mason hit him with a classic double jab, a cross, and then another uppercut. By the time he had finished, Bullion was sinking to the floor, lights out. The knife slipped away from his nerveless fingers.

Mason stepped over the unconscious figure. On the makeshift stage, Moloch was gazing at the shadows, the smoke. Candles were blazing on several tall concrete plinths. He was holding the foot of the struggling figure in one hand, the sword in the other. His eyes were wide, like dinner plates, his face slack with reverence.

'*Ave Satanus,*' he breathed.

Mason realised he could hear the man. The noise in the room had diminished greatly. He didn't have time to check why. He ran at the dais, vaulted up on to it.

Moloch wasn't as far gone as he looked. As Mason landed, he whirled, swept the sword around in an arc. Mason saw it flash before his eyes, the blade glinting. He leaned back, unbalanced, actually feeling the passage of the weapon close to his neck.

Moloch, driven mad with rage, desperate to summon his dark master and enlist his help, leapt not at Mason, but onto the tied sacrifice. He brought the blade slashing down.

Mason screamed. He was too far away to help. He saw another innocent victim about to die in agony. The victim's eyes bulged in terror.

Moloch was bellowing, chest heaving, every muscle a taut sinew.

Mason couldn't at first follow what happened next. He saw the sword fly out of Moloch's clenched fist. Then he saw several of Moloch's fingers tumbling through the air. Then he heard a gunshot.

Looked back. Saw Roxy standing with legs apart, holding a gun in front of her.

Mason didn't waste any more time. He ran to the altar, grabbed Moloch, heaved him off, and dragged him to the floor. He let the guy's forehead hit the floor first, then rolled him over and straddled him.

And punched him unconscious.

Mason left the unmoving figure, then ran to the sacrifice. With a knife, he slit the bonds that held her arms and legs. He looked into her eyes.

'You're safe now,' he said.

Tears sprang from her eyes. Mason turned away, looked down across the room. The sight was both stunning and surreal. His team stood among masses of fallen black-robed bodies, most of them horribly masked. It looked like a scene from hell, as if his team were surrounded by dark demons, some creeping, some crawling across the floor. There was blood too, lots of it, seeping into the floorboards and pooling across the wood, splashed up against the wall. The cops stood around, their eyes horrified.

Mason helped the woman sit up. He checked Moloch was still out cold, then took another look at the incredible scene that filled most of the room. It made him think of a malign, creeping Hell.

With that, though, he looked up at the ceiling. The smoke still roiled there as he knew it would. It was the smoke of candles. Nothing else. Moloch had been sure it was the appearance of his dark master. Perhaps, in some warped way, he had seen much more than smoke.

Something far worse.

Mason shuddered. He wanted to be far away from this basement, this scene, this moment. He looked down as his team walked up to the foot of the platform.

'You're bleeding,' Roxy said.

Mason had forgotten the slash across his face. The blood ran freely. His shirt was soaked. He shook his head. 'It's nothing.'

There were a few injuries. Roxy had broken a finger. Hassell had injured his knee and been slashed across the stomach. Everyone would need a paramedic. At that moment, Bullion, lying at the foot of the platform, started coming around and began to groan. With an effort, he sat up, shaking his head.

'Where . . . ' he began.

Without even looking at him, Roxy launched a boot at his head, struck his skull, and sent him back into oblivion.

She grinned. 'Back where he belongs,' she said.

'Nice kick,' Mason said.

'I have my uses.'

'This is over now,' Sally said. 'And we also have Professor Taylor stashed away so that he can give evidence. So, even if all these people here somehow collectively lose their memories, Taylor can tell everyone what really happened during those Masses.'

The cops started rounding up the fallen civilians, disarming them, cuffing them where they could. Using the comms system, they found out that the guards had eventually surrendered outside and were also in custody. Ambulances were on the way, as well as a horde of authorities. It was going to be a long night.

Mason just wanted to get out of the room, away from the robed Satanists, away from Moloch and the terrible altar and all the rest of the diabolical paraphernalia. He nodded towards the door.

'Shall we make a break for it?'

They walked away from the chaos, crossed the outer room, and didn't look back at the fiendishly carved door. They climbed the stairs back to the kitchen. Through the comms system, they learned where Moloch had stored the Hellfire and went to pay it a visit.

They walked through rooms, under archways and along passages before coming to a vast chamber. Mason entered first, his hand held to his cheek to staunch the blood flow. He found himself in a circular room with a domed ceiling and framed prints on the wall. The centre of the room was stacked with unbelievable wealth.

The Hellfire was a tall, glistening pile of gemstones. Every facet sparkled at them, reflecting a billion lights. It was all colours, greens and reds and golds and blues, and it seemed to drip with glitter as small diamonds and rubies tumbled from top to bottom.

Sally cleared her throat. 'This kind of wealth,' she said, 'will make men and women do crazy things.'

Mason winced. 'I've never seen anything more crazy in my life than what I just witnessed,' he said. 'It was like they were all under a spell.'

'Satan's spell,' Roxy said with a grin.

Mason gave her the finger.

'But we're all alive to tell the tale,' Quaid said. 'Alive to take on the next mission.'

Mason stared at him. 'Give us a chance to get over this one, mate. I feel like my feet haven't touched the ground in weeks.'

But he knew what Quaid meant, knew what he was getting at. Their lives were all about moving forward, about embracing the next thing. It was what kept them at the top of their game, what kept the real demons at bay.

Demons. Now there was a topical thought.

But there were no demons here tonight, not in this house. No Satanic masters. No dark presences that couldn't be explained. There was relief and triumph and satisfaction. They had unmasked a great wrong and were sending countless evil individuals to prison, including Moloch, a man who would have spread his malevolent influence far and wide.

Roxy held up a bottle of whisky. Mason realised she must have grabbed it on their way through the house.

'A toast,' she said. 'To beating the bad guys.'

She raised the bottle to her lips and took a gulp, passed it on to Sally. Again, the bottle was raised. Sally repeated the toast, passed it on to Hassell. Quaid drank next, and then the bottle was with Mason.

'To Roxy's incredible skills with a gun,' he said. 'You saved that woman's life. I couldn't even get close.'

'But you were there,' she said. 'You stopped him before I did. And together we succeeded. As a team, we got the job done.'

He felt uplifted and drank the toast. What had started out as an anxious, dark, inscrutable day was turning into a happy ending with friends.

It was how every day should end.

You've met Jack Reacher.
You've met Jason Bourne.
Now it's time to meet Joe Mason . . .

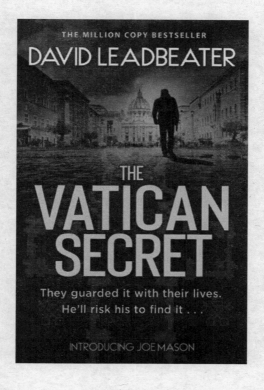

Go back to where the adventure began with
***The Vatican Secret*.**

Available now!

The adventure continues . . .

Don't miss the second action-packed and adrenaline-filled instalment.

Available now!

In this game of cat and mouse, the rules are simple:

kill or be killed . . .

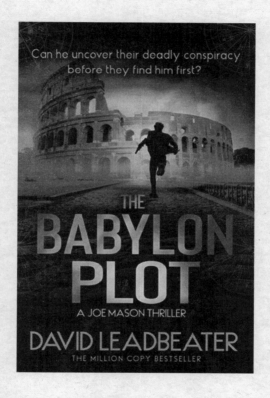